THE
THIEF WHO
Loved ME

New York Times & USA Today Bestselling Author

CYNTHIA
EDEN

I0714697

This book is a work of fiction. Any similarities to real people, places, or events are not intentional and are purely the result of coincidence. The characters, places, and events in this story are fictional.

Published by Hocus Pocus Publishing, Inc.

Copyright ©2022 by Cindy Roussos

All rights reserved. This publication may not be reproduced, distributed, or transmitted in any form without the express written consent of the author except for the use of small quotes or excerpts used in book reviews.

Copy-editing by: J. R. T. Editing

CHAPTER ONE

He hated being bored. When Remy Stuart felt bored, he had the tendency to do rash things like...steal million-dollar necklaces. Screw over the CIA team that mistakenly *thought* he was some sort of reformed bad guy who they had on a leash. Or maybe, just for the hell of it...being bored made him want to forge a few new pieces of artwork that he could then sell to unfortunate fools who needed to be parted with their wealth.

Remy sat in the corner of the rundown bar, not touching his beer. He'd made the mistake of sipping it earlier and was pretty sure the beer had to be modeled after battery acid. The beer bottle—and beer inside said bottle—grew warmer, his mood took a sour turn, and Remy decided that being on the right side of the law just was not for him. Being good was simply too boring.

The bar's door opened with a creak. He'd picked his spot deliberately so that he would be able to see every single person who entered and left the bar. A personality quirk, he liked to look at faces. He actually *never* forgot a face. A talent Remy possessed. As soon as he saw someone, he did a mental sketch in his mind. The image stayed with him.

So as the door opened, he tilted his head and...

Wrong bar, sweetness. Wrong man. Wrong night.

The woman who peeked inside didn't belong in the bar. Her face was all angelic grace and ethereal beauty, with dark, arched brows over the deepest, greenest eyes he'd ever seen. Even across the room, her eyes were stunning. Her lips were unpainted, a pale pink, but lush. And her hair was a tangled tumble of darkness.

His eyes narrowed. Was that a *leaf* in the darkness of her hair?

No music played in the bar. Not exactly that kind of place. The floors were dusty, the service was nonexistent, and a flickering light bounced over the one pool table in the joint. Remy had spent plenty of time in places one hell of a lot better.

He'd also spent too much time in places that were worse.

The lost angel stood in the doorway, one delicate hand gripping the edge of the door far too tightly. Probably trying to decide if she should come fully inside or turn away and run.

Turn away and run. That would be the smart choice.

Instead, her emerald eyes locked on him. She swallowed. Her whole body trembled, as if the woman was utterly terrified. But she let go of the door and stepped toward him.

Such a poor life choice. But Remy arched a brow. His gaze also slid down her body. She wore a white dress. Long and flowing, it hid entirely too much of her body. The bottom of her dress was dark and spattered with what appeared to be mud. The dress was spattered and so were her bare feet.

Remy straightened. She had cute toes. Red toenail polish adorned them. So did a great deal of dirt, as if the angel had just walked—or run—through the muddy woods in order to reach the bar at the edge of town.

Halfway, Georgia, wasn't exactly a tourist mecca. Sure, it was nestled in the Blue Ridge Mountains, and the views were phenomenal, but this town wasn't like the others in the area. It was more of a pitstop—thus, the name. The few locals in the area liked to joke that when you reached the town, you were *halfway* to one of the more entertaining cities.

No one ever stayed in Halfway. Nothing ever happened in the small speck of a town. So, yes, it had seemed like the perfect hiding place for Remy.

The woman in white had almost reached his table. He could feel a frown pulling at his brows. He would have turned to look around the bar to see if maybe she'd confused him with someone else, but, other than the bartender, he was the only other person in the bar. Well, he had been. Now she was there so—

She stopped right at the edge of his wobbly, wooden table. "I need your help."

Remy smiled at her. "Sweetness, you obviously have me confused with someone else."

"No, I-I understand that you don't know me..."

He leaned forward. Studied her. Did the usual mental sketch in his mind. *Oh, how I could paint the hell out of her.* "Your eyes are quite spectacular. A very strong, vivid shade of green." He'd seen a meadow in Ireland that shade once.

"What?" Even as she asked the confused question, she darted a look back toward the bar's entrance. Her thick hair trailed over her shoulder.

He saw a second leaf. His lips pursed. Someone had definitely spent time in the woods. And that white dress of hers—though dirty—was certainly interesting. If he didn't know better, Remy might think he was staring at a runaway bride.

But I don't know better, do I? His night had certainly perked up.

Her head jerked back toward him.

He studied her face. The angles. The softness. The slopes. In his mind, Remy continued his sketch. "Great nose. Very elegant. Heart-shaped face. Bow lips. And your skin has a golden tint. I'm thinking...Italian? Maybe Italian on one side of the family and either Irish or English on the other?"

Her bow lips parted. She blinked.

Remy shrugged. "It's okay to say I'm right. I'm really good at things like this."

She slapped her hands down on the table. At the sudden movement, his bottle of beer shook and began to topple. Casually, Remy reached out his hand and caught it before the beer could do anything *fortunate* like shatter and spill all over the floor.

"Please." Her voice was nice. Husky. Warm. "I need your help."

Again with the H-word. Tragic. Remy released the beer and rose. He tossed a twenty onto the table. The bartender was staring at a football game on a miniscule TV, not paying them any attention. "This is where I think the confusion originates. You seem to believe I am someone who helps. I'm not." But, well, he *could* give her helpful advice. He edged around the table toward her.

The angel backed up a quick step and sucked in a breath.

Average height. Maybe five-foot-six or so. She tilted her head back to look up at him.

"Rodney over there follows the rules of most local establishments." Remy pointed to the bartender.

Her gaze flew toward the back of Rodney's gleaming head. Rodney made a habit of shaving his head clean every three days. Like clockwork.

"What rules?" she whispered.

"No shirt, no shoes, no service." Remy pointed downward at her adorable, though dirty, toes. "Don't know if you've noticed, but you appear to have lost something."

She grabbed his shirtfront. Fisted the fabric beneath her hands. "I need to get out of here!"

Remy raised his hand and plucked a leaf from her hair. "Did you run through the woods?"

"*Yes.*" She shivered. Clutched his shirt even tighter. "I saw the big, black truck outside. Tell me it's yours."

Technically, it wasn't, but he lied all the time so... "It's mine."

"Take me away in it."

Now Remy realized that he was going to say words that he *never, ever* had thought he would say, especially given his previous type of work. "You seem to be having some sort of incident."

"What?" Her glorious eyes doubled in size.

"Your clothes are muddy. You have leaves in your hair. You've lost your shoes." He shrugged. "And you're approaching a complete stranger for help. I'm assuming all of this means you're in some sort of danger."

"Yes."

And here were the words. The ones he couldn't believe he was about to utter but... "I would suggest calling the cops. The local sheriff is surprisingly adequate." He reached for her hands. Closed his fingers around her wrists and...

Heat slid up from his fingertips. He frowned but didn't pry her hands from his shirt.

"Don't turn me over to the cops!"

Interesting word choice from his mystery lady.

"Please..." She looked over her shoulder once more. She kept doing that, as if she feared that someone had followed her. But no one else had entered the bar. "I just need a ride. Take me out of here. Act like—act like we're together."

A sigh slipped from Remy. "Didn't your mother ever teach you that strangers can be dangerous? You should not approach them. You should not ask for rides from them." He considered the matter. "I think you're also not supposed to take candy from them."

Her head whipped back toward him. Those deep, deep green eyes locked on him. Such big eyes.

"I don't have candy," he murmured. "Sorry to disappoint."

"Are you dangerous?" she squeaked.

Ah, well, at least she'd paid attention to that part of his little speech. "In so many wonderful ways, yes." A thousand times, yes.

The mystery lady immediately freed him. She stepped back. Shoved her hands behind her body.

Fabulous. Now they were making real progress. He pointed to the oblivious Rodney. "He has a phone behind the counter. Call the sheriff." There. Remy had done his due diligence. Time to be on his merry way back to his cabin in the woods. Except...

He plucked the second leaf from her hair and put it on the table. He also didn't leave.

She swallowed and made no move to approach Rodney as he continued to watch his game. "Please." Barely a breath. "I just need to disappear for tonight. Just one night, that's all I'm asking."

Do not do this... "And you want to disappear with me?" Her skin was truly lovely, and she had amazing bone structure. Not conventionally pretty, but something so much more. *Arresting.* No, entrancing. There was something about the way her features flowed together...

I want to paint her. No, more than that. *I need to paint her.*

Remy stiffened as the thought registered.

"Look, it's not like I have a whole lot of choice." Now she sounded disgruntled. "You're the only guy with a ride."

Not true. "I'm sure Rodney has a vehicle out back." It was actually a bicycle, but that still counted as a vehicle, didn't it?

Her lush lips pressed into a line. Then, she said, "If I ask for his help, your friend Rodney will probably call the sheriff you keep talking about."

"Oh, that's quite possible. Especially since they're brothers. And he's not my friend. We're barely acquaintances." He liked Rodney's bar because Rodney didn't give a shit about him. Rodney didn't ask questions, and Remy didn't have to deal with a crowd when he came to the bar.

A gasp tore from her. "*Brothers?*" She turned to run—

But he caught her hand. Easily, casually, he pulled her back toward him. Remy also noticed that she didn't try to resist his pull at all. "Have we been involved in something illegal tonight? Not judging, mind you. I'm just vaguely curious." More than vaguely.

"I haven't done anything illegal!"

"That's disappointing." Until that low but passionate response, she'd been livening up his night. At her frown, Remy continued, "Oh, sorry, I guess I was judging." A little illegal fun would have amped up the stakes.

A furrow lingered between her delicate brows even as she wet her lips. A quick, nervous swipe of her pink tongue. "I really, really need a ride." She trembled again. "I can't be found. I *can't*."

Fear seemed to roll from her. He could feel her pulse racing beneath his touch as his fingers circled her wrist. A delicate wrist. Fragile. Too easily broken. As were so many things in this world. "What's your name?" Why had he asked? He didn't care.

"Jacqueline." A slow exhale. "Jacqueline Peters."

He liked her name. *Jacqueline*. Elegant. Classic. Remy peered down at her bare feet.

"It's been an incredibly bad night," she confessed as her shoulders hunched. "I hitchhiked almost to town, but the truck driver wasn't coming to Halfway, so he had to let me out."

"You hitchhiked..." His lips wanted to curl. "In a wedding dress?"

"I—it's...It's *not*—"

"Guessing it looked better before you ripped the hem out of it and lost nearly all the pearls that had been around the front?" He could still see one or two pearls dangling, as if they were holding on for dear life.

Her lower lip trembled. Her eyes filled with tears.

Shocked, oddly horrified, Remy immediately dropped his hold on her hand. "Don't do that."

"What?" Jacqueline sniffed.

Cry. Do not cry. "Get all watery."

"What?" She swiped her hand over her cheek where—sure enough, she'd *teared up.* "Do you mean cry? Did you just tell me not to cry?"

"I did, yet you are." He snagged an ancient napkin from the middle of his table and stuffed it into her hand. "I would appreciate it if you would stop doing that." Because now his chest felt uncomfortably tight, and surely that was not a conscience trying to rear its head inside of him?

Usually, his conscience was dead quiet on most things. But, with her...

I don't like her tears.

"It's been an incredibly stressful forty-eight hours for me, okay? I can't help it." She dabbed at her eyes.

"Fuck." There was no choice. He was going to do this...

She peeked at him from beneath the napkin.

"I will give you a ride," Remy heard himself say.

She hurtled herself at him. Remy grunted at the impact because he had not been expecting her to hit him with the force of a mini tornado. For someone seemingly so delicate, she had a very strong grip.

"Thank you." A heartfelt sigh of gratitude. "You have saved my life."

His hands hovered in the air. Was he supposed to hug her in return? Give her a reassuring pat on the back?

Grab her tight and not let go?

Whoa. That last thought had come out of nowhere and was absolutely not the right response in this situation. So Remy went with option two. His left hand awkwardly patted her on the back. "There, there." That seemed appropriate enough. "Though, I hardly think a ride equals a life-saving deed."

Her head lifted. Tear drops clung to her long lashes. "It does to me."

Uh, huh. "Were you this grateful to the truck driver?"

She still held him. Still gazed up at Remy with her desperate gaze. "Even more so. He got me out of—" Jacqueline stopped. Didn't tell him exactly *what* she'd gotten out of, before adding, "So I paid him with the ring. I didn't want it, and he'd been so kind that it was the least I could do." She swallowed and seemed to finally realize that she was gripping Remy too tightly. That her body had pressed closely to his.

He could feel all her curves. Her lush breasts. Her warmth. He could—

She jerked back. "The ring was the only thing of value I had on me. I-I can't offer you anything else as payment." Her hands twisted in front of her.

"Sure, the ring was the only thing. Totally makes sense to me." He headed past her but paused long enough to reach out to capture her hand once again. Remy had discovered something rather odd. He liked touching her. His fingers threaded with hers as if it was the most natural act in the world. It wasn't. He wasn't normally big on touching. But, well, he needed to pull her along, didn't he? If he was being the big hero of the night, they should get moving.

Before whoever was chasing the lost bride came running in after her.

They were almost at the door—Rodney still hadn't glanced their way—when she suddenly dug in her bare heels. "Wait!"

Sighing, he swung his head toward her. "Wait for what?"

Jacqueline bit her lower lip. Released it. Bit it again. Didn't speak.

"Ahem." He gave an encouraging nod. "There something you need to say?"

"I'm not going to sleep with you in order to pay for a ride." The words were so low that he almost missed them.

Almost, but not quite, and laughter erupted from Remy.

Red flashed in her cheeks.

Because the laughter was ever so booming, it even caught Rodney's attention. He spun toward them. "Hey!" Rodney called. "What's going on over there?"

She shuddered and pushed close to Remy once more. He realized that her back was to Rodney, and Jacqueline had just positioned herself so that her face was tucked toward Remy's body. Other than seeing the white dress and dark hair, Rodney wouldn't be able to say much about the woman *if* he were to be questioned by someone later.

Remy rolled one shoulder in a shrug. "My lady came to get me tonight. Made a joke about me being late for our date." It was close to midnight, so, yeah, that had to count as late. "See you around, Rodney."

Grunting, Rodney focused on his screen once more.

Remy took a still-blushing Jacqueline outside. He unlocked the truck and hoisted her up into the high seat because the vehicle had some very big-ass tires. Big-ass everything, come to think of it.

Perched in the passenger seat, she looked down at him as the vehicle's interior light illuminated the scene. "I'm sorry if I assumed the wrong thing inside." Now she sounded miserable. "You're obviously a good guy—"

More laughter. Damn. She was cracking him up. Very unusual. He had some acquaintances who would swear he never laughed. "Watch the foot. Don't want those toes getting banged when I close the door."

Her foot whipped away from the door. He slammed it, and, whistling, made his way around the vehicle. But before he climbed inside...Remy paused to glance around the area. The road appeared deserted. No other vehicles. No people at all. The main street in Halfway seemed as deserted as always.

But appearances could be deceiving. Remy knew that. So he took a moment. Looked for anything out of the ordinary.

The night was still, tinted with a hint of a growing fall chill. The cold came faster in the mountains. You could always hear better in these quiet spaces. Sound could travel for miles and—

A growling engine. Coming closer. His head tilted as Remy tried to decide just what was approaching. Nodding, he opened his door. Jumped inside. "Did you marry him?"

Jacqueline stopped tugging on the seatbelt that she'd been positioning across her chest. "Excuse me?"

He sighed once more and hooked the belt for her.

"Thank you." A breath from Jacqueline as he leaned over her. The breath blew lightly over the shell of his ear, and once more, Remy felt a flood of awareness course through him. His head lifted, and he stared at her. The interior light had gone dark since he hadn't cranked the vehicle but had shut all the doors.

"Did you marry him?" Remy repeated. "Is that why he's chasing you? You said yes and then cut out on the bastard?"

"No."

"Good to know." He eased back into his seat. "You ran before the 'I do' part, huh?"

"I don't know why you think I was marrying..." Her words trailed off. "It was an engagement. Sort of."

How did one have a "sort of" engagement?

"Everything was a total mistake. I never wanted to marry him. You don't know what was involved."

Nope. He didn't know. They were strangers. He was just giving her a lift. Playing his hand at being a Good Samaritan. Trying to understand why some people enjoyed doing random good deeds. So far, the good deed bit seemed like a pain in the ass. "Most people don't run from an ex—at least, not as fast and as desperately as you seem to be running." His hand moved toward the ignition.

Her fingers touched his. "Most people don't have the trouble after them that I do."

When she touched him, his skin heated. A definite attraction burned between them. Or at least, it burned on his end. Did she feel it, too? He'd be finding out. "Where am I taking you?"

"I..." Jacqueline stopped.

Nothing.

He started the engine. "We've got a motorcycle heading this way. Probably want to be moving soon because something tells me the rider is searching for your sweet ass."

"*OhGod.*" She immediately started looking all around for a motorcycle.

"So...about that destination?" There had to be some sort of karmic gold stars coming his way for this night. But then, considering his past, he could probably do a million good deeds and never balance the scales.

And that is why sweet beauties like her shouldn't walk up to me in a bar and ask me for a ride...

"Please drive. *Please.* Like, drive super, super fast."

He reversed the vehicle. "Driving 'super, super fast' isn't safe on these narrow mountain roads." Someone should probably tell that to the motorcycle driver. "You don't have a destination in mind, do you?"

She peered through the passenger side window. "No."

"Didn't think so. There's a motel at the edge of Halfway. It looks like a hole in the wall, but it's got clean rooms, so don't be fooled by its exterior."

"He'll look there. I-I can't stay in a motel." Jacqueline swung toward him.

Oh, no. Nope. "Don't say it." He began driving. Slowly. "My newfound goodwill only goes so far."

"Do you…happen to have a spare room?"

She'd said it.

His hands tightened around the steering wheel. "Do you have any self-preservation instincts at all? Like, a single one?"

"Yes."

A fast slant her way showed that Jacqueline had lifted her chin.

"It's why I got away from him and why I'm with you now," she continued as a determined edge entered her husky voice.

He hated to shatter her illusions but… "Yeah, sweetness, for all you know, I could be a serial killer. One who has lured you into my ride. I could have fixed the locks so you can't get out, and now that you're trapped, I'll take you away to my home in the woods where you will never, ever be seen again."

Silence. The kind of stark, uncomfortable silence that told Remy he'd probably just scared his runaway bride nearly to death.

"I think I'd like to be let out," she stated, her voice incredibly polite. She also reached for the door. Grabbed the handle and yanked—

He laughed again. Shit. He probably shouldn't have laughed but… "I wouldn't tell you my plans in advance. That would make me a shitty killer."

"Oh, God. *Are you a killer?*"

Remy didn't plan to touch that one. "Not tonight, I'm not. Tonight, I'm playing the role of the hero. Uh, want to do me a favor and shut the door?" He could see the headlight from the motorcycle up ahead. It barreled straight toward them.

"Tell me you aren't going to kill me."

"I am not going to kill you." An easy enough statement to give. But he couldn't resist adding, "I only kill pretty would-be brides on Tuesdays, and, as you clearly know, today is—"

"Don't."

Okay. He should stop playing with her. "My name is Remy," he told her, tone deepening because there had been real fear shaking in her words. "I have no intention of hurting you. I actually have a younger sister, and if she showed up in the middle of the night, desperate and afraid, in a rundown bar, I would want someone to help her." Absolute truth. "You are safe with me." He had no intention of hurting the woman beside him.

Jacqueline shut the door.

"And, sweetness, if you don't mind, how about you put the screwdriver that you are clutching in your left hand—how about you put it *back* in the glove compartment? Don't want to be worrying that you're going to stab me with it while I'm driving."

Her hand moved, sliding from beneath the loose fabric of her dress. "How did you know I had it?"

A simple enough deduction. "Because you don't trust me. Smart not to since we just met. And it made sense that you'd want a weapon in case you needed to defend yourself. I knew the screwdriver was in the glove box, you had access to it…" He let his words trail off. "It would have been my move, too."

She hadn't put up the screwdriver.

He considered the matter as the motorcycle's headlight kept barreling closer. "You know what? If it makes you feel better, keep it."

"It does make me feel better."

The motorcycle light seemed brighter.

"Just promise not to stab me with it," Remy added as his eyes narrowed against the approaching glare.

"I promise." Soft.

"Good." But even if she tried to come at him, Remy had no doubt that he could disarm her. Not that he'd share that bit of info with her. If the screwdriver made her feel better, he'd let her have that moment of peace. "I'm thinking you should slide into the floorboard, at least until we pass our friend."

She unhooked the seatbelt and slid down with a whisper of her dress.

The motorcycle roared toward him and—

The sonofabitch driving it suddenly turned his bike into the middle of the road. Drove *into* Remy's path and braked with a squeal of his tires.

Remy had three choices.

He could drive around the dumbass, but that would just make the guy follow him.

He could hit the dumbass, but then there would be blood. And death. And he was trying to avoid that lifestyle. The whole murder scene really wasn't his gig.

Or three, he could stop.

He stopped.

"No, please," Jacqueline begged from her crouched position in the floorboard. "Don't—don't let him take me! I will do *anything* just—"

"Yeah, hold the thought." He rolled down his window with a press of a button. He also turned on his bright lights to blind the bastard. "Hey, asshole!" Remy shouted. "You've got ten seconds to get that piece-of-shit ride out of my way, or I'll be rolling over it and you!" There. He'd issued a fair warning.

The man kept straddling his bike. He wore a battered jacket and had a black helmet—with the face shield down—on his head. "I'm looking for someone," the guy shouted back.

"Like I give a shit. You have five seconds." Remy gunned his engine.

"Let me search your ride—"

"Fuck you!" Remy called back cheerfully. "Gonna be a shame to total that bike, but a man has to do what a man has to do!"

The motorcycle driver craned his head to peer into the truck. Remy turned on the interior lights to show that he was the only person in the cab of the vehicle. He also counted down, loudly, "Five, four, three, two..."

The motorcycle blasted away, zooming in the direction of Rodney's bar—and the motel that was a few blocks away from the bar. Nice. Exactly what Remy had thought the jerk would do. "Stay down a bit longer," he told his damsel in distress, "just in case." They only had a bit to go before their first series of turns. A few turns, and the SOB wouldn't be able to find them, not once they started snaking through the old roads that twisted through the mountains.

Remy rolled his window back up. Turned on his radio. And drove slowly back to his cabin.

Jacqueline stayed in the floorboard. Curled all in tightly around herself. Still clutching that screwdriver and that pissed him off. Jacqueline was well and truly afraid.

He began to sing along to the song on the radio, wanting to put her at ease, and he kept glancing back to make sure they weren't being followed. That was the thing about this particular cabin, unless you knew exactly where you were going—and you had a powerful ride with four-wheel drive to *get* you to the destination—you'd miss it. Especially in the dark.

He pulled into the twisting drive. Took the truck around to the back of the cabin in order to hide it and then… "Okay, it's time to get out."

She didn't move. Frowning, he leaned over her. "Jacqueline?"

Her head had tipped forward. Her hair fanned over her shoulders, and she was…

He touched her lightly. She didn't move—because she was out cold. Sonofabitch. She'd fallen asleep on him. Remy exited the ride and went around to her side. Carefully, he opened her door. Not like he wanted her spilling out onto the ground. When she slid back, he caught her in his arms. Hoisted her up against his chest.

"Wh-what…" A sleep-slurred whisper.

"Don't stab me with the screwdriver," he warned, but it was an unnecessary warning because he saw she'd dropped it. He snagged it, slid it into the back of his waistband, then focused on her. *Sleeping Beauty.* He lifted her up, cradled her against him, and carried her toward the cabin.

She felt good against him. Almost right which was freaking ridiculous. He was obviously spending way too much time alone in the mountains if this stranger felt *right* to him. No one had ever felt right. His life was a lie. Half the time, he was surrounded by criminals, and he should *not* be carrying this woman into his home.

But he was.

Into his home, up the stairs, and all the way into his bedroom. As he carried her, the light scent of vanilla cream teased him even as the loose fabric of her dress trailed down his arms. Whatever else his lost bride had been through, she still managed to smell absolutely delicious. A wondrous feat. She smelled delicious. She looked beautiful. And...

Innocent.

Too trusting.

Because when he put her down, Jacqueline just cuddled into the covers of his bed. Didn't even open her eyes again. Sure, she'd been running for forty-eight hours by her own account, so she had to be exhausted but...

He brushed back a lock of hair that had fallen over her brow. Remy straightened and left a small present on the nightstand. If his friends—and enemies—could see him now, they would probably be stunned. After all, Rembrandt "Remy" Stuart was hardly known for his good deeds.

This wasn't actually a good deed, though.

What he'd done...

He'd just stolen someone else's bride. Not a bad night's work for a thief. Smiling, he headed for the door. "Good night, sweetness."

Best thief ever.

CHAPTER TWO

A gunshot seemed to echo in her ears even as Jacqueline jerked awake. A gasp tore from her lips, and she grabbed for the—

The silk sheets around her? Yes, black silk sheets covered the enormous bed. A bed that did *not* belong to her.

Her breath sawed in and out even as the last vestiges of the nightmare left her. Jacqueline sat up, slowly, and took stock of her situation. She was still in the white dress. An exceedingly dirty dress because of her frantic run through the woods, but the white still stuck out in sharp contrast to the dark bedding. *His* bedding? The man from the bar. The stranger with the too-handsome-to-be-real features. Movie-star perfect in the middle of nowhere. Thick, lustrous hair that had tumbled over his forehead and a devil-may-care grin that had made her heart race even as she silently prayed...

Please, please help me.

And he had. Jacqueline slid her legs to the side of the bed and grimaced when she got a look at her feet. She'd gotten his bed all dirty and felt bad about that. Though she tried to pull up the memory, she didn't even recall coming into the bedroom. But they must have walked in there together after they'd arrived...*Wait, where am I?*

Her gaze darted around. Gleaming, wooden walls. Big windows that were covered by rather sheer curtains. Heavy furniture. No pictures. No real hint of softness in the room except for those curtains and...

Her eyes fell on the screwdriver that rested on the nightstand. Jacqueline vaguely remembered clutching tightly to that screwdriver and crouching in the floorboard of Remy's truck. She'd been utterly terrified because he'd stopped the truck, and someone had been in front of them. She'd feared Remy would turn her over to the guy. After all, why *wouldn't* Remy give her up? Not like he knew her. Not like he understood why she was running. For all he knew, she was some sort of terrible criminal who was being hunted for her crimes.

But Remy hadn't betrayed her. He'd gotten her out of there.

And she couldn't really remember much else. Once more, she surveyed her surroundings. She spied a bathroom and scampered inside. Surely, he wouldn't mind if she borrowed his toothpaste, would he? After she washed her hands, she put a bit of toothpaste on the tip of one finger to clean off her teeth and when she was done...

Jacqueline couldn't help it. She used more of his soap and one of his white, fluffy towels to clean off her mud-covered feet. She was still stuck in the mud-spattered and torn dress, but she was better. Definitely better. Squaring her shoulders, she exited the bathroom. Then the bedroom. A few moments later, she found herself standing at the top of the stairs, and again, she had zero memory of climbing those stairs. Her hand curled around the banister as she began to tentatively creep down the steps. "Remy?"

No answer, but she could hear something. Sounded like...pounding? Vibrations? Her steps were a little faster as she hurried down and, as she descended, the pounding grew stronger. When she reached the bottom of the stairs, she didn't turn toward the den and its truly massive fireplace. Instead, Jacqueline spun for the right. She followed the pounding that was starting to almost feel like a throb that vibrated through the cabin. She slipped through a kitchen. Went past high-end appliances and, as she drew closer to the source of the sound, Jacqueline realized that she was following the hard, pounding beat of rock music.

The trail led her to a closed, red door. Her hand lifted, and her knuckles knocked lightly against the door. "Um, Remy?"

Nothing.

She knocked again. A little harder and louder. "Remy?" She needed to talk to him. To come up with some sort of plan. To see if maybe— hopefully, magically—he had a pair of women's shoes somewhere in the cabin that she could borrow.

But he didn't answer her.

Her fingers curled around the doorknob. When she twisted, Jacqueline realized it was unlocked. She opened the door a few inches so she could peek inside. "Remy?" Even louder. "Remy, are you—"

Naked from the waist up. Showing off a truly fabulous chest and rippling abs as the music blared around him. Specks of what appeared to be black and green paint dotted his powerful arms, and he gripped a long paint brush in one hand as he stared with complete and total focus down at the canvas in front of him.

She stepped forward, and the floor beneath her gave a long creak. The sound could not have been louder than her knocks at the door or her calls of his name, but for some reason, that creak had his head snapping up, and his dark, deep chocolate eyes locked on her.

All the moisture seemed to leave her mouth.

She had been desperate the night before. So very afraid. She'd been aware of the fact that he was ridiculously handsome, but in the light of day, Jacqueline had thought that maybe she'd imagined some of that perfection. By the time she'd seen him in the bar, adrenaline had been the only thing keeping her going.

Nope. Did not imagine how hot he is. Remy was absolutely gorgeous. Probably not what she should be focusing on considering the nightmare of her life but...

He was.

"Ah." Remy smiled and flashed his perfectly straight, white teeth at her. "You and your screwdriver are inseparable again. Nice to see that some things haven't changed."

Jacqueline looked down and was vaguely surprised to see that she gripped the screwdriver in her left hand.

"You're not here to try and do wicked harm to me, are you?" He didn't seem particularly concerned as he put his paintbrush in a white cup. He stepped away from the table and the canvas and strolled toward her. On his stroll, he paused to turn off the music.

The silence that followed felt deafening.

Too good-looking. Too muscled. Her head shook in a *no* motion because she needed to respond to him. It certainly wouldn't be good form to attack her hero. Jacqueline slapped the screwdriver down on a nearby shelf. "J-just bringing it back to you." Because it was his. The whole place was his. Her gaze whipped around, and she realized that she was standing in an art studio. Canvases were everywhere. They peeked from beneath heavy cloths that had been draped on top of them. The room smelled of paint, and she could see dozens of paint tubes and containers on other shelves. The sunlight poured through the floor-to-ceiling windows on the right, sending in what had to be incredible light for an artist. And that was clearly what the man stalking toward her was. An artist.

He stopped about a foot away. Crossed his arms over his powerful chest. His paint-spattered jeans hung low on his hips. "You have adorable feet."

Her head snapped down to look at her ever-so-average feet.

"Not that I have a foot fetish or anything."

Her head whipped right back up.

"But it was hard to tell much about them last night since you'd been running barefoot through the woods and they were covered in mud."

Yes. About that run... "I'm not a criminal."

"Um, did I ask if you were?" He sent her another smile. This one seemed oddly gentle. He also uncrossed his arms and brushed past her as he made his way to the door she'd left open.

She hadn't been able to see what he was painting. The canvas had faced him, not her. Curiosity had her edging toward one of the covered canvases nearby, and her fingers curled around the fabric as she prepared to take a peek at his work.

"Hardly worth a look," Remy dismissed without glancing back. "How about breakfast?"

Her stomach growled to remind her that other than the two candy bars she'd gotten from the truck driver, Jacqueline had not eaten much in a very long time. "I...thank you. Breakfast would be wonderful." She let the cover fall as she followed him.

"How very polite you are." Mocking amusement filled his voice. Remy's voice was like the rest of him—beautiful. Deep and rich, and it seemed to warm her from within, even if he was mocking her.

"I figure polite is the least I can be," she replied when he stopped in front of some sort of extra gleaming coffee maker that looked as if it might have cost more than her first car. "Seeing as how I forced myself into your home."

After pressing a few buttons, he turned away from the machine and rested his hip against the counter. "Hardly forced. In fact, I'm pretty sure I carried you in."

Jacqueline stiffened. "Excuse me?" She had no memory of him carrying her. Zero.

"There you go, being all polite again." He winked at her. "For shits and giggles, why don't you try saying, 'Remy, what the hell do you mean?' I bet you'll like that better. It will roll off the tongue easier."

She could only shake her head. "You carried me inside?" She wanted to get back to that part of the conversation.

"Yes, I did because I am ever so gallant. And strong. Ask anyone. They'll say that Remy—he is *the* best." A pause as his gaze raked over her. "You know, I do come with references. Impeccable ones, I assure you. If you're suddenly terrified because you woke up in my bed and you're wondering if you're safe, I can let you talk to a few people who will vouch for me."

"I was in your bed?" She'd suspected as much, but the confirmation made her stomach do a funny dip. Jacqueline took a tentative step forward. "You carried me inside and put me in your bed?"

"And when you were snuggled up like the sweet angel you are, I promise all I did was brush back a lock of your hair. Thought I saw another leaf." A shrug. "I can assure you, it was an imminently boring night for everyone concerned. Your virtue was completely safe."

Excellent to know. But... "Having a complete stranger approach you in a bar and beg to stay with you is boring?" If that was the case, she had to ask, "What are your normal nights like?"

His lips twitched. "Best to not go into that part right now." The machine was already brewing and hissing behind him.

Her stomach growled again. "I am so sorry."

"For what? And again, don't waste manners with me. How about saying, 'Could you hurry up and fix me some fucking food? I'm starving.' Try that." He ambled toward the stove. "Let's start with eggs. Scrambled, fried, over easy…?"

"Scrambled, please."

Remy paused. Looked back over at her. "A good girl to your core, hmmm?"

What was so wrong with being polite? "I owe you, and I don't have any way to repay you." Humiliating to admit, but she couldn't lie.

"So wrong. But we'll get to that. You look pale so you eat first, then we can talk about our arrangement." He cracked some eggs. Went to work. Pointed to her with a utensil. "If anyone asks, this never happened."

The eggs smelled like heaven. Her toes curled against the floor. "Who would ask? Aren't we the only ones here?"

"Yes, but for future reference, I have a rep, and my rep does not involve me cooking breakfast on demand for strangers, no matter how gorgeous said strangers may be."

Remy thought she was gorgeous? No way. She had to look like warm hell. No, correction, she *did* look like that. Jacqueline had caught sight of her reflection in his bathroom mirror, and even though she'd tried to finger comb her hair a wee bit, she was as far from runway ready as a person could be.

But...he'd called her gorgeous. And he was cooking her breakfast. She did not know what to make of this man. *A real-life hero.*

Moments later, she was seated at his table, eating eggs that were the lightest and fluffiest eggs in the entire world and sipping the best coffee she'd ever tasted. "Heaven."

"I'd try again on that one."

Her gaze darted toward him.

He smiled as he sat in the seat across from her. Sipped his coffee. He hadn't pressured her yet for details about how she'd come to appear in that bar last night. Remy had just let her eat. Been a warm, reassuring presence. And he'd even tugged on a t-shirt. One that stretched across him because it was too tight. Or because his muscles were too big. Something. She should probably not be noticing his muscles or how toe-curling that smile of his was. Not in light of her current circumstances. But she did.

Oh, she did.

Jacqueline put down her fork. "I should get ready to leave."

"Um." Another sip of his coffee.

"I don't suppose you have a...girlfriend who might have left some clothes around here? Things I could borrow? Shoes?" Shoes would be amazing.

"No girlfriend."

Her breath released. Holy crap, had that just been a *sigh* of relief that escaped her?

"But there are some clothes that would probably work for you. The previous occupant just boxed up stuff and left it. I was gonna donate it but didn't get around to it. Not yet. I think there are some sweatpants and tops upstairs." His gaze seemed to twinkle. "Maybe you'll get lucky and find some shoes."

"I don't tend to get very lucky." Such a true statement. "My luck is more the opposite." The worst ever. Case in point? Her mad escape from New Orleans all the way to Halfway, Georgia. A rush that had included taking nothing but the clothes on her back and the ring that had been shoved on her finger.

But she'd ditched that ring. Now she could start again. It wouldn't be the first time she'd started over from scratch. Perhaps it would even be the *last* time. But before she could begin that new life plan, she had to make sure the people following her lost her trail. "Bad luck follows me," she murmured. *Just like that creep last night.*

"Hmm." Very noncommittal. Remy sipped again.

She felt twitchy. "I know I've already asked for a ton, but after I search for the clothes, could you...is there any way I could get a ride to..."

He lifted his brows. Waited.

Jacqueline dropped her stare to the table.

"Where do you need to go, Jacqueline?"

"You can call me Jackie. Lots of people do."

"Where do you need to go, Jacqueline?" Remy repeated.

Okay, obviously, he was not lots of people. She cleared her throat. "I don't technically have a place in mind. A destination, I mean." Not yet.

When you were running blindly, you didn't plan. You fled.

"Uh, huh." Another sip. How much coffee was left in his mug? "So you don't have a place to go...and I noticed you didn't exactly have a purse or wallet on you."

No.

"Do you have access to a bank account?"

If she accessed her account, *he* would find her. Or his goons would. She had to go off-grid and stay there for a while.

"Do you need money, Jacqueline?"

Again with that sexy rumble. When he said her full name, her stomach clenched. Odd because she'd always hated her name. So formal. Stuffy. But Remy made it sound sensual. Beautiful. Jacqueline pushed a lock of hair behind her ear. "I'm not taking money from you."

"Last night, you said if I got you away from the bastard on the bike, you'd do *anything* to repay me."

Her stomach didn't just clench. It dropped. She also leapt to her feet and her fast movement sent her chair slamming down onto the floor behind her. It hit and sounded like a whip cracking. "I'm not sleeping—" Jacqueline began hotly.

His soft laughter cut through her words. "You are obsessed with that. I told you before, not on my agenda. I don't routinely pay women for sex." A wink. "I don't have to do that."

Right. Sure. Now she could feel the burn in her cheeks. No way would Remy be paying for sex. Not a guy who oozed hotness and sex appeal the way he did. She needed to calm down and be grateful to the man who had literally been her hero the night before. "I'm sorry, I misunderstood, I didn't—"

"Ever done any nude modeling?"

Her jaw hung open.

"I'll take that as a no."

It was a no. Her mouth snapped closed.

"Are you *interested* in doing some nude modeling?"

She backed away. Forget the clothes, she should probably make another fast getaway.

"I'll also take that as a no," he said. "Pity. I bet your body is perfection beneath that hideous dress. By the way, tell me you didn't pick it out."

Jacqueline kept inching back. "Look, if you have some kind of fetish, I am not your girl."

Remy didn't rise from his seat. He did put down his coffee mug and lock his dark and intense gaze on her. "You are most definitely mine."

Goose bumps rose on her arms.

"My muse," he continued carefully. "I'm sure you noticed that I'm an artist."

"Hard to miss all the paint." And canvases.

"I'd been going through a bit of a dry spell, then you fell into my life. So to speak." His words were so easy and casual, an exact match for his expression, but Jacqueline could have sworn that a thread of tension hummed beneath that light surface. "I saw you and felt inspired."

"I'm not sure what that means." She'd inched so far away that her back hit the counter.

"You don't need to be afraid of me." He rose but didn't approach her. Just stood there, all towering and tall. Remy had to clock in at a few inches over six feet, and he was solid muscle. She knew, she wouldn't be forgetting the sight of his bare chest anytime soon. "Hurting women isn't a hobby I have."

"That shouldn't be a hobby anyone has."

"Agreed." His head dipped toward her. "I want to paint you, Jacqueline."

For clarification, she noted, "You want to paint me...naked."

"Nude." His lips twitched. "And, yes, that would be nice, but since you seem a bit...prudish...about the situation, feel free to keep your clothes on for the process."

Her chin jerked up. "It's not prudish to be uncomfortable getting naked in front of a stranger. That's totally normal behavior."

His broad shoulders rolled back. "If you say so, but I've never had a problem getting naked."

Of course, he hadn't. "Who are you?"

"Told you my name before. It's Remy."

Yes, she knew that. What Jacqueline had meant was—

"Part-time artist. Part-time hero. At your service."

He kept disarming her. "Remy," she tasted his name and liked it. She'd actually known a Remy or two in her day. "Are you, by any chance, from New Orleans?" She probably shouldn't have asked but... "Popular name there," she added quickly. "You know, because it has a French origin and so many people in New Orleans are..." She stopped.

His brows wiggled. "You're an expert on names?"

"No. I remember random facts. I-I read that some place. I do a lot of reading."

"Do you now?"

Hadn't she just said as much? Besides, she owned a small bookstore. Reading went with the territory. As long as she could remember, she'd always loved escaping into books.

"Not from New Orleans," Remy added as he continued to stand by the table. "Remy is a nickname."

Okay. "So you won't call me Jackie, but I'm supposed to use your nickname?" Hardly seemed fair.

"No one calls me by my full name."

Curiosity pulsed inside of her. "And that full name would be what?"

He took a few steps toward her. "Rembrandt."

She blinked. "Like the artist?"

His jaw tightened. "Just call me Remy."

But he wasn't Remy. He was Rembrandt. And he was an artist just like his namesake. An artist who wanted to paint her.

He stopped right in front of Jacqueline, and she could have sworn that the heat from his body slipped out to wrap around her. "You're clearly running from something."

More like from someone. "What gives you that idea?"

His hand lifted, and he brushed back a lock of her hair. The same lock she'd tucked behind her ear moments ago. The dang thing had slipped forward once more. When his hand drew close to her face, she stiffened. A move Jacqueline couldn't help. She stiffened. Maybe even flinched.

His jaw locked. "Who hurt you?"

"I haven't been hurt." *Yet.* That would be why she was running. "I just wanted to start over." She would miss her old life. She'd worked so hard to get it.

A faint line appeared between his brows. "You wanted to run away in your wedding dress—"

"*Not* a wedding dress. It was just a white dress, okay? And I didn't know the engagement party was going to happen. That was sprung on me. Before I understood what was happening, the ring was on my finger, everyone was clapping and..." And she needed to stop talking about this. "It wasn't going to happen. There was never going to be any marriage."

"Because you didn't love the groom?"

Dammit. "Because he utterly terrifies me. Happy?"

"Not in the least." Anger seemed to churn in his voice. "I don't want you terrified."

Remy didn't even *know* her. "If it makes you feel better, I don't particularly like to be terrified. I think most people feel the same way."

A muscle jerked again along his jaw. "I have a deal for you."

"A deal? I was sort of hoping for a ride."

"A ride to a destination that you haven't even decided yet. Doesn't sound like the best plan to me." His gaze pinned hers. "We've now established that you were running *from* someone. I'm offering you protection."

This couldn't be happening. She opened her mouth to tell him that very thing, only to hear the loud, echoing ring of a bell. A doorbell.

"Company," Remy murmured. He didn't look away from her. "What are the odds that our early-morning visitor is here for you?"

She lunged toward him. "Please, do *not* turn me over!" Her hands curled over his arms.

"As far as I know, you're running from a man who terrifies you."

The doorbell rang again. Yes, she was running from a man who utterly terrified her.

"Maybe we should talk about our deal a bit more," Remy added.

"What's the deal?" Frantic, she looked toward the den. And the door that was just beyond that den.

"You be my muse—my model. Don't worry, you can keep your clothes on. If that's what you want."

Her grip tightened on him. "Remy..."

"I'll give you room and board in exchange for you being my model, and, depending on how long I need your services, we can also work out an hourly pay scale. But you must know, I'm demanding."

The doorbell chimed again.

"I'm also a bit of a bastard," he continued, not seeming to be bothered at all by the chiming bell that grated on her nerves. "I keep odd hours. I don't take breaks, and I will expect you to hold the same pose for extended periods of time."

"You won't turn me over?" To whoever was at the door. To whoever had been sent after her.

"Not if we have a deal."

The doorbell seemed to be ringing constantly now. "Yes! Yes! Please, just—don't let him know

I'm here. Say you've never met me. Just...help?" A plea.

Remy nodded. "Why don't you go back up to the bedroom? I'll handle our visitor. While I'm dealing with him, check the closet up there. You should find some clothes in the brown trunk."

She didn't let go of him. The bell echoed around them.

Remy's lips thinned. "Our visitor is quite persistent. And obviously, a total asshole. Good thing I know how to handle his type."

"Promise you won't turn me over?" A breath. A whisper.

He leaned toward her. His mouth moved to her ear. "I promise." A whisper in response. His breath teased the shell of her ear.

A shiver slid over Jacqueline. "Then we have a deal." Her head turned and, because they were so close, when her head turned, their mouths were almost touching. It would take no effort at all to brush her lips against his...

The doorbell chimed again.

She jerked back.

Remy sighed. "Perhaps we shall revisit that little near development later, hmm? But for now..." He marched for the den. "I have an asshole to send on his merry way."

CHAPTER THREE

Remy waited until he no longer heard the sound of Jacqueline scurrying up the stairs, and when he was sure she'd safely made it to the second floor, he glanced through the small peephole in the door. He also made a mental note to install one of those doorbell security cameras, ASAP. He hadn't exactly been planning to stay in the cabin long term, so he hadn't taken many security precautions. With Jacqueline's arrival, things needed to change.

A man in a cheap brown suit glared at Remy through the peephole. The man's hair had been buzzed, and he wore black-framed glasses. He was also reaching out to ring the bell yet again.

Remy swung open the door. "Morning, sunshine."

The man froze with his hand extended.

"Want to tell me who the hell you are and why you're on my doorstep at..." He looked at his wrist. No watch. "Helluva-early-thirty?"

The man jerked his hand down, only to shove it toward his coat.

Remy stiffened, anticipating an attack, but the guy just shoved up a wallet. No, an ID.

"FBI," the man said as he jutted out his slightly pointed chin. "Special Agent Tim Palmer."

Remy took the ID. Studied it. "Wow. A real, live FBI agent. I've got goose bumps."

"What took you so long to answer the door?"

"Took me so long?" He looked up. Furrowed his brow. "How long were you ringing the bell?"

Tim's lips tightened.

"Sorry." Remy wasn't. Not even a little bit. "I was working in the back. Painting." He had the flecks of paint on him to prove it. "When I work, I tend to turn my music way up. Didn't realize you were even out here until I took a break to grab some coffee." He smiled his most innocent grin. "Something I can do for you?" Then he whistled. "The FBI. Man, must be something to work for them. Are you like, a real badass?"

"Yeah, I'm a badass." Tim poked his ID back in the coat.

I don't think you are, my friend.

"I'm looking for a wanted fugitive," Tim announced as he jutted his chin up a little more.

"Is there any other kind?" Remy wanted to know, genuinely curious.

"Excuse me?" Tim's brow furrowed.

"A fugitive," he explained easily. "Aren't they all wanted? Doesn't that go along with being a fugitive?"

Anger tightened Tim's features.

"I'll take that as a yes." Remy nodded. He also rocked back on his heels and casually took in every part of the man's appearance. Cheap brown coat and pants. Too tight dress shirt. Tennis shoes.

Tim attempted to peer around Remy. Remy moved his body to make sure that just wouldn't happen. "I'm happy to inform you that there is no fugitive in my home."

"I'd like to search the premises."

Remy laughed. "Yeah, that's not happening. My artwork is everywhere, and I'm not letting you prance around inside and potentially damage my masterpieces. You're just gonna have to take my word for it—no fugitive is hiding inside." Conspiratorially, Remy couldn't resist adding, "I think I would have noticed him."

"Her."

"What?" Remy scratched his chin.

"I'm looking for a woman. About five-foot-six, one hundred thirty-five pounds. Dark hair. Green eyes." He reached into his coat once more, and this time, he hauled out a picture of Jacqueline. A picture that showed her from a bit of a distance, as if the photo had been taken without her knowledge.

The plot thickens. Remy let loose a low whistle of appreciation. "I would know if a woman like her was in my cabin."

"She's dangerous."

And it thickens even more. "No? That little thing?" He laughed. "What'd she do?" He would really, really like to know.

"Let me search your place."

Remy arched one eyebrow. Someone was being very adamant. Time to up his game. "Let me see your warrant, and maybe that will happen."

Tim glared at him. "What do you have to hide?"

Everything. "Oh, you know, the usual."

"Is she inside—"

"Look, I don't have any fugitive in my cabin. Not like I tucked the woman in my bed or something and then scrambled her some delicious eggs for breakfast. I mean, seriously, is that what you think is happening here? That I've snuck some dangerous predator in my cabin and I'm now treating her like a queen?"

"You think this is a fucking joke?" Tim's features had reddened. More of a reddish purple, technically. Very unhealthy looking.

Remy considered the question. "I don't find myself laughing so I guess it's not a joke."

Tim surged toward him. "I know you took her away from that bar."

Remy didn't even blink. "What bar?" He also didn't back down. No way was Tim getting inside.

"Last night, you were at the bar in town. I talked to the bartender—"

"You mean the owner, Rodney?" Remy supplied in what he thought was a helpful manner. "FYI, Rodney is actually the bartender and owner."

"You *left* with a brunette. Where is she?"

"She went back to Atlanta. Headed out at sunrise."

The reddish-purple blotches spread for Tim.

"Look, you have this all wrong. I left with my girlfriend." Tim still gripped the picture, so Remy pretended to focus on it. "I guess her hair is kind of similar to my girl's. My lady met me at Rodney's like she always does. We came back here. Had fantastic sex for a few hours, then she returned to Atlanta."

Tim's mouth opened and closed.

"Did Rodney *tell* you I left with the woman in the picture?" Remy shook his head. "Why would he lie about that? His brother is the sheriff. Rodney should know better than to make up stories."

Tim took a quick step back. "He didn't actually say it was her. He didn't see her face." He tucked the picture back into his coat. That coat of his sure did seem to have lots of pockets. "Sorry to disturb you. Obviously, there was a communication mistake."

"Obviously." And obviously, Tim had quickly changed his tune as soon as Remy had mentioned the local sheriff. Not at all suspicious. "You have a good day now, special agent." A shark-like smile. "Oh, and don't come back to my door again anytime soon." A hard order. "I've got work to do, and I don't have time to waste."

Tim's features twisted with anger.

Remy slammed the door shut on him. Then he locked it and glanced up the stairs. He could all but feel Jacqueline. No way had she gone into the bedroom. Odds were high that she'd just ducked behind the railing on the second floor. Since he'd left the door open the entire time, he was sure she'd overheard his whole conversation.

Once more, he turned and fired a quick glance through the peep hole. Tim had stalked away. Remy had the feeling he'd be seeing that guy again, despite his request for the man to stay away, but for the moment... "The coast is clear." Wasn't that the fun expression that people liked to use? "My dear fugitive..." Remy called as he made his way to the stairs and climbed up a few steps. "You can come out now."

She appeared at the top of the stairs. *Still* wearing that dreadful dress. When she finally ditched it, he might just have to burn the thing.

"He's lying," Jacqueline announced.

Remy kept climbing up the stairs. His hand trailed along the smooth surface of the wooden banister. "Are you suggesting that an FBI agent would lie?" Mild. Curious.

Her hands fisted at her sides. When he reached the landing, she stepped back. He'd noticed she did that quite a bit. Retreated. She didn't trust him. Wise. He wasn't overly trustworthy, but her retreat still had a faint frown pulling at his brows.

"I'm not dangerous," she said, voice thick. "I swear, I'm not."

He nodded.

She stared expectantly at him. The green in her eyes seemed to burn a little brighter. As she kept staring at him, Remy wondered if he was supposed to give her the same reassurance. Was she waiting for him to say he wasn't dangerous, too? He usually lied as easily as he breathed but lying to her just then felt wrong. So he compromised and said, "I'm not dangerous to you." There. Safe enough.

She blinked. "You...what?"

"You really need to get out of that dress." He leaned toward her. Inhaled. "*You* smell like vanilla, but it smells...poorly."

Jacqueline gasped. "Did you just tell me I stink?"

"No, I said your dress smells poorly." And he'd only said that to distract her because fear had been gleaming in her eyes, and he did not like her fear. "Thought you were going to change. And maybe shower. Showering is good."

Her lips tightened. "I couldn't. I had to make sure you were not going to turn me over to him!"

As if that had ever been an option. "Who was he?"

"He...he said he was...I heard him tell you he was a special agent with the FBI."

"Yes, but that was a lie, so I thought you might know the truth." He turned away from her and strolled toward his bedroom.

He heard the rush of her steps as she gave chase. "How do you know it was a lie?"

Because I've worked with plenty of Feds. Because I've even been a Fed. Sort of. But it didn't seem like the moment to go into all those details—and he'd never been big on sharing anyway—so Remy kept striding forward. He went through his bedroom and into the bathroom. Total luxury. The shower would easily have been big enough for two. Though he suspected she was not at the sharing-a-shower point with him just yet. Pity. He still turned on the water for her.

"What are you doing? Remy?"

"Getting your shower ready." He was being *nice* again. More karma points must definitely be heading his way. "You'll feel better after you shower and, while you're in there, that will give me a chance to burn your dress—I mean, get rid of it." He turned back toward her. "You have to take it off first, though."

She clutched the damaged dress as if it had been made of gold. "I'm not stripping in front of you."

A long-suffering sigh escaped him. "Fine. I'll just go outside and stand in the bedroom. You toss the dress to me, and I'll have other clothes waiting when you're done. Happy?"

Her delicate nostrils flared.

He supposed that meant she wasn't happy. Some people were hard to please. Remy brushed by her on his way out.

Jacqueline's hand flew out and caught his. "How did you know he was lying?"

"Because I've seen real IDs that belong to FBI agents. I know a fake when I spot one." He also knew FBI dress protocol. Everything about the man—and the profuse way he'd started to sweat at the mention of the sheriff—had screamed that he was shady.

Her eyes widened. "Are you serious?"

"One hundred percent." Her fingers were sliding lightly along his wrist, and he was liking her touch way too much.

"I'm not dangerous," she said again as she slowly released him.

His hand slid under her chin. The water was pounding, and steam filled the room. He tipped back her head. Lowered his mouth toward hers. "I wouldn't care if you were."

"Remy?"

He wanted her mouth. But he wanted *her* to make that move. The move that brought them together. Because there was something about her eyes...and the way she retreated...*Fear*. "Enjoy your shower." He eased away. Headed for the door. Had almost exited when he remembered. "Oh, yeah, there is plenty of soap under the sink if you need—" Remy spun around as he talked.

She'd already yanked the dress over her head and dropped it to the floor. She still had on white panties. A white bra. Her back was turned to him, and his gaze locked on her.

Or rather, his gaze locked on the dark bruises around her shoulders. Bruises that looked like fingerprints. "What. The. Fuck?" A snarl that broke from him.

Jacqueline instantly whirled around. Gasped. She bent and grabbed for the dress.

"Fuck the dress." He yanked it from her. "Who the hell put those bruises on you?"

"I-I fell when I was running through the woods—"

"Lie." His own hands had fisted around the fabric of that shitty dress. A rage burned through him, dark and hot. "I know fingerprints when I see them. Someone grabbed you, hard. Tell me the bastard's name, and he's done."

"Wh-what?"

Get your control back, now. "No one will be putting bruises on you again. That's a guarantee."

Her wide eyes searched his. "You don't even know me."

"Yes, I do." A truth that burned just as hot as his rage. "You're mine."

Her lips parted.

"My muse," he added grimly. "And no one hurts you. No one."

"Remy..."

"Who was it?" *Give me the name, and he is a dead man. I will make him beg before I end the bastard. Just a name. Tell me.*

"I need to shower. Let me shower, and then…"

Oh, *now* she wanted to shower. He'd had to practically trick her into the bathroom, and now she was trying to kick him out. His eyes narrowed on her.

"I'll be your muse," she whispered. "I want our deal to work. I want to stay here with you."

He jerked his head in agreement. "Fine. Shower. Be my muse. And *then* you'll tell me what I need to know." He did an about-face and headed for the door.

"Is it…is it because of the man who came to the door? Because of what he said? Do you think that I'm a fugitive? Is that why you have questions now? Remy, answer me!"

"It's because some bastard put his hands on you and left bruises. That won't happen again." He stalked out. Dragged the door shut behind him. Sucked in one deep breath. A second. The rage still blasted through his veins.

Someone had gripped her hard enough to leave bruises. And she'd run away because she'd been terrified. Run off into the middle of the night and now some fake FBI agent was searching for her.

If Jacqueline hadn't found him in the bar last night, if Remy hadn't taken her out of there, what would have happened?

And what would happen when the people searching for her finally *did* find her?

No one hurts my muse.

Breath heaving, he made his way out of the bedroom and double-timed it down the stairs. When he reached the first floor, he grabbed the phone he'd left on a table and dialed a man that he damn well knew he could count on. Unlike Remy, his contact was one of those true-blue assholes who always did the right thing.

Eric Wilde answered the phone on the second ring. "This is Eric."

Yes, Remy had the personal number for one of the richest men in the US. Big deal. He'd done a few side jobs for Eric Wilde over the years, and the man who owned *the* most elite protection and security firm in the whole freaking world just happened to be stored on his contact list. "It's Remy." That was all he said. Eric wouldn't have his number stored because Remy switched phones as often as he switched identities.

And sometimes, he did that one hell of a lot.

Silence greeted his announcement. Then, "What's the trouble?"

"That's what I need you to find out." Keeping his voice low, Remy glanced toward the second level of the cabin. "Just got paid a visit by a Fed."

"So? You get lots of those visits."

"Not the real deal this time. I had a fake Fed on my doorstep."

"Okay, now you have my attention."

"Don't I always?" His hold tightened on the phone. "He was looking for a woman who he claimed was a fugitive."

Silence. After a bit, "Why is she wanted?"

How very like Eric to cut to the chase. Remy could almost imagine the man stalking around his high-rise office and peering out at the city below. "If I knew that, then I wouldn't be seeking the services of Wilde now, would I?"

A quick inhale. "Are you calling to *hire* me?"

What the hell else would he be doing? Calling to talk about the freaking weather? "I need you to do a quick and dirty background search on a woman for me. Her name is Jacqueline. Find out everything you can about her."

Eric cleared his throat. "My Wilde team isn't exactly known for being quick and dirty."

"Nah. You're more overpriced and fancy. Got it. Noted."

"*Remy...*"

"I need the intel ASAP. I don't want this getting out, understand? So put someone you absolutely trust on this case, and I'll pay you double." Wait. What the hell had he just said? But, he meant it. He'd pay whatever was necessary in order to get the information he needed. *Bruises on her soft skin...*

Remy could practically feel Eric's surprise even before the guy slowly replied, "She must be quite important to you."

"No, she doesn't matter at all." The words sounded hollow. He felt hollow saying them. What. The. Hell? He'd met the woman yesterday. "I think someone hurt her, and I want the bastard's name." *So I can end him. Slowly. Painfully.*

"And when you get that name? Will you be going to the cops?"

"Ah, Eric..." He kept the phone to his ear as he made his way to the art studio. "You know me. I like to handle things with my own two hands." He pulled out his sketch pad. Snapped a pic. "Sending you her image now." He sent the text.

"That's...a sketch," Eric informed him after a beat of time.

"Damn, man. You are astute." His gaze had locked on the sketch. Just a charcoal work. He'd like to do her in—

"Why are you sending me a sketch instead of an actual picture of the woman?" Eric grumbled. "Do you know how hard tracking her down is going to be based on just a sketch and a first name? Tell me you have her last name, at least. I'm good, but I'm not exactly a miracle worker over here."

Remy closed the sketch pad. "I thought you liked a challenge. My mistake. If it helps, start the search in New Orleans. Does that narrow things down for you?"

"Remy..."

"And her last name is Peters."

"Why not just tell me that to begin with? Now I can work faster. Thanks so much."

Remy ignored the sarcasm. "There's a chance I could need backup. I'll send you my current address. I strongly suspect the fake Fed might make another appearance soon." *Despite the fact that I told him to keep his ass away.* "I plan to stick close to Jacqueline, but if he comes back with a team, I need someone on my six."

"Oh, so you can't just magically take down a whole team on your own? So disappointed. Your skills are slipping."

Remy considered the situation. He was glad Eric had said something. "You know what? You're probably right. Scratch the backup. I can handle these jerks in my sleep." He ambled through the cabin and back to the base of the stairs. Looked up. "The chitchat has been fun, but I've got a dress to go and burn."

"*What?*"

"Not like she has a lot of other clothing options, unfortunately. She had to cut out of New Orleans in a hurry."

"Back up, man. Did you say you were burning a dress?"

That was the plan. A bonfire at the earliest opportunity. "Kiss that beautiful wife of yours for me, will you?"

"Forget my wife—"

Smiling at the snarl of anger from Eric, Remy hung up.

***

"Sonofabitch," Eric growled as he glared at the phone in his hand—and the sketch of the woman that now filled his screen.

"What's wrong?" Piper asked as she appeared in his study's doorway.

At her voice, he looked up. He wasn't at the Wilde office today. He'd been at home, intending to enjoy some quality time with his family. Then, of course, Remy had called. *Kiss that beautiful wife of yours for me, my ass.*

"Got a last-minute client," he told Piper. The sketch he had was incredibly detailed, probably better than any photo would ever be, but that was Remy for you. The man had mad artistic skills, and he generally chose to use those skills in illegal endeavors.

Or, he *had*. But Remy was supposed to be turning over a new leaf.

A frown pulled at Piper's brows. "You seem worried."

He was. When Remy was involved, Eric worried. But in this instance, he knew exactly who to put on the case. He could get a tech agent to trace down the woman's background info and, as far as having someone on Remy's six... "I have it handled."

Piper crossed to his side, moving with grace even as she put a hand to her rounded belly. Almost at the seven-month mark.

"God, you are beautiful," he said, momentarily forgetting Remy.

"I'm waddling like a drunk duck. I lost my ankles weeks ago, and you're an insane man." She cupped his chin. Leaned up and kissed him. "But I love you."

He kissed her back. Sensually, tenderly, with all the love that he felt. Piper was his world. Had been for as long as he could remember. Always would be. Piper and the kids—they were his joy. He would do anything to protect them and preserve the life he had with them. *Anything*.

Piper eased back but blinked when she caught his expression. "What's wrong?"

He forced a smile for her. "Nothing." He'd just realized that for the first time since he'd known Remy, the guy had reached out *directly* for help.

Not help for his family—Remy's family was a twisted and dark story of its own—but for a woman. Was the mighty Remy falling?

"Take care of your client." Piper turned away. "But you'd better hurry. Don't forget your brother is due to stop by any minute for breakfast."

He typed out a fast text to a new Wilde agent. A hire he'd made personally. Remy wanted someone he could trust on his six? Eric had the perfect guy in mind. Eric sent out the job order, the location address, and their client's name to the new hire.

The response was immediate...

You are shitting me.

Eric glowered at the screen. Someone didn't know how to talk to the boss. He fired off a quick follow-up. *I think you meant to say, I can handle it. Consider the job done. Thanks for the opportunity, boss.*

He waited for a reply. And then, it came. *That means you aren't shitting me.*

The new hire definitely needed to work on his interpersonal skills.

But...Nope, Eric was not shitting him. Before Eric could text back, another response came from the new agent.

Consider the job done. I can protect Remy in my sleep.

Eric wasn't so sure Remy needed protecting. He was a bit more concerned about who might be coming after Remy—and Remy's new friend, Jacqueline. So he warned, *Don't let Remy go rogue.*

Unfortunately, that warning was probably too little, too late. Most people believed that Rembrandt had gone rogue years ago, just like his father had.

CHAPTER FOUR

"So I'm just supposed to sit here?" He'd seen her bruises. Jacqueline hated that he'd been able to catch sight of them on her shoulders. The shower water had just been so tempting, and she'd wanted *out* of that horrible dress. She'd thought that he'd already left the bathroom, but then he'd called out about soap and—

"Try to sit *still* if you could." Remy stared at her but seemed to see *through* her.

And as if on cue to that magic word of *still,* she rolled back her shoulders.

His eyes narrowed. He put down the paint brush in his hand and stalked toward her. Music played again. Not the blaring rock music of before, but softer, sensual music. An elegant, classical refrain. She didn't know much about classical music, so Jacqueline had no idea what the song was, but she liked it.

Remy stopped in front of her. "You don't need to be afraid."

Oh, he was so very wrong in that regard. "I'm being hunted. I left everything I knew behind. I think I have a reason to worry." Why was she oversharing with him?

And, better question, why was he helping her? But he was. Opening his home to her. Lying to protect her. Putting himself at risk for her. "You should tell me to go."

"Not happening." His head cocked to the right. "When I said you didn't need to be afraid, I should clarify. I meant, you don't need to be afraid of me."

Her mouth opened. Closed. Then she told him the truth, "I'm not."

"No?"

"You've been nothing but good to me. An absolute hero."

His brow furrowed. God, would she ever quite get used to how gorgeous this man was? Because it was truly startling when you looked at him. People were not supposed to be this attractive in real life. A face like his was supposed to be due to a whole movie magic trick process or something that involved lots of soft lighting.

"I hired you to be a model. Hardly what I'd call heroic."

She shifted slightly on the stool. She'd found a pair of sweatpants that mostly fit and a loose t-shirt. With two pairs of socks, the shoes she'd discovered in the bottom of the trunk had stayed on her feet. Her hair had dried after the shower, and it tumbled over her shoulders. She had zero makeup on her face. Why the man thought she was any kind of model, Jacqueline had no clue.

"When you're afraid, it shows in your eyes."

It did? "Sorry. I'm not sure how to fix that." She wet her lips. Jacqueline saw his gaze dip to her mouth. Was it her imagination, or had his stare just heated? *Had* to be her imagination. A guy like Remy wouldn't be seriously thinking about...

What?

Kissing me? No, no, she was the one thinking about that—about kissing *him*—and she should not be. She certainly had enough problems going on without adding this weird attraction to her list, but...

She *was* attracted to Remy. Incredibly, overwhelmingly attracted. The kind of attraction that you felt with a touch. One that made a spark of electricity zing from your fingers through your whole body. The kind of attraction that she hadn't thought was real, not until she'd first touched Remy.

Rembrandt. She liked his name, even if he didn't. She pretty much liked everything about him. She especially liked the way she felt so safe with him.

"I will not hurt you." His voice had gone extra deep. So rumbling and strong. Sexy. As if there weren't already enough sexy things about the man.

"I didn't think you would," she returned.

His lips curled. "No? Then why did you steal that screwdriver shortly after we met?"

Steal. "I was just taking precautions."

"Um. You can tell me all your secrets, you know."

She could not. She'd already put him at enough risk.

"I'm a vault. I'll keep your confidences for you."

How utterly wonderful would that be? To have someone she could trust. "You just met me. Why would you care about my secrets?"

He leaned forward. Reached his hand out and tucked a lock of her hair behind her right ear. His fingers brushed over her cheek, and sure enough, Jacqueline felt that maddening zing again. The one that flashed through her whole body and had her breath shuddering out a little too quickly.

And, observant Remy stilled. "Jacqueline?"

"It's a little, ah, warm in here, isn't it?" She fanned herself.

"Not in the least."

Really? He couldn't have given her that, just said that it was hot?

"But you are flushed. You have a tendency to get the most delightful pink in your cheeks."

Now he was calling out her embarrassment? Wonderful. "I have no idea why you want me to be your model. I'm sure you could call up someone who is way more experienced at this sort of thing."

His hand lingered against her cheek. "I don't want anyone else."

Her heart slammed hard in her chest. *He's talking about modeling. Not sex. Settle down.*

But was she *leaning* toward him? Guilty. She was.

"I only want you," Remy said, voice rumbling even more. "You're the one who inspires me."

That was probably the nicest thing anyone had ever said to her. "I used a shoestring to help keep these pants in place around my waist. I finger combed my hair, and I'm wearing two pairs of socks with my shoes."

He glanced down at her feet. "I hadn't noticed the double socks."

"I am not inspiring."

His stare returned to her face. "That's the problem."

She swallowed.

"You believe that, and it's making you nervous. I'm gonna need you to reframe."

"Excuse me?"

"Reframe. See yourself as I do."

"How do you see me?" She shouldn't have asked. Too late.

"Your hair is thick and dark and beautiful. I want to run my fingers through it and pull you close while I brush my mouth against yours."

"Um..." It was definitely hot in there.

"Your lips are perfectly sculpted, and they look so soft. Tempting. Everything about you is tempting." Rougher. "You have an innocence that lurks in your eyes, but your sensuality is clear to me. When you want someone, you want him with your whole body. You need and you yearn, and when the desire gets strong enough, the control you have wrapped around yourself will shatter."

She caught herself just before her hand could lift and start fanning her face again. "You say this to all your models?"

"You're actually my first model. I've never paid someone to sit for me before." Abruptly, he turned away. "It's not about the clothes, if those are what make you uncomfortable. That's why I suggested you be nude. The clothes are just fabric. It's about *you*. Nothing else. You don't need fancy clothing or makeup in order to be beautiful."

Easy for him to say. The man was walking perfection.

He'd gone back to his easel. Picked up a brush. Once more, his eyes were on her, but this time, he wasn't seeing through her. Jacqueline had the uncomfortable feeling he was seeing every single bit of her.

"Why hide?" Remy asked simply.

Her tongue swiped over her lower lip. "Because hiding is safe."

"You're safe with me. You can show me the real you."

Exposing her real self would be too risky. *You don't know him.* A cautious whisper from within.

She remembered that Remy had said he would give her references who could vouch for him. People she could call so that they could tell her what a great guy he was. "Who are the references?"

His brush slid over the canvas. "What references?" Now he seemed distracted. Just that quickly.

She held her body still. Kept herself turned toward the light, just as he'd instructed when she first hopped onto the stool. "You said you had references. People I could talk to about you. Who are they?" A question she should have asked before.

"Oh, you know, the usual. The head of the FBI. A few well-placed members of the CIA. And Eric Wilde. You ever heard of him?" More light brush strokes on the canvas. "He runs—"

"Wilde," Jacqueline said as every single bit of moisture dried from her mouth. Of course, she'd heard of Eric Wilde. The man was stupid rich, and his security and protection firm was in the news every other week.

Trouble. I'm in big, serious trouble.

"What's wrong?"

Jacqueline focused on keeping her breathing nice and steady. Well, she hoped it was nice and steady, anyway. But absolute fear and panic had just flooded her, and *clearly* Remy had picked up on her change of expression. "Why would the head of the FBI be able to give you a reference?" Except she suspected, and this was *bad.*

The FBI big boss would give him a reference because...

Remy works for him.

"Your flush is going darker," he noted.

She leapt off the stool. "I need some fresh air." What she needed was an escape plan, stat. "Can we take a quick break?"

His dark eyes narrowed. "Jacqueline?"

"Just need to stretch. Five minutes, tops." With an effort, she tossed him a quick, broad grin. Then, before he could argue, she double-timed it to the door.

She could feel his stare on her, but he didn't stop her. Her shaking fingers curled over the knob, she yanked it open, and then she...

Practically ran through the cabin. Went straight for the front door. She hauled it open and bounded down the porch steps.

Get away. Run. Her frantic gaze swept the area. She had *zero* memory of arriving at his cabin the night before, and when she looked around, Jacqueline could see pine trees stretching for what looked like miles and sweeping arches of mountains in the distance. No other cabins. Just a graveled drive. She could follow that drive and probably get to the main road, but if she stuck to the drive, she'd be easier to spot if Remy decided to give chase.

So she flew toward the woods, knowing they were her best option as—

"Really? Going to take your chances with the bears and wolves instead of staying with me? Do I frighten you that much?"

He was behind her. Very, very close behind her. Too close. She spun around and found Remy about a foot—*a foot*—behind her. "How did you do that?"

"Do what?" One eyebrow lifted.

"Get...*here*. Behind me. Without me hearing you."

"You were running—stomping very loudly—so I doubt you would've heard anyone." He didn't touch her. He could have. He could have reached out and grabbed her. His hands remained at his sides. "Why did I scare you?"

"You didn't." *You did.* "I was just running out for a quick bit of air. I told you, it was hot in there."

Remy shook his head. "We both know you're lying."

Jacqueline backed up half a step.

"Bears, sweetness. Wolves. Maybe some coyotes. That's what you'll be facing if you run off into the woods. Of course, you also have to worry about dehydration because you have no water on you. No food, either. And unless you have some fantastic knowledge of the area, you will be lost within about ten minutes because there is no trail in those woods. This is a very secluded spot." Now he glanced around. "When I first arrived, I thought it would probably be a serial killer's paradise." His gaze slid back to her. "I'm not one, so you can unclench your fists."

She hadn't realized they'd clenched in the first place. "Serial killers don't work for the FBI."

"You sure about that? It's been my experience that they have all sorts of unusual people on their payroll."

How could he be so calm and mocking? "I should have never come home with you." Big, massive mistake. "You're FBI, aren't you?"

He laughed. But, she noticed, Remy also didn't deny her charge.

I am so screwed.

Her head dipped forward. "I tried to do the right thing, for a very long time, I swear, I did." *Too late now.* After sucking in a deep breath, Jacqueline forced her head back so she could see him. "I really did not want to wind up in a jail cell."

"Ah, sweetness, what could you have ever done that would make you—"

A twig snapped.

And just like that, Remy went from his cool, casual pose to something entirely different. She'd been staring straight at him, so she saw the transformation swipe over his face. His gaze immediately sharpened. Went hard. Almost feral. As did his features. No longer was he movie-star perfect. Instead, a rough, primitive rage tightened his features. Hollowed his cheeks. Had his jaw hardening. *His* hands clenched at his sides. "Get inside."

"What?"

"I want you to run back into the cabin. Make certain all the doors are locked."

"Um…" She glanced toward the woods. She'd heard that twig snap, too. "You think it's a bear?"

"I think I want your sweet ass in the cabin, *now*."

Maybe it was a bear or maybe one of her hunters had come back. She suddenly felt like prey, and her stare swept over the thick growth of trees. She couldn't see anyone out there, but that snapping had sure seemed close and it had—

Remy swung her into his arms. The move was sudden and fast and then she was being bounced and jostled as he raced back to the cabin. One of her arms flew up and curled around his neck. "Wait, what are you—"

He put her down on the porch. "Inside. *Now*."

Nothing easy going at all about him any longer. He didn't even seem to be the same man. "Remy?"

"Get the fuck in the cabin, sweetness." He whirled away.

She grabbed his arm. "You can't go after him!" *Him*. As if she now fully believed that a man was watching them from the woods. A man, and not a bear or a—a racoon or…

"Trust me. I can. I will." And he did. He pulled away and ran straight for the woods. She stood staring after him, her whole body shaking, as he rushed out to confront one of the monsters that *she'd* brought to his door.

***

The growl of the engine seemed to echo through the woods. Remy bounded after that sound, swatting branches out of his way and jumping over fallen limbs even as he knew that he'd be too late. A growling engine meant his prey was already fleeing.

And, on foot, Remy would not be able to reach the bastard in time. The knowledge didn't make him slow down. If anything, Remy just sprang forward faster. Faster and faster and—

He saw the curving edge of the old road. Caught the flash of taillights as the motorcycle disappeared around the bend. Had to be the same motorcycle from last night. And now, the jerk had proof that Jacqueline was with Remy.

Only she isn't with me. I left her at the cabin. On her own. Remy whirled and began running back for her. It looked like he was dealing with two perps—one on the motorcycle and the other who'd pretended to be an FBI agent that morning. Partners? Probably. Two bastards for Remy to handle instead of one. Not exactly a hard job, but, if the duo had just worked a divide-and-conquer strategy on him, then he was screwed.

Because while the guy on the bike was fleeing and I gave chase, the other SOB could have stayed at the cabin in order to get his hands on Jacqueline.

Remy burst through the woods, breath heaving as the cabin came back into sight. There was no sign of Jacqueline. Maybe she'd followed his orders. Maybe she was safe inside. Or...

Maybe she's been taken. He didn't bother calling out her name. He surged straight for the cabin.

Or maybe she ran away. She was trying to run from me before, but then I heard the twig snapping. Jacqueline had become absolutely terrified when he'd mentioned that she could talk to the head of the FBI. Her whole body had trembled. And she'd tried to escape.

His sweet angel was afraid of the Feds. Which probably meant...

She's not nearly as sweet and innocent as I thought.

He grabbed for the doorknob. Found it locked. His fist pounded against the door. He didn't call out her name. Just pounded and—

The door swung open. Her eyes—so wide and that unforgettable green had filled with fear—met his.

"You're okay!" She threw her arms around him even as he kicked the door closed. "I was so worried. Do *not* do that again, okay? You don't need to put yourself at risk for—"

He pulled back from her. Glared down at her. He flipped the lock on the door and was aware of a faint tremble in his normally rock-steady fingers. What was up with that?

Jacqueline swallowed. "R-Remy?" Fear, vibrating softly in her voice.

Fuck it. Just...*fuck it*. His emotions were spinning out of control. He was out of control. He didn't know her. They were strangers. Nothing should matter. Nothing ever mattered to him. He didn't get involved in other people's problems. He stayed away from personal connections. Other people did not matter and she—

"Please," Jacqueline whispered, and the word trembled. "Don't get hurt for me. I'm not who you think I am."

Fuck. It. His mouth crashed down on hers.

CHAPTER FIVE

Remy's arms closed around her, he pulled her up against the burning heat of his muscled body, and his mouth took hers. Stunned surprise held Jacqueline immobile. Her mouth had dropped open when he first hauled her close, and his tongue thrust past her parted lips.

Stunned.

She couldn't believe this. He—they—

I'm kissing him back.

She was. Her hands flew up to clutch his powerful arms, and her tongue eagerly met his. She should *not* be doing this. Bad guys were on her trail. Probably on the *literal* trail near Remy's home. And she was stopping to make out with him.

But...

Damn, the man could kiss. Inside her two pairs of socks and the oversized shoes, her toes were curling. She rubbed eagerly against him, opened her mouth a little wider, and felt heat and lust surge through her entire body. Remy kissed her with a single-minded determination. As if nothing else mattered in the world. As if he'd been hungry for her a very, very long time and he was going to explore all of her now that he had her in his arms and—

What am I doing? What am I thinking? This was...wrong. This had to stop.

Yet, nothing had ever felt this right before. She'd never wanted to melt into a man as he kissed her. To just forget everything else—including the threat at the door—and simply let go. Passion never swept her away. She wasn't that type. Practical, reliable, *boring*. That was her. Not this...this woman who was moaning and twisting and trying to get *more*.

He nipped on her lower lip. She could actually feel arousal flood through her at that sensual bite. Another moan came from her and...

His head lifted.

It took her a moment to realize he'd stopped kissing her. Her eyes flew open, and she stared up at him, aware that her heart raced far too fast. "I..."

Lust blazed in his eyes. *Blazed.* Wow. She didn't think any man had ever gazed at her with that much lust. It looked as if he wanted to pounce. Amber sparks burned in the darkness of his eyes.

"He got away."

"You kissed me."

Wait. Wrong thing to say. Obviously, he'd kissed her. Remy would have been aware of that pertinent fact, and clearly, he wanted to stay on a topic that mattered. He'd been talking about the bad guy. She'd been talking about making out. Her lips pressed together. *I can still taste him.*

"Damn right, I kissed you. And I would be doing one hell of a lot more if it weren't for the fact that the bastard got away. It was the prick on the motorcycle." His hands slid over her shoulders. His grip tightened. "I was afraid the fool pretending to be the FBI agent had come back and gotten—"

She winced when his fingers slid over a bruise.

Swearing, Remy let her go and jumped back. "I hurt you."

"No, I—" Okay, yes, it had hurt. "Not your fault. My shoulders are just a little, ah, sensitive—"

"Because some fucker put his hands on you." Low. Lethal. Promising all kinds of hell in retribution.

She inched back a step. This was...scary Remy. Intense Remy. Still way-hot Remy, but...*stranger Remy*.

"Don't." A growl from him. "Don't be afraid of me. I would *never* hurt you."

She licked her lips. Could have sworn she still felt his kiss. "Because...you're a Fed? And Feds don't hurt people?"

His eyelids flickered. "Sure, let's go with that story."

"You *are* a Fed, aren't you?" Her stomach was twisting but it was no longer due to the excited butterflies that had been spinning around when he'd kissed her. Instead, fear caused the churning. "That's how you knew the man at the door was a fake when you first talked to him. You're the real deal." *And I am in so much trouble.*

"I've worked with the Feds."

Confirmation. Her shoulders slumped.

"And the CIA," he added with barely a pause. "You can say that I get around with my services."

The news just got worse and worse. When she'd first seen him in that rundown bar, she'd thought he was the answer to a prayer. Now she realized that...

Maybe this is how it ends for me. Her stare locked on the floor.

"Is it fascinating down there?"

Her head snapped up. Her eyes met his.

"Didn't think so," he muttered. His hand ran over his face. "I want answers. Didn't think they fucking mattered, but these jerks aren't giving up. We need a plan of attack. We need—"

She knew exactly what they needed. With her shoulders hunching even more, Jacqueline lifted her hands toward him. She turned them over, so that her wrists were up. "You need to arrest me."

One of his eyebrows slowly rose. "Why would I do that?"

"Because..." She choked down the lump in her throat. "I'm a thief." There. Said. Done.

His hands rose and curled around hers. No— around her wrists. That same crazy spark surged through her at his touch, and she wondered how she could still feel that burn when he was about to call his *real* FBI buddies and lock her away.

His fingers lightly caressed her skin.

"Remy?"

"What a coincidence," he murmured and flashed her a killer smile. "So am I."

***

"Confirmation," Nate Lark said into his phone. He'd braked his motorcycle on the side of the godforsaken road. *Nature*. He freaking *hated* being out in nature. His left hand slapped at a mosquito that was attempting to drain blood from his neck. His right kept gripping the phone. "I saw her with my own eyes." Jacqueline had been standing right next to the big bruiser near the cabin. "She's at his place."

"Dammit, I thought so," his partner Tim seethed back. "When he wouldn't let me past the front door, I knew he had her in there."

Yeah, yeah, whatever, Tim should get a gold star or some shit for being right. "It's just the two of them. We can take them whenever you want."

"He knows the sheriff."

Another mosquito buzzed around his neck. So the guy knew the sheriff. Big deal. "And that matters because...?"

"Because if we get the local law involved, our asses will be in trouble."

Tim was such a worrier. Always had been. They'd been partners since they were barely legal, and the guy always fretted. *Dude, we just need to get the job done. Make our delivery and get paid.* End of story. "I don't like nature."

"I know." A long sigh. "But I'm in Halfway, and I did some checking. The sheriff is supposed to hit some charity event at a nearby town this evening. When he's gone, we'll attack."

"No. Waiting is a bad idea." They needed to move, now.

"Uh, no, it isn't. It's genius."

Tim had never gotten a genius idea in his life. "I think he saw me."

"Who? The sheriff?"

Jesus. Nate rolled his eyes. "The guy hiding Jacqueline. He chased me through the woods."

"If he chased you, then he *definitely* saw you."

Smartass. "Yeah, fine, he definitely saw me. Happy now?"

"I'm not gonna be happy until we get paid."

That made two of them. But Nate could tell that Tim had started to consider other attack possibilities. Being spotted meant that now their new enemy would be on alert. The big bruiser would be watching. Ready.

"What do we know about him?" Nate asked. "Other than the fact that the hoss is big."

"The bartender in town told me that the guy is some kind of artist."

Nate grunted. "Didn't look like an artist to me." He'd looked like trouble. "And the way he was acting with her—I think they're involved." There had been something about the way the big jerk had positioned his body near Jacqueline's. And he'd sure hauled her into his arms fast enough and rushed with her back to the cabin.

That was when I made my exit.

"Bullshit. They can't be involved. She just met him. I found the truck driver who dropped her off, and he said she didn't even have a destination in mind. She's here by chance and—"

"If the guy is not fucking her already," Nate cut in to say. "He will be." Utter certainty.

"The truck driver is not fucking Jacqueline."

Nate had to squeeze his eyes shut and count for patience. "Were you dropped on your head when you were younger? Or maybe just straight slammed down on your head? Something like that?"

"That is not funny," Tim huffed.

"I didn't mean the truck driver," he gritted out as he exercised supreme self-control. *This asshole drives me crazy. This will be our last job. The last.* "I meant the artist. I suspect they're cuddled up in the cabin as we speak. They're either fucking or they will be fucking."

"You think that's how she got him to give her shelter? She offered to screw him?" A low whistle. "Oh, Preston is not gonna like that."

Understatement. Nate could all too easily imagine their boss's rage. "Maybe we leave that out of the report?"

"Uh, I don't think so. He finds out we lied to him, and *we'll* be the ones hunted."

Tim wasn't wrong. "Preston is gonna lose his shit."

"Yeah, he loses his shit every other day. But he pays well." A beat of silence. "Only one road leads to the cabin."

And they'd switched to a new topic. Typical Tim. "Yeah."

"So we just stake out the end of that road. We don't let them leave. And if they haven't run into us by nightfall, *then* we make our move. The sheriff will be gone, so we'll be free and clear." No mistaking the smugness in Tim's voice. He was proud of his plan.

Tim had overlooked a point or two. Typical. "And what if they *do* run into us by nightfall? What if the dude comes charging out in that big-ass truck of his?" That truck could have destroyed his motorcycle when they'd had the faceoff on the road. "You need to get that piece of crap rental you have out here. Use that as a roadblock." Not his bike.

"I'll come meet you. And if the *artist* protecting her comes to meet us before nightfall, I'll flash my badge again."

That fake badge. "Didn't seem to do much good before," he muttered.

"What?"

"I said..." He cleared his throat. "You gonna fake arrest him?"

"Yeah, I'll slap some cuffs on him, scare the would-be hero to death, and feed him a line about Jacqueline being a criminal. He'll beg us to take the woman off his hands."

Maybe. Maybe not. Either way...

They had a job to do. And a shitty plan to follow.

*****

Already fast, Jacqueline's pulse jerked even more beneath Remy's touch. "Are you making fun of me?"

No, he'd been giving her a confession. Not that he'd ever been one to jump on that whole "Honesty is the best policy" bit, but he'd been trying. "Wouldn't dream of it." He kept caressing her wrists. "I also would never dream of putting cuffs on you. Unless, you know, it was a foreplay sort of situation."

Her eyes narrowed right before she snatched her hands back from him. "You *are* making fun of me."

Again, no, but he *was* battling an almost painful erection and wishing that she was still in his arms. She wasn't though, and they had some problems to address. His aching dick would have to wait. "What did you steal?"

She backed up a step. He did not like it when she retreated from him, and, to stop himself from reaching for her, he crossed his arms over his chest and locked his feet to the floor.

"It...I didn't know I was stealing something. I should start by saying that."

"Um."

"My grandfather was Fabian Fletcher."

The name surprised a laugh from him. "Fingers Fabian?" Ah, damn, talk about a small world.

Her lashes fluttered. "You know him?"

"More like know of him. Never had the pleasure of meeting him." The man was a legend.

A grim nod from Jacqueline. "You never knew him because the Feds never caught him. He used a ton of assumed names."

Oh, this is hitting way too close to home. Remy kept his expression neutral.

"And he was wanted for way too many bank robberies and...safe cracking incidents."

"Incidents?" That was a fun word choice. "You mean Fingers Fabian was *the* best safecracker out there. When you wanted someone who could make a safe spill every secret it had, you turned to Fabian." An ace cracker, some had sworn that the man had a magic touch—and magic ears—when it came to his work. Sure, he could be old school and listen to all the clicks and light pops that came from prying the secrets out of a combination lock, but stories said he seemed to *feel* the vibrations when he worked a safe. He would press his hands to the safe, get them near his target...and *voila*. The safe would open.

"I'm sure the FBI had quite a file on him." Her lips curled down. "He wasn't just a criminal, okay? He raised me after my parents died. Showed up at every dance recital I had. Took me fishing every Sunday. And he..." She bit her lower lip.

He'd bitten that lip, too. Nipped it. Had her moaning. Remy wanted her moaning again and again. But, nope. Not the time. She was spilling the deep, dark secrets of her past. He knew what else was coming. Just as he knew—*this is gonna be bad*. Remy kept his arms crossed over his chest. "He taught you the trade."

A miserable nod. "But it was just a hobby for me, I swear! I-I liked spending time with him, and when he got older, he couldn't walk so well. So we would sit in his office, and we'd work with safes and with his tools for hours and hours. I promise, I never intended to do anything illegal. I own a bookstore in New Orleans. I live a quiet, safe life. Everything was so normal for me. And then I met *him*."

Remy rocked forward. Caught himself. So much for his damn feet being locked to the floor.

"This the part where you say you fell in love with some asshole and broke into a safe for him?" *The fucking wedding dress*. Though she'd said it wasn't a wedding dress.

She'd said that, but...

Had she lied?

I've lied. He'd omitted plenty of truths from her, led her to believe he was someone he wasn't, so why the hell would he hold a lie against Jacqueline? And why the hell did he feel so freaking jealous when he thought of the bastard who'd—

Put bruises on her.

The jealousy stopped. Twisted. Transformed into hard rage. "He's the one who hurt you. The bastard you were going to marry."

"I was *never* going to marry him! I told you that already!" She blew out a hard breath. "He tricked me, all right? He came to my shop, said he knew about my grandfather, that he'd heard there was no safe that Fabian Fletcher couldn't open."

From the tales Remy had picked up over the years, that was probably a true statement. Word on the street was that no one had ever been able to match Fabian's skills.

"Preston's father had passed away. There was a safe that he desperately needed to open..."

Oh, fuck, Remy got where this story was going. He also got that he hated this Preston prick.

"Preston asked if my grandfather had ever taught me anything about his craft." A roll of one delicate shoulder from Jacqueline. "I told Preston that I knew a little. I'm certainly not on my grandfather's level. Preston said he just wanted to see if I could open it. That the only things inside were of sentimental value to him."

"Bullshit." A snarl.

Her eyelids flickered. "Well, yes, but I didn't realize it at the time. I believed Preston was a nice guy. He came in wearing an expensive suit. He was well-known in the area. A philanthropist who volunteered his time and money—"

"Stop singing the jackass's praises. He wanted you to break into a safe so he could steal the contents. You were too trusting, and you let the bastard use you." Each word was bitten off.

"*No.*" A hard snap. And just like that, Jacqueline surged toward him. "I was not there to steal anything! It was *his* safe. His father left it to him. Preston said he wanted me to open it."

Too trusting. Too naive. Dammit, she reminded him of his kid sister. Back in the day, Iris had been just like her. "Right, because if the safe *belonged* to him, then he needed to go straight to the granddaughter of a master safecracker instead of, I don't know, just using a freaking blow torch or something to get inside himself."

Her lips tightened.

"He didn't need you." *He used you, sweetness. But don't worry. I'll make him pay for that.*

"I got that, later. At the time, it was…" A long exhale. "He took me out to dinner. Seemed interested in me. I refused to take the job at first, but he kept coming around."

His hands fell to his side. "The bastard seduced you." The jealousy was back. Jealousy and rage and what in the hell was happening to him? He didn't get jealous. Didn't get furious over the idea of some slimy SOB taking advantage of a stranger—

She's not a stranger. She's my muse.

"He didn't seduce me, Remy. Despite the fact that I just kissed you as if my life depended on it, I don't normally fall into bed at the first sign of interest from a man." Ice dripped from her words. "I did *not* sleep with Preston."

The universe shifted and centered directly on her. "I like the way you kissed me." He'd like for her to do it again. Now. *I just kissed you as if my life depended on it.* He didn't think anyone had ever kissed him that way.

He realized that he'd kissed her as if...as if...*I'd been starving for her.*

"I've...ah, I don't usually kiss men I've known for less than forty-eight hours." Quiet, not as icy. Pink fluttered over her cheeks.

He grinned at her. "You can make an exception for me. I can be the exception to all your rules."

"Because you're a good guy." A nod from her. "You're an FBI agent."

Ah, yes, about that... "I don't really work with the Feds any longer." Not since he'd told them all to go fuck themselves, and he'd technically never been an agent, more freelance, working on some task forces so...

"Oh, you're retired?" Her eyes lit with understanding. "That's why you're not arresting me!"

She was way too eager to be arrested. He should probably tell her that the first rule of criminal behavior was to try and *not* get yourself locked away. He opened his mouth to do just that and then remembered another important point. "You haven't told me *why* you should be arrested yet."

"I opened the safe for him." A rather miserable confession. "Preston just kept saying he wanted the items inside so badly, that they meant so much because they were all he had left of his father."

Yes, mental note. Jacqueline was entirely too *kind* and sympathetic to others. Bad people would use those traits against her.

Bad people like me?

"I don't have a whole lot left that belonged to my father, either. He and my mother—they died a long time ago. That's how I wound up with my grandfather. He took me in when I was just three years old so I wouldn't wind up in the foster system."

A career criminal—probably the best safecracker in the world—with a lost little three-year-old girl. Hell. "I'm sorry," he heard himself say, and Remy meant the words. Sympathy was as unusual for him as the jealousy had been. All of a sudden, he was getting hit with these new feelings and emotions left and right, and he did not like them one damn bit.

She reached out and took his right hand. Squeezed it. "Thank you," Jacqueline told him softly, her eyes all big and warm with that gorgeous green color shining. "I know we all have our pain, don't we? Everyone carries some kind of burden, but usually people don't notice. I'm sure you have plenty of sadness, too."

If by sadness she meant a fucked-up past with a monster of a father who'd been intent on using his kids for his own criminal gain then, yes, sure. Remy had plenty of that. But Remy didn't talk about his past. Ever. And he wasn't gonna overshare now just because he was staring into the most amazing eyes he'd ever seen. He pulled his hand away from her. "What was in the safe? Wait, let me guess. Diamonds? Cash? Drugs?" All of the above?

"Nothing."

Not what he'd expected. "Come again?"

"I think it was just a test. He wanted to see if I could do it. Of course, I didn't realize it at the time, I was all apologetic because I thought he was disappointed his dad hadn't actually left him anything, but then Preston told me not to worry. There was another safe. He was sure *this* was the right one."

"Oh, sweetness, tell me you didn't open it."

"He took me to what I thought was his estate. Showed me the safe behind the painting in his study."

Remy's eyes squeezed shut. "Not his estate. Not his painting. He took you on a B&E test run."

"Not like I knew, okay? It was my first crime!"

"Too trusting. Too naive. Your grandfather was a damn criminal, you should have known better!" His eyes flashed open just in time to see the pain sweep over her face. *Shit*. "I didn't mean that."

"Preston had a key to the estate's front door." A stark whisper. "He knew the code to the security system. I didn't realize what was happening."

Because she'd trusted the wrong bastard.

"He had a key to everything," she murmured.

"What in the hell does that mean?"

"Preston was given the key to the city. Literally. The key! He led one of the Mardi Gras parades last year and everyone cheered for him. He's a local hero. Why would I think he was lying to me? Why would I possibly think he was getting me to do something illegal?"

Because some people were just too good at lying.

"He watched me open the safe. Later, I learned he timed me."

"How fast did you open the safe?" Idle curiosity. He should probably be focusing on something—

"I did it in under two minutes."

Damn. His spine straightened. She had skills.

"This safe *did* have a diamond necklace inside. Lots of big, glittering diamonds. Cash was in there, too. He didn't touch any of that. He took what looked like a journal out, and he also took a ring. One with a circle of emeralds on it, and big ruby in the middle."

He stiffened at that description as a memory stirred. *And now we are getting somewhere.*

"He shut the safe, and Preston told me we had to get out before we were caught. Caught," Jacqueline repeated with a wince. "See, that was the big tip-off that he wasn't who he pretended to be."

"Not Prince Charming."

"I freaked out. Said he had to put everything back, but he just laughed. He told me not to worry, that he'd disabled the security cameras, so we were good." A shake of her head. "When I tried to take the ring from him, he pulled out a gun."

What. The. Fuck.

"He said we were leaving. Right then. I'd never had a gun pulled on me." A hollow note entered her voice. "I was scared to death."

"How did you end up in the wedding dress?" He was trying to connect all the dots, but big chunks still seemed to be missing from her story.

"It *wasn't* a wedding dress." An exhale. "I told him that I wanted to go home. To just take me home, but Preston said that wasn't happening. That he'd been looking for someone with my skills, and he had no intention of losing me now. The next thing I knew, we were pulling up at a club he owned. He kept me at his side and told me he really didn't want to use the gun..."

Preston, I am going to enjoy meeting you. Meeting you, then hurting you.

"The dress was waiting in his office. He—he told me to change. Made me change in front of him. He kept the gun on me the whole time. I was terrified that I'd hear it firing at any moment."

I will hurt you so much, Preston.

"When I had changed, he took me out in front of everyone and announced we were getting married. The ring he'd taken? He put it on my finger while everyone watched him and smiled."

Remy's shoulders stiffened even more.

"He told me that we were going to be an incredible team. That he had so many plans. I was terrified, and I wanted to get away from him." She dragged a hand through her hair. "When I told him that I was going to the cops, that was when he grabbed my shoulders and shook me. Preston said that he had more cops on his payroll than I could imagine, and if I went to them, they'd just bring me back to him. He said he owned me now, and he wouldn't let me go."

I will find you, Preston. "No one owns you."

"No." Soft but certain. "That's why I left the minute his back was turned. Why I ran and kept running. My grandfather restarted our lives over and over while I was growing up, so I planned to do the same thing. Start over. I needed to get away. I did. I gave the ring to the truck driver as a thanks for helping me—I know it was stolen, but I had to give him something! I didn't look back. I kept running until..."

"Until you found me." He'd never been so grateful to have been in a rundown bar with a shitty beer in his entire life.

"Until I walked straight up to a former Fed." Some of the tension seemed to leave her body. "Someone he can't control?" Hopeful.

"Sweetness, no one controls me." Not any longer. "I want his full name."

"Are you...are you gonna call in some of your Federal friends?" Hesitant and, again, hopeful.

"I was thinking I'd handle this personally." And get some grim pleasure out of the act. Preston sounded like an absolute prick who thought he was gonna be playing in the big leagues. He could think again. Remy would stomp him back into his proper place in the world. "A full name."

"Why do you call me sweetness?"

Oh, this was easy to answer. Since she still stood right in front of him, he lifted his hand. Curled his fingers under her jaw and leaned his head toward her. "Because the first time I caught sight of you, I thought you were the sweetest thing I'd ever seen."

"I-I was a mess. A total wreck."

"You smelled like sweet vanilla."

"I use that lotion. I'm surprised you could smell it at all after my trek through the woods."

"When I kissed you, you *were* the sweetest thing I've ever tasted." He wanted her mouth again. Wanted *her*. "Like your life depended on it, huh? That was how you kissed me?" *How I want you to kiss me again.*

"I don't understand what's happening between us," she confessed. "Everything is crazy, and when you touch me, things just get crazier. *Why?*"

He could break this down for her. "Attraction. The hot kind that makes you want to rip off your clothes and fuck for hours." Blunt. Truthful. "Sometimes it happens when you least expect it. You see someone, and the primitive response is just there. No fighting it." You saw someone and things clicked into place for you.

You saw them and thought...*Where the fuck have you been? And why are you wearing a wedding dress?*

"I've never felt a primitive response to anyone else," she murmured. "You're the first."

She was freaking *adorable*. And so honest that it almost hurt. It was like the woman had no shields up at all. Her grandfather had taught her how to crack safes like a pro, but he hadn't bothered to make sure she was savvy when it came to the predators out there?

Guys like that bastard Preston?

Guys like...*like me?*

"It kind of scares me," Jacqueline added breathlessly.

That gave him pause. "I scare you?" She didn't even know half the secrets he was holding. If she did, if she knew the truth, Jacqueline would go running into the woods. Then he'd have to rush after her and carry her back. Not like he could let the bears or wolves get to her.

I'm the big, bad wolf.

"No, not you," she rushed to say. "I feel safe with you. Finding you was the luckiest thing that ever happened to me."

Funny. I was thinking the same thing.

"I get why you didn't jump to help me when I first walked in that bar. You thought I was a criminal. I mean, I *am* a criminal—"

"You aren't. Preston used you. Then he held a gun on you. You're a victim, sweetness, and you don't need to worry any longer because you've got me on your side." As to why he'd hesitated when he first saw her... "Sometimes, you know certain people are just going to change everything for you. They'll screw things to hell. Obliterate your world. You can try to walk away, but that doesn't work."

"I ran away."

Ah, she was talking about Preston. She'd run from him. *And found me.*

And as for Remy...he was talking about *her.* "Give me his full name." He still cupped her cheek. Still wanted her mouth. Still intended to have it—and her.

"Preston Guidry." Anger hummed in her voice. "But it will be my word against his. Like I told you, he's well-respected, and if what he said about the cops is true, he'll have a mini-army on his side. I don't want you getting hurt because of me. Just turn this over—turn *me* over—to your old supervisor at the FBI. I'll cooperate. When I ran out of your art studio, that was me panicking. I promise, I won't panic again. I'll tell the agents everything. I just...I don't want you hurt. That's the bottom line for me. I don't want you to be hunted. And if it's not too much to ask, I'd like my old, quiet life back, please."

So polite. And so not going to happen. Turn her over? No way. He'd just gotten her. "I don't think that's going to be a possibility."

"Why not?"

"Because I'm not ready to let you go." And his mouth took hers.

CHAPTER SIX

Remy was a selfish bastard. But, occasionally, he could do something good. Very, very occasionally. More like rarely. It did happen, though. Hadn't he worked all those years to protect his sister? He'd tried to stay away from Iris so that the danger would be focused solely on him.

Then he'd fucking *tried* to right all the wrongs in his past. He'd done what the CIA wanted. Played nicely with the FBI. Joined their joint task forces. Pretended to be different people over and over again for them. Hell, his hair still wasn't even back to its natural color yet. For one of his last cases, he'd had to dye his normally dirty blond hair black. He'd had to become someone else, yet again. He'd done all that shit over and over. Didn't that mean that he deserved something good of his own? Didn't it mean that when he found something he wanted, he should hold on tight?

Her lips had parted for him, her tongue met his, and again, Jacqueline was by far the sweetest thing he'd ever tasted. She had a flavor that was just her. There was an innocence that clung to her. One that he could all but taste, and innocence was something he had not known in a very, very long time. If forever.

He savored her. Remy kissed her and knew that he would be taking her. Not yet. No, not yet...*Soon, or I will lose my mind.*

Because sometimes people came along and changed everything. Yes, when she'd first walked into that bar, he'd thought to turn her away. But it was far too late for that now. There would be no going back for him.

He couldn't. She'd obliterated the world he knew.

She needs me, and, dammit, I will be exactly what she needs. He wasn't going to let her down. He couldn't.

Remy's arms moved to wrap around her. To pull her closer. Not good enough, though. The kiss had started gently. More about a tasting than anything else because he'd already come to crave her taste. He had the feeling nothing else would ever satisfy him.

But the more he kissed her, the more those soft moans slipped from Jacqueline. She rubbed her body against him, and he wanted her even more. He could feel the thrust of her nipples against him, through her shirt. Through his. She wasn't wearing a bra, and her round breasts pushed against his chest. He wanted to strip the shirt away. Wanted to put his mouth around her nipple and see if she tasted as sweet there.

He'd bet that she did. He'd bet that she was even sweeter down below. Between her thighs. He could strip her. Spread her. Taste her everywhere, and when she climaxed for him—against his mouth—then he'd be tasting the hottest part of her.

I want all of her.

He gripped her hips. Lifted her up. Her legs locked around him like it was the most natural thing in the world. And that was the truth—kissing her, touching her, wanting her with the insane need that he felt—it all seemed *natural.* Like he'd been waiting for this.

For her.

Turn her over? Give her up?

Never. She was his muse, and he'd like to see some foolish bastard try to pry her away from him because that shit was just not going to happen. Ever.

Remy took a few lurching steps forward and pinned her against the wooden wall. She was trapped—the wall behind her and him in front of her. The damn shirt of hers was in his way because he wanted to see her breasts. To touch them. He wanted to kiss every inch of her, and he was going to do exactly that. Until she cried out in release for him. Until she begged for more.

Until he gave her everything.

But Jacqueline tore her mouth from his. "I-I..." A shudder. "How do I feel this way?"

Desire. Need. It was pretty basic as to the how.

"I was running for my life. Now all I want to do is rip your clothes off!"

Remy *loved* her honesty.

"Is that normal?" A squeak. "It's not. I'm not. I shouldn't be jumping you, not with everything that's happening." She looked down at their bodies. At her legs locked around his hips. "I literally jumped up on you." Red burned in her cheeks. Not a little pink. A dark flush of red. She started to slide her legs down.

He kept her in place. "I lifted you," Remy said. "You didn't jump. And who cares if this is normal or not? Normal is boring. Screw that."

"*I'm* boring! I have a quiet—"

Laughter rumbled from him.

"What are you laughing at? Wait, are you laughing at me?"

"Yes." Sorry, he was. "If you think you're boring, then I am laughing at you." His chest felt warm as he told her, "I can assure you that you are one of the least boring people I've met."

Her eyes blinked a few times, and Jacqueline seemed a little bemused. "It's only because I have a crazy guy stalking me with his goons. And because you met me under extreme circumstances. I can assure you, my life is normally far from exciting." A pause. "I like it that way. I like safety."

He wasn't the man to give her safety. He wasn't a man to give her a quiet, ordered life. What he could give her? Passion. And pleasure. As much pleasure as she could stand. More. Enough to have her screaming and clawing her nails down his back.

He could also give her protection. Remy planned to protect her from every threat that came her way.

"You should put me down." Her hands fluttered around his arms.

Maybe. "But I like you where you are."

Her hands stopped fluttering and gripped his shoulders. "I like where I am, too." The bright red had faded, but a pale pink still dotted her cheeks. "You're not going to arrest me?"

Not a power he possessed. "Not planning on it."

"You're going to help me stop Preston?"

He nodded. If stopping Preston was what she wanted, then, yeah, Remy would do it. *Some people are only stopped when they're in the ground.* This guy had pulled a gun on her. He'd sent his men after Jacqueline in order to hunt her like prey. This wasn't some man who was going to magically change his behavior. When Remy started to dig on the fellow, he knew all sorts of skeletons would come spilling out of Preston's closet.

"How can I repay you?"

Lots of wonderfully naughty ways popped in his mind, and Remy opened his mouth to say, "You don't have to."

Wait. *What?* What the hell had he just said? He'd meant to say she could fuck him into oblivion. He was sure that was what he'd meant. He opened his mouth again and told her, "I just want to help you."

Again. *Wait. What?* Was he having a psychotic episode? What. The. Fuck?

Jacqueline's lips trembled before stretching into a wide smile. Her eyes lit up. Such a vivid green. She looked at him like he'd just given her the world.

He hadn't. At all.

Her expression had gone all soft. "I would expect an FBI agent to say something like that. You just want to do the right thing, don't you?"

Uh, sure. They could go with that. "The right thing. That's what I always do. No hesitation."

She leaned forward and brushed a kiss over his cheek. "Thank you."

His dick shoved against her core. She had to feel the long, thick bastard pushing against her. A few minutes ago, he'd been sure her hips had rocked, and she'd been riding him. At the little kiss on his cheek—one of the least sexual things *ever*—his hips surged against her in fierce arousal. Dammit. He had to get his control back.

Now.

He had work to do. Remy had some criminal mastermind wanna-be to destroy. A good girl to save. Damn. His to-do list was exhausting.

When it's done, I'll have a good girl to fuck. Oh, but he hoped.

Jaw locking, he lowered her until her feet touched the floor. When they touched, he glared at the oversized shoes. "We're getting clothes for you."

"I have clothes. I found a lot of items I can use upstairs. Thank you for letting me borrow this stuff."

Her thank you seemed to grate in his ears. "No, we're going to town. We'll *buy* you clothes that fit."

"That's really kind of you."

Kind?

"But I don't have any money, and I'd rather not be more of a burden to you than I already am."

She hadn't just said that. "You *aren't* a burden."

Jacqueline pulled her hands away from his shoulders. "Well, sure I am. I burst into your life, you had to give me a place to stay, you had to feed me, and you even had to offer me some fake job as a model. I think I am pretty much the walking definition of a burden."

He leaned toward her. Slapped one palm on the wood behind her head. "You're *not*. I like having you here." Sonofa—what the hell was wrong with him? He truly must have lost his mind. Why did he keep saying such crazy shit? His back teeth ground together. "The modeling job is real. You'll keep being my muse. I have work that needs to be done. For the first time in longer than I can remember, I'm painting things of my own."

Her lips were slightly swollen from his mouth. "What do you usually paint?"

Do not say it. "Things I shouldn't." No, that wasn't guilt. He never felt guilt. But looking into her eyes...

She doesn't see who I really am.

"I'd love to see your work, Remy. It was all covered up earlier, and you didn't let me peek beneath the tarps."

No, he hadn't. "It's not worth seeing."

Disappointment swept over her features.

"When I'd done with my first painting of you, I'll let you see it."

"The first painting?" Surprise flashed on her face. "How many do you plan to create?"

"As many as I can. Until I'm no longer inspired." But first... "We're heading to town." Because they needed to get out of the cabin. He needed to get his thoughts together. And he needed to start the investigation on Preston Guidry. Remy shoved away from the wall and turned from her.

"We're going to town? Now? But I thought you didn't want me to be spotted by the men Preston sent."

"Yeah, that cat is out of the bag."

"What?"

Remy glanced over his shoulder. "They know you're here. No point hiding any longer. So we might as well get our asses to town and get you some clothes that fit." They also needed to be ready for what was going to happen next. They couldn't stay at the cabin forever. And Remy had always believed in not waiting around for the enemy to strike. He was more of a kick-them-in-the-dick-first kind of guy. "Before we head out, I need to make a few phone calls."

"To the FBI?"

He should explain about his exact position— or lack thereof—with the FBI, and he would, later. When he could find a tactful way to tell her that he'd been forced to work with the Feds because he'd been given the choice to either use his talents to help them or get tossed into jail. Because, *surprise, surprise, sweetness*, he was a criminal. Or he *had* been. "I'm going to contact the people who can help us." This part was going to be important. "Do you trust me?" He would probably have to convince her to—

"Yes." Instant. Confident.

"Dammit, don't." He whirled back around to fully face her. "Stop being so trusting! You don't know me! You didn't *know* Preston and look how that shit wound up for you!"

She sucked in a breath. "But you're not him."

No, plenty of folks would say he was one hell of a lot worse.

"You even told me I could talk to the head of the FBI, and he would back you up."

He'd been a lying bastard when he told her that. A toss-out line that had gotten him a reaction he hadn't expected. "Listen..." Maybe it would be better to just rip off this Band-Aid right now. "There are things you need to know about me."

She rushed forward and caught his hand. "I already know plenty. I know you helped me. I know you're still helping me. And I know that I can count on you."

Yes, she could. Because looking into her eyes right then, he knew he would do just about anything to keep her safe. "You can." Gruff.

"Go make your phone call. I'll, um, hit the kitchen again, if you don't mind. I'm starving. The last forty-eight hours have been rough, but things are better now." She leaned up and brushed another kiss over his cheek. Like that was the most natural thing ever.

Why the hell did it feel so good?

She turned and made her way back to the kitchen. The woman had *run* away from him before, when she'd thought he was an FBI agent who might arrest her.

Now she was humming—humming!—as she walked through the cabin.

Hell. He yanked his phone out and put it to his ear. His foot tapped as he waited for Eric to answer the call. On the third ring...

"Two calls in one day?" Vague alarm. "Is everything okay?"

No, nothing at all was okay. A woman was kissing him on the cheek—the freaking cheek—and now he wanted to take on an army of bad guys for her. Obviously, he'd gone way too long without getting laid. A situation that would change, ASAP. He could not keep thinking with his dick. His dick was an extremely poor planner. "Preston Guidry."

"And that would be...?"

"The man who is causing trouble for Jacqueline." He kept his voice low as he stalked toward his studio. He'd left on his music, and the classical strains drifted in the air. Mozart's *A Little Night Music*. Mozart always helped him to focus. "He's in New Orleans. One of those jerks who pretends to be squeaky clean, but he's rotten inside. Get your people to find out everything you can on him. And from him, you'll learn about her."

"Your Jacqueline."

She is mine. He'd stopped in front of the painting he'd started. Her amazing eyes stared back at him. Her eyes were all he'd done so far. Capturing the expression in her beautiful eyes had been one of the best challenges he'd had in ages. "She owns a bookstore down there." And there was more he had to say. "The last name I gave you before is probably bogus. Turns out, she's the granddaughter of Fabian Fletcher."

"*What?*"

He had to pull the phone a few inches away from his ear. "Jeez, man, get a grip."

"You have Fabian Fletcher's granddaughter with you?" Eric seemed stunned.

Join the club. "Yes." Hadn't he already said as much? "That Preston ass found out who she really was, even with a fake last name, so I'm sure you can connect the dots with your team and get the intel we need, too."

"Fabian Fletcher," Eric repeated the name. "You know..." Eric cleared his throat. "I'm sure you know it's rumored he turned on his last employer. That he stole twenty million dollars, all supposedly in one hundred dollar bills."

"And hid the money in a safe that only he could crack. Yeah, yeah, I've heard the story." Plenty of people had. "Total urban legend," he dismissed.

"Maybe. Maybe not." Speculation filled Eric's voice. "I would think a guy like you would be very interested in this, ah, particular urban legend."

Remy stared at the eyes he'd painted. Jacqueline's eyes. "A guy like me? You mean someone incredibly heroic and kind?"

"Uh, no, that wasn't what I meant."

Remy hadn't thought so. "I'm hurt."

"Are you?" Doubtful. "Or are you using this woman who fell out of the sky and straight into your lap like a gift from above so that you can get yourself a twenty-million-dollar payday? Damn. You always did have the craziest luck in the world."

That luck had saved Remy's ass more times than he could count. His left hand lifted. His fingers hovered over the eyes he'd painted. "Told you, that story about the cash is just an urban legend." The music kept playing. "Don't worry about it. Just focus on getting me the intel I need."

"Remy…"

"I'll have to leave this cabin soon. It's been compromised. I'm sure I saw one of the bastards sent to hunt her in the woods earlier." *And I think he saw Jacqueline.* "I figure I'll just go straight to New Orleans and kick Preston's ass for Jacqueline, but I would like more intel before I stage my war."

"War?"

"Um." Noncommittal. "So how about you get that info, ASAP, would you? Thanks so much." He hung up the phone, put it down, and reached for his brush. He didn't have her eyes just right. He hadn't captured the emotions that could blaze so vividly in them. He dipped the brush in the paints on his palette. Tried to add the flecks to her gaze.

Are you using this woman who fell out of the sky and straight into your lap like a gift from above so that you can get yourself a twenty-million-dollar payday?

Eric's question echoed through Remy's mind. The paint brush snapped in his grip.

CHAPTER SEVEN

He was acting as if their frantic kiss of moments before had never happened.

When she and Remy climbed into the truck, he seemed all cool and collected. He boosted her up, and she could have sworn his touch singed her. A pang of longing went through Jacqueline, and she sucked in a breath.

But he just let her go. Slammed the door. Strolled away without a care.

Get it together, Jackie.

By the time he climbed into the driver's seat, Jacqueline thought she might have a controlled mask in place. Sure, it probably wasn't as good as Remy's but she was making an effort. So what if the kiss had blasted through her and shattered the memory of every other lover that she'd ever had before. So what if those encounters now seemed clumsy and cold. Apparently, the scene had been no big deal for Remy. For all she knew, he might kiss a woman nearly to orgasm every single day.

He reversed the truck, didn't say a word, and turned to take them back out the twisting drive.

She *had* been nearly to climax from that kiss, and it was an excruciatingly embarrassing fact to face. She'd been grinding her sex against him and, even through their clothing, she'd felt the long, thick length of his dick. She'd ridden him. Had felt pleasure hum through her. Normally, it was hard for her to climax. Took forever. But she'd been about to come with him, right then, right there, with their clothes on. Just from kissing and grinding against him.

So embarrassing. No wonder he wasn't talking about it.

"Why are you blushing?"

Because her skin loved to betray her?

"What are you thinking about?" he pushed.

Oh, the usual. Orgasms. Falling for someone she shouldn't. The danger stalking her.

"Jacqueline?"

He made her name sound so sexy when he rumbled it that way. Fine. If he wanted to know so badly, she'd tell him. "Orgasms."

He slammed to a stop. Her hands flew out and hit the dashboard. "Remy!"

"Sonofabitch."

Her head swung toward him. "Excuse me?" There was no missing the fury in his voice.

"Company." His eyes had narrowed. He was looking ahead and to the left, just a little off to the side.

She leaned forward in an attempt to see the same company he did. She couldn't spy anyone through the trees, but...wait. Light had just glinted off something. Someone?

Remy threw the truck into reverse. "Don't want a shootout when you're in the truck with me."

Her head swung toward him as her mouth hung open. After two stunned seconds, she managed to snap it closed. "How about we don't have a shootout at all? Is that a possibility?"

"Thinking they are going to make that hard for us." The faint lines near his mouth deepened. "Should have figured they'd try to block our exit. Bet they believe they're making sure we can't cut out and escape them."

It wasn't just about believing. "Uh, they *are* making sure of that, aren't they?" She fiddled with her seatbelt. "Maybe we should just try to rush by him. How fast can this thing go?"

"If I were them, I would have put down spikes to blow out my enemy's tires. I can't barrel through over there without checking to make sure they haven't used the same tactic. The last thing I want is to break down directly before them with you in the vehicle." He'd spun the truck back around as he headed for the cabin. "They are *not* taking you."

"Do you..." Jacqueline cleared her throat. "Do federal agents often toss out spikes onto the road? I didn't know that was a thing."

"If you want to blow out someone's tires, hell, yes, it's a thing. Cops use them to end high speed chases. You throw down a strip of spikes, and you can take out all four tires on the perp's car, if you're lucky."

Jacqueline glanced in the mirror on her side of the truck. "Do you think they saw us? Or heard us?" Not like the truck was silent. And as big as the ride was, it would be hard to miss. *Probably saw us. Most likely saw us.*

"Doesn't matter. We'll get back to the cabin. Get you secured inside, and then I'll go back to handle them."

No one was giving chase, at least, not that she could see in the mirror. "I don't like the sound of that."

"Sounded pretty good to me." He whipped the truck behind the cabin. Back to its hiding spot. "Not as good as your orgasm talk, obviously, but what could compete with that?"

So he *had* heard that confession from her.

Remy killed the engine. "Inside, now."

Well, someone was certainly barking out orders, but since she feared the men after her might spring and attack at any moment, she wasn't in the mood to argue. Getting inside sounded like a brilliant plan to her. She scampered out of the truck, double-timed it to the cabin, and when the door locked behind her and Remy, Jacqueline finally let out the breath she'd been holding.

Only to lose it in the next instant when Remy headed to a tall cabinet, unlocked it, and pulled out a gun.

"Remy!"

"This one is for you," he said. "I have another for me."

He did? Where—

And his arm moved. He'd put on a light jacket before they left, and now she could see that he had a holster under one arm. *Holy crap.* He was wearing a gun right then! Remy caught her hand and pushed the gun he'd taken from the cabinet into her fingers. "I'm assuming you know how to use this."

The weapon felt heavy and scary in her grip. "Your assumption would be very wrong."

A furrow appeared between his brows. "Fingers Fabian didn't teach you how to shoot?"

"He was a safecracker! Not a-a—" she floundered.

"Just because you know how to shoot, it doesn't mean you're a killer." His voice came out flat. Hard. "You need to be able to protect yourself. The world is a dangerous place full of very dangerous people."

Her lower lip trembled. "Do you know what happened to my parents?" The gun seemed too cold and heavy.

A shake of his head. "I'd heard about your grandfather, but not your parents." His fingers still trapped hers around the weapon.

"That's because they didn't live long enough to make the FBI's Most Wanted list." A joke that just wasn't. The gun felt so heavy in her hand. "My mom got pregnant with me when she was seventeen years old. By twenty, she and my dad thought that the best way to get fast cash was to rob a bank." She blinked quickly so that she would not cry. Jacqueline hadn't learned the truth about her parents' death until her grandfather had passed away. He'd always told her that they'd been killed in a car accident. Why would she not have believed him?

He lied to protect me. "Even when you have the best of intentions, lies still hurt."

Remy's shoulders stiffened. "Where did that come from?" His fingers released her.

She was left holding the gun. "It's the truth. Lies can be told to protect you, but they still rip you apart." An exhale. "My grandfather lied about what really happened to my parents. Said they'd been in a car accident. I didn't learn about the robbery until much, much later." When she'd been all alone.

His head dipped toward her. "Tell me."

"My dad took a gun into the bank. My mom had one, too." She'd never told this story to anyone. Her shame. Not like you wanted to brag that your parents were would-be bank robbers. Would-be, because they hadn't succeeded. "A guard shot them both."

"Fuck."

Yes. Fuck, indeed. "My mom's gun wasn't loaded. Neither was my dad's. They were kids who didn't understand that life wasn't some game." She put the gun down on the nearby table. Took a few steps away from Remy. "My grandfather wasn't in my dad's life. He'd thought that by staying away, he was protecting his son." All those good intentions...*for nothing.* "With me, he said things would be different."

"And he didn't ever want you near a gun."

No, he hadn't. *Yet here I am.* "He didn't want me near anything illegal. He raised me to follow the straight and narrow. Told me over and over not to make the mistakes he had." He'd wanted her safe. And now...

I want to be safe again.

Remy's body and warmth seemed to reach out to her as he slowly edged closer once more. "Your grandfather wanted you out of the crime game, yet he taught you how to crack safes. Not like that was the best hobby for a law-abiding citizen."

Now she was the one to stiffen. "Cancer had weakened his body at the end. He wanted to spend time with me. I wanted to be with him. Teaching me about the safes kept him busy. It made him happy. Not like he expected me to start my own safecracking business on the side."

"No, I'm sure that's not what he expected at all. I'm sure—" Remy broke off then squinted at her. "Are you *crying?*"

Yes. She swiped her hand over her cheek. "I don't talk about my family with a lot of people."

"*Don't* cry."

"It's not like I can control the tears at will!" She swiped again. "When I get upset, I cry sometimes. It's a normal thing."

He lumbered toward her, eliminating the last bit of distance between them. Frowned more. Squinted more.

"I miss them," she said. "I miss my grandfather. He was the only family I ever really knew. I hate that I didn't get to know my parents. I hate that they thought they needed to take guns into a bank and..." A sob. Dammit. She shoved her hand to her mouth to muffle the sound.

Meanwhile, Remy stared at her with abject horror on his handsome face. Wonderful. Jacqueline huffed out a breath. "I'm sure your family was lovely." Those picture-perfect families that she saw in TV specials. "Your mother and father probably are extremely proud of you." How would they not be proud of an FBI agent who so willingly helped people over and over again?

But bitter laughter poured from Remy. "Proud is not the word my father would ever have used."

She didn't understand. "Remy?"

"My parents are dead, too. My mother died a very long time ago, and she was wonderful. An angel with a smile that lit up a room." His nostrils flared. "She had the misfortune to marry the devil. He made it a habit to get involved with the wrong crowd and do dangerous, illegal shit every chance he got."

Her hand reached out. Pressed to his chest. "I'm sorry."

"Why be sorry that he chose to be a bastard? And that he wanted me to be just like him?" A bitter smile tugged at his lips. "Always the disappointment, that's what I was. And in the end, he even died because of me. Died to save my ass, though I'm sure he probably regretted the choice."

What? Shock rolled through her. His father had died protecting Remy? She could hear the echoes of pain and anger in his voice, and Jacqueline wanted to throw her arms around him and hold on tight. No, more than that. She wanted to take away his pain. To help him, as he kept helping her. "Remy, I'm certain your dad loved you. If he died saving you, surely you see that? We protect the ones we love. Those who matter."

"Very little mattered to my father. He trained me from a young age. Had an idea of what I was supposed to be." Clipped. "I didn't turn out how he wanted."

"Of course, you did! Remy, you're *good*. I'm sorry he didn't get to live long enough to see how wonderful you are. You're strong and brave and you help people."

"Sweetness, you don't know me."

She fisted his shirt in her hand. "I do. I know you're the man who has been my hero when I needed someone at my side. You are *helping* me. I will never be able to repay the kindness you have shown to me." And...*he needs this*. She surged closer and threw her arms around him. She hugged him as tightly as she could.

His whole body tensed. "What are you doing?"

It should have been obvious. "Hugging you." Also, she was trying not to touch his holster or gun.

"Why?" Gruff. A little ragged.

"Because you need to be hugged." Clearly.

His arms slowly closed around her. "You were the one crying."

"Sometimes, it can feel good to cry."

"I'd rather you never cried again."

An odd statement. She hugged him tighter. "And I'd rather you not be sad."

"*That's* why you're hugging me? Because you think I'm sad?" More bitter laughter. "I'm not. My old man was trouble. My life got a lot easier when he was gone."

She didn't let go of him. "You can lie to yourself, but you don't need to lie to me. I'll take you exactly as you are."

And suddenly, he was hugging her back. Tightly. Almost crushing her. "No," he muttered near her ear. "You won't."

Why would he say that? Her head tilted back so she could stare up at him. "Why won't you think that you're a good man?"

So many emotions flashed across his face.

She hated his doubt. So her hands moved up, cupped his face, and Jacqueline pulled him toward her even as she rose onto her toes. Her mouth brushed against his. "You're good."

"Sweetness..." A growl. "I am *trying*, but you make it hard."

He was hard. Literally. She could feel his dick pushing against her, and her body rubbed back against him. "Then you know what?" Jacqueline whispered back. "Let's be a little bad." They could both use some bad.

She could certainly use some.

Preston's goons were blocking the road. Fear wanted to beat hard and heavy inside of her, but for the moment—this one moment—they were safe. They were secure in the cabin. She had her armed protector right in front of her. Jacqueline had no idea what might happen in the next ten minutes, the next hour, the next day. But that didn't matter.

This moment did. Her tongue slid along his lower lip. "Be bad with me."

"I don't think you know how to be bad."

Granted, maybe she didn't. "Then show me." She nipped his lower lip. Felt him jolt. "Show—"

His mouth took hers. Need and lust erupted inside of her as he kissed her with a frantic passion. Hunger and desire and demand. His tongue thrust into her mouth. He tasted her, and he drove her aching body to a fever pitch. Being bad had never been her game plan before. But right now, she'd take it—and him—anyway she could get him.

No one has ever made me feel this way.

She suspected that no one ever would again. His touch alone electrified her. She'd almost been coming just by rocking against his cock earlier. What would happen when he was inside of her?

She had to find out. Before the goons came swarming. Before she was separated from Remy. Before her life could go to hell.

She'd take a slice of heaven, please.

His hands curled around her hips. His touch felt possessive and strong, and he lifted her up. His power was a heady aphrodisiac. She sucked his tongue. Heard his growl even as she curled her legs around him. She began to rock. To slide. He was fully turned on for her, and she'd never had a man react so strongly. For the first time in her life, she *felt* sexy. Like she could seduce him. Like she could just let go and have pleasure pour through her.

"Sweetness, I am going to taste every bit of you."

Oh, that would be new. They could certainly try that but... "Can't you just fuck me?" She nipped his lower lip. "Right now?" While she was still surging on this powerful tide of arousal? While she wasn't thinking about embarrassment or doubt or all the other problems out there?

"I'll do both." He carried her up the stairs.

A startled cry burst from Jacqueline when she realized what he was doing. Her legs tightened around his hips even as her fingers dug into the muscles of his arms. "No! I can walk! You'll drop me." Or he'd hurt himself. Go tumbling down the stairs right in the middle of this amazingly romantic gesture.

No one had ever carried her anywhere. Well, technically, Remy had before. When she'd tried to flee, he'd caught her outside, and carried her back when he'd thought the bad guys were close. And then there had been the instance when he first brought her to the cabin. Though she'd been fast asleep and didn't remember a bit about that encounter...

This was different. This was heady. Sensual. Powerful.

But don't drop me. Stairs are crazy.

Remy laughed. "The only place I plan to drop you is into my bed." He kept climbing. His muscles barely rippled against her. The man acted like carrying her up a flight of stairs was the easiest thing to do in the world.

It wasn't.

But it was stupid hot to her.

Since he seemed so secure, she moved her head toward his neck. Pressed her lips against him in a gentle kiss. Then licked.

"*Jacqueline.*" A warning as a shudder worked over him.

"Don't drop me."

"Never."

She licked him again.

He moved faster up those stairs. "Don't play."

"Wouldn't dream of it." Her usual shyness had vanished. "Can I taste you everywhere, too?" The shyness and hesitation had vanished because this was Remy, and everything was different with him.

"Fucking hell, *yes*."

She smiled. "Good. Because I've never done that before, and I really want to try it with you."

"*Sonofa—*" They were at the top of the stairs. He lunged for the bedroom. Kept a tight grip on her as he thundered toward the bed. He didn't drop her onto the bed. They both sort of tumbled down together, and when she blinked, he had her pinned beneath his much bigger body. His mouth took hers in a devouring kiss. Powerful. Possessive. Her legs still twined around his hips, and she arched against the long bulge of his cock. His clothes were in the way. They needed to go. So did his—

"Gun," Jacqueline gasped as she pulled her mouth from his. "You have to get rid of the gun! I don't want it going off while we're—you know." Her breath panted.

He heaved up on his arms. Stared down at her with his dark eyes. "Baby, don't worry about anything going off prematurely."

Oh. She licked her lower lip.

"I'll handle the gun. You get rid of your clothes."

Okay. Fair. Fine. Doable.

He slid off her. Stepped away from the bed. Stripped off his jacket, then the holster. He put the gun on the dresser and hauled his shirt over his head.

Jacqueline feared she might be doing a wee bit of drooling. His chest was the stuff of dreams. Like, exceedingly hot dreams about men with perfect pecs and abs that went on for days. His long, lean fingers went to the top of his waistband even as he kicked off his shoes.

Jacqueline jumped up and crouched in the middle of the bed—her knees digging into the mattress—so she could have a better view.

But he hesitated. "Weren't you supposed to be doing something, too?"

Something. Yes, right. Something new to try. Jacqueline bounded out of the bed. Rushed toward him. Her hand went to the button of his jeans, and she opened them. Carefully pulled down the zipper. Her fingers were shaking but she got the job done.

His cock spilled into her fingers. Thick and hard and *warm*.

"*Not* what I meant," he rasped. "But, sweetness, you do you. Go for it."

She was. "If I do something you don't like, tell me."

"Yeah, sure, that will happen. *Never*."

Her knees hit the carpet. Just seemed like a better position. The move put her right in front of him. She still carefully held his cock, and her head moved toward him. "First time," she whispered.

"*Fuck*." Almost savage.

Her lips feathered over him. Licked the tip. Hesitant, but, she liked it, liked his taste, so she did it again.

"*Fuck*." Even rougher.

Jacqueline opened her mouth and took the head of his cock inside. She sucked lightly and swirled her tongue over him.

If possible, his cock seemed to get even harder in her mouth. So she took a little more of him. Her head bobbed toward him, and she was sure that her rhythm was terrible, but she didn't care because she was getting more and more turned on as she took and tasted and—

"No more."

She'd done it wrong. Horror filled her as she let him go and fell back onto her ass. Jacqueline blinked and swallowed. "I am—"

His hands fisted and released at his sides. "Good thing the clothes aren't valuable because I am totally ripping them off you."

He was?

Remy reached for her. Lifted her up. Pretty much ripped her top off.

He was.

He jerked off her too big shoes and both pairs of socks. He did stop to frown at them, but then he was yanking down her sweatpants. Her panties went with them, and she was naked when he lowered her onto the bed.

"I was the first?" Remy demanded. "The first in your mouth?"

A nod. "Was it...okay?"

A muscle flexed along his jaw. "I'll be the only." Then he caught her legs and pushed them apart.

This was it. Wow. He was going right for her sex, and she should tell him that this was a first for her, too. That no one had ever gone down on her before. "Ah, Remy, I need to tell you…"

His mouth was already on her. Too late to say anything. Well, she tried to say something, but the words came out as a moan, and she grabbed tightly to the bed covers.

He pushed her thighs apart even wider. His tongue stroked over her clit, fast, warm strokes even as he slid a finger inside of her. Remy seemed to know *exactly* what he was doing. No novice here, and she found herself lifting up her hips to give him even better access as he worked that incredible, magical tongue of his on her. *In* her.

"Delicious." A rumble that went through her.

His tongue slid into her body, and she would have jumped off the bed, but one of his hands held down her hips. In the next breath, he licked her clit again. Again. Again.

She couldn't hold back. Pleasure surged through her, and her head tipped against the pillow as she gasped out his name. The orgasm had her eyes squeezing shut and her heels digging into the bedding. Jacqueline couldn't catch her breath. The drumming of her heart echoed in her ears as wave after wave of release seemed to surge through her.

"Are you ready for me?"

Her eyes opened.

Remy smiled at her, but his smile held a sharp edge. "Because I want inside. *Now*."

Inside was where she wanted him.

He reached over to the nightstand. Opened the drawer and hauled out a small packet. As she watched him and tried to calm her frantic breathing, he ripped open the packet and then rolled the condom over his dick.

Remy watched her even as he positioned his cock at the entrance to her body. She had been feeling all boneless and replete, but when that broad head nudged at her, Jacqueline began to tense.

He stilled. "Change your mind?"

"Absolutely not." Was that husky voice hers? "It's just...been a bit."

"Good." He caught her hands. Twined his fingers with hers. Didn't look away as he surged inch by careful inch into her. Slowly. Deeply. Filling her so tightly with his thick length.

She watched him, too. Jacqueline found herself helpless to look away. He stretched her. Seemed to claim her. And the expression in his eyes was so primitive and hungry. Demanding and deep.

Did she look at him the same way?

When he was fully inside of her, Jacqueline's breath released in a rush. He was being so careful, waiting on her...

Her inner muscles clamped around him.

He jerked. *"Jacqueline."*

"You were the first man to go down on me. I was too nervous with anyone else." This was not the time to overshare, yet here she was. "Why? Why do I feel like this with you? Why do I feel like everything is right?"

"Simple." He kissed her. Deep. Drugging. "Because you're mine."

Then...

Then he withdrew, only to plunge deep. The careful restraint seemed to have shattered, and his thrusts became increasingly stronger. So strong that the bed rocked against the wall, and she loved every minute of the pounding, furious, *frantic* lovemaking. Her hands curled along his sides. Her legs rose so that her knees could press to his hips. In and out. Over and over, he plunged into her.

One of his hands slid between their bodies. He went straight for her clit. Stroked her with his easy skill, over and over, and she cried out when the sudden climax broke through her.

He thrust faster. Deeper. He grabbed her legs and lifted them over his shoulders so that she took even more of him. The new position sent aftershocks of pleasure humming through her, and Jacqueline greedily clamped her inner muscles around him, wanting more.

He gave her more. He thrust and thrust and his fingers worked her and when he came...so did she. Or maybe she'd never stopped coming. She couldn't tell for sure. All Jacqueline knew was that when Remy bellowed her name in release, she cried out his, too.

***

When she opened her eyes, the bed was empty.

Jacqueline jerked upright. The last thing she remembered was...pleasure. So much bliss streaming through her entire body. Remy's dark gaze locked on her. And then...

Then they'd kind of collapsed. She'd sunk into a deep sleep. She'd *fallen* asleep after sex with Remy. Now she was alone in the big bed, and Remy was...

"Don't make a sound," he warned her.

Her head whipped to the right. She was *not* alone. The blinds had been lowered. The curtains closed, but when she squinted, she could make out Remy's shadowy form near the window on the right.

"We have company," he added, his voice whisper soft. "Bastard is coming for the back door right now."

Company? While she was stark naked in the bed? Automatically, Jacqueline yanked the sheet up to her chin.

"I want you to stay up here. Lock the door behind me." Again, his words were so low they seemed to be barely a breath.

Stay there while he...what? Faced the bad guy on his own? Dragging the sheet with her, Jacqueline climbed from the bed. She managed to roughly loop the sheet around her, toga-style, as she tiptoed toward him. Her bare toes pressed into the floor. "You need backup."

"You're not trained. Didn't we cover this already?"

Yes, they had, and then they'd gone to having hot, incredible sex, and, afterwards, she'd apparently passed out on the guy, and now she had no idea how much time had passed. It just felt late and scary and the hunters were closing in on them. "I want to help."

He brushed a kiss over her forehead. "Help by staying up here. By staying safe."

She reached for him. Her hands touched his clothes. Fully dressed. Had he been awake the whole time she slept?

"Don't worry." A low rasp from Remy. "I can handle these guys in my sleep. I just need to know you're safe."

She wanted to know the same thing about him. His safety was of major importance to her. "Don't get hurt."

"Not on my agenda." His fingers curled under her chin. "Just in case, hide in the closet for me, will you?"

Hide in the closet? "In case of what, exactly?" But she knew.

In case they get past Remy. In case Remy gets hurt. Or...killed?

No. Not happening. Not.

"If anyone but me comes through the bedroom door and gets to the closet..." He reached down and...

The gun.

He put a gun in her hand again.

"Got this one from downstairs for you. The safety is on, but you take it off by doing this." He moved her fingers. Showed her. "If anyone but me comes through the bedroom door and gets to you in the closet, you shoot, got it?"

This plan had her stomach twisting.

"I'll be back before you can even miss me."

He was wrong about that. So wrong. When the bedroom door shut a moment later, she already missed him.

***

The sun had set. Remy had fully expected the bastards to wait until nightfall before they came at him with their pitiful attempt at an attack, and yes, the pricks were acting just as he'd predicted.

Remy had gotten an alert through his security feed—a few motion cameras that were on the perimeter of the cabin. The guy was closing in from the rear.

Or, correction, the fool *thought* he was closing in. Coming up for a sneak attack.

Not happening.

Remy had slept far longer than he'd realized. Sleeping hadn't been something he intended to do, not with the clusterfuck surrounding him and Jacqueline, but he'd fallen into a heavy, contented sleep after the fucking mind-blowing sex with her. He'd awoken suddenly, senses humming, with the certainty that danger was coming.

He always got that adrenaline kick right before something bad happened. Probably because he spent too much time *with* bad things occurring in his life. Even before he'd reached for his phone and checked the footage, he'd known that he needed to prepare.

There were lots of ways that he could play the scene. He could send a warning shot outside that would make the fool scamper back. He could rush out and attack his prey head on. Or...

Or I could roll out the welcome mat.

He rather liked to do the unexpected, so Remy figured he'd go with the third option. Once Remy reached the first floor of the cabin, he marched straight for the back door. He unlocked that door.

That should make things easier.

He made certain all the lights were still on in the kitchen. After all, he wanted a nice view of his visitor. Remy glanced around and picked the perfect spot to wait for the prick—uh, his guest. The waiting spot was a few feet to the right of the door.

He took up his position, he pulled out his gun, and he kept it aimed at the door.

Sure enough, less than five minutes later, that door swung open. A man rushed inside. He didn't even slow down when he entered the kitchen, but barreled forward.

Remy advanced from his hiding spot and kicked the back door shut. "Yeah, dumbass, you need to freeze."

The dumbass did *not* freeze. Instead, he whirled to face Remy.

And the dumbass *smiled.* "Aw, come on," he chided as he ducked his head toward Remy. "Is this really the best way to greet your best friend in the entire world?"

CHAPTER EIGHT

Hell.

Remy glared at the man before him. "Constantine."

The light hit his dark hair as Constantine Leos dipped his head forward. "The one and only." His brows wiggled as he took note of the gun. "Want to tell me why you're aiming a gun at your bestie?"

"You shouldn't be here." He did not lower the gun. "You should be far, far away from here."

"Oh? Really?" Constantine pretended to ponder that. "Far away, you say?"

"Yes," he gritted out from between clenched teeth.

"That why you ditched my ass the last few months? Why you seemingly vanished on me without a trace? After all the shit I did for you? You wanted to be *far away* from me? *Me*? The man who always had your freaking six no matter what?" Anger broke through what had been a mocking mask on Constantine's face. "You might as well have been my fucking brother. I *bled* for you, man. Then you turned your back on me. You left me. You—"

"You don't need to be here." He could not deal with this situation right now. "I don't know how you found me, but you need to take your ass back out and get on your motorcycle or your four-wheeler or whatever you used to get through the woods and go away. It's not safe here."

Constantine laughed. "Since when have either of us cared about safety?"

Since the time I thought you'd been killed because of me. Remy studied the man before him and tried to figure out what the hell he should do next.

"You got Fabian's granddaughter stashed somewhere in the cabin." Constantine nodded. "You think she's gonna lead you to the twenty million? Figure you'll just keep it all for yourself once you get it and disappear into the mist? *That* why you don't want me around?"

"No, dumbass." Remy surged toward him. "I want you gone because I'm tired of you getting hurt and having your life thrown to shit because you have the misfortune to be my friend."

"Your *only* friend," Constantine pointed out. But he frowned at Remy. "Wait...are you...oh, hell, no. No." A hard, negative shake of his head. "You didn't ghost me because you were playing a martyr."

Constantine needed to get out of there. "Look, I'm kind of dealing with some shit right now. Bad guys are coming—"

"I thought you *were* the bad guy."

Too loud. Constantine's voice could be way too loud, and it could carry entirely too far. "Would you lower your voice?" Remy rasped. "I do not want to be overheard."

One eyebrow cocked. "By the granddaughter? You don't want her to know...what, exactly?"

Only everything. And how the fuck had Constantine even known about Jacqueline? Alarm bells began to ring in Remy's head.

"We worked to stop the bastard who killed your dad." Constantine turned grim. He also lowered his voice. "We got your sister free and clear. Even had her settled in all nice and happily-ever-after like with that bodyguard of hers."

Yes, they had done that. Iris *was* happy and safe.

"Then the next thing I know, you're gone." He jabbed his index finger into Remy's chest and completely ignored the gun Remy still held. "Friends don't do that crap to friends."

They did when they were *protecting* a friend. "You have no record. You are not wanted on *any* outstanding charges. Not for anything."

Constantine's brow crinkled. "I'm pretty sure someone is after me. Someone *usually* is."

Not any longer. "No, because your slate was erased. You were only *in* trouble because of me. So when the CIA came to me and said they had another deal..." Hell, everyone had been working deals with him. The Feds. The CIA. Even certain very well-placed criminals that he would not be discussing. "I took it. In exchange for doing a few more jobs, I made sure that you were erased from their system. They won't be calling you in any longer. You don't have to play their games." A pause. "Their game or mine. You're free."

"Is that what I am?" Constantine's gray eyes studied him.

"Yes." A hiss. "Now can you get your ass out? I have company coming."

"The kind of company you prefer to greet with a gun."

"Dammit, you were *left for dead* because of me! If you hadn't been wearing a bulletproof vest, you would have died. For years, you've been pulled into trouble over and over again because of your friendship with me." Remy's breath heaved out. "So, yes, I *tried* to do the right thing for you. Getting me out of your life? That's the right thing. Now, just...dammit, go, would you? Just—"

He heard the squeak of a stair. Instantly, he bolted around Constantine and flew back through the cabin. Stair number six squeaked. He knew, he'd made note of that fact the first time he'd climbed the stairs.

Did someone come in the front door while I was distracted by Constantine? Is someone trying to get Jacqueline?

"Stop!" Remy snarled as he burst onto the bottom of the stairs and aimed his weapon.

A sharp cry emerged from Jacqueline as she froze. Her eyes were huge. Her expression taut with fear. And she also had a gun in her hand.

"What the hell?" Remy immediately lowered his weapon. "You were supposed to be upstairs!" In the freaking closet where it was safer.

"I know." A quick, breathless response. "But I heard voices, and I was worried you needed backup. I couldn't leave you on your own."

Yes, she could. He jumped up the steps. "I'm the one with experience. You're the one who has never held a gun until today. That means *you* stay hidden. I'll do the fighting."

"I just don't want you hurt. I pulled you into this mess, and I bet you wish that you'd never seen me step into that bar—"

A low whistle. One that came from the bottom of the stairs.

Hell.

He looked back—and down. Remy knew Jacqueline's gaze also flew to the source of the whistle.

Constantine gave a casual wave. "Hi, there. I'm Constantine, and, please, let me assure you, I think that is the last thing he wishes." His gaze took her in—and the fact that Jacqueline was wearing jogging shorts and a loose t-shirt. Items she'd probably scavenged from the closet after Remy had, ah, ripped the others. The shorts were super short and displayed her toned legs to perfection, and the thin top clearly showed the tight outline of her nipples.

Remy shifted to block Constantine's view.

"Is he one of the bad guys?" Jacqueline asked softly.

Not softly enough. That single eyebrow of Constantine's quirked again. "Aren't we all?"

Remy started to speak.

"Remy isn't. He's FBI," she defended instantly.

Constantine's other eyebrow rose to join the first. "Right. How could I have forgotten? He's a Fed, and I'm his backup."

Remy heard Jacqueline's breath expel in a long rush of relief. "Thank goodness because I was afraid I'd wind up shooting myself instead of the enemies. I am not much good as backup."

Yes, that would have been why Remy asked her to stay hidden.

"But I couldn't leave Remy on his own," Jacqueline continued doggedly. "Not after dragging him into my mess."

Constantine stared straight up at Remy. "I don't think he minds in the least. Playing hero is his favorite thing in the world to do."

Remy sent Constantine a grim smile. One with a lot of teeth. *Be careful what you say, friend.*

"Got some clothes for you," Constantine announced with a casual roll of his broad shoulders. "They're right outside the back door. Shoes, too, because I figured you needed some of those. Heard you had to cut out of your town in a hurry, and I suspected that meant you'd had to leave everything behind."

Wait, wait...wait. *Heard*...Remy bounded back down the stairs toward him. The alarm bells that had rang in his mind earlier were now blasting. *Should have realized...* "You're working for Wilde?" At first, he'd thought that Constantine had just managed to track him down, but, no, more was clearly at play. A whole lot more.

"Did I not mention that fact?" Constantine blinked innocently. "I didn't tell you about my new job in one of our *many* conversations over the last few months?"

Remy locked his back teeth.

"You asked for backup," Constantine reminded him. "You called Eric and told him to send in his best agent."

No, he hadn't used those words exactly.

Constantine lifted his hands and gestured toward himself. "Well, wish granted. Here I am."

***

Being in clothes that fit, having a new bra and matching panties, not wearing two pairs of socks and still having the shoes slide up and down her heels...actually having shoes that were comfortable and her size...oh, the joy. Jacqueline practically hopped down the stairs and rushed to meet the men as they waited in the den. "It's all perfect, thank you so much!" Jacqueline felt so exuberant that she *almost* wanted to hug the stranger who'd brought the clothes to her.

Constantine.

He turned toward her with a broad, warm smile on his face. His gray eyes crinkled a bit at the corners. "You are most welcome. Though, I have to say, I liked what you were wearing before just fine, too—ooof!"

Remy had elbowed him in the ribs. "My bad. Didn't realize we were standing so close." His gaze swept over Jacqueline. "Everything fits perfectly." He looked over at Constantine. "How did you know her size?"

"I just did a little investigating. It's what I do at my new gig with Wilde."

There was an odd tension between the two men. Her hands shoved into the back pockets of her jeans as she tried to figure them out. "Were you two partners at the FBI?"

"Sure. There, everywhere." Constantine's answer seemed...off.

She bit her lip and focused on Remy. He'd tell her the truth.

A muscle flexed along his jaw, then Remy said, "Con and I have known each other a long time."

"Seems like forever," Constantine murmured.

Remy sent him a hooded glance. "We got into plenty of trouble together back in the day and we tried—"

"Tried to get out of that trouble together," Constantine finished. "Sometimes, we succeeded. Sometimes, we just wound up raising more hell." He threw his arm around Remy's shoulders. The two men were roughly the same height and had the same strong, muscular build. "This guy knows every secret I have, and, until recently, I was sure that I knew his, too."

Remy seemed to tense. "You're gonna be the backup?"

"Isn't that what I said already?" A grumbly response from Constantine.

Remy turned his head to frown at him. "And you won't get your ass *shot?* Can you work on that for me?"

"That was hardly my fault!" Constantine snarled, indignant.

"I know, it was mine," Remy snapped right back. "So you should be staying out of the line of fire, but, nope, here you are, rushing straight into danger—"

"My fault." She had to say it. They all knew it.

Both men immediately turned their attention to her.

"I was running blindly," she added because if Constantine was going to be pulled into this mess, he deserved an explanation. "I don't know what all Remy has told you yet..."

"Act as if he's told me nothing. Zero. Go from that point," Constantine urged as he released Remy and stepped toward her. "Just tell me everything."

"Ah..." Fair enough. "A man named Preston Guidry is after me. I think he wants me to break into a safe for him."

"A safe, you say?" Constantine rubbed his chin. "Do go on."

"Oh, for shit's sake," Remy growled. "She's Fabian's granddaughter, you know that, and this prick named Preston is after her because he wants to use her. She had to flee from him in the middle of the night. The bastard left *bruises* on her." His hands fisted at his sides. "She came to me at a bar and asked for a ride, and I—"

"Brought her into your home, became her protector, and now plan to hunt down the man who left bruises on her." A nod. "Absolutely sounds like something you'd do." An exhale. "My buddy Remy always has been the type with a major hero complex. If there is an option to do the right thing, he does it. Every single time."

Remy's eyes narrowed. "Stop being a prick."

"Don't be a jackass," Constantine tossed back.

The two men whirled to face each other. Fury tightened their faces.

Jacqueline laughed. "I get it. I see what you were holding back from me."

They both swung their heads toward her once more.

"You do?" Remy's voice had gone tight.

Yes, it was pretty apparent. "You're not just friends. You're brothers, aren't you?" Jacqueline nodded as she studied them. "I think I can see the resemblance. It's around the chin. And you both kind of carry yourselves the same way."

"We are *not* brothers," Constantine denied. "Why would you think that?"

They weren't? Oh. "Best friends." Her second guess. "And I thought you might be brothers because you two fight like family. Not that I'm speaking from personal experience or anything, but...sort of what I've seen other people do." She was not explaining this well, and she was pretty much going by her gut. "You fight with family, but you love them, and you stand up for them no matter what. Remy called in for backup, and you came running." Like a brother—or a best friend— would do. "And now you're here to help me, too, because of Remy." She paused. "Thank you."

Constantine thrust back his shoulders. Some of the tension seemed to leave him. "You found her in a bar, you say?"

"Uh, huh." Remy swiped a hand over his face.

"And you kept her? Good choice."

"She didn't have on shoes," Remy muttered. "Couldn't let her just continue wandering around. She just would have found more trouble."

Constantine nodded. "Makes perfect sense to me."

The tension seemed to have completely vanished. Instead, there was now an easy camaraderie between them, one that told Jacqueline she'd been right. These two men were close. They cared about each other.

What would it be like to have someone in your life that came running when you were in trouble? That was just there for you, no hesitation? She imagined it would be pretty amazing.

"You've got two assholes blocking the road to your cabin." Constantine began to pace.

"Yes, I'm aware." Remy didn't seem concerned.

Jacqueline figured she was concerned enough for the both of them.

Remy added, "Not like they're doing a good job of hiding their presence. More like they just wanted to set up a roadblock to stop us from leaving."

Constantine peeked out the nearby window, edging the curtain a bit to the side. "I'm sure there is an obvious answer to this question, but I'll ask it anyway." He looked back over at Jacqueline. "Why didn't you just go to the cops?"

She opened her mouth—

"Really?" Remy drawled. "That question is gonna come from you? Of all people, *you?*"

"Yeah. I know. Crazy, right? But I still needed to ask it."

"Preston is well respected in New Orleans." She didn't think Remy and Constantine understood just how powerful her enemy was. "No one there will think he's a criminal. He has the police on his side—"

"Working for him," Remy translated.

"And *I* was the one to break into the safes."

Constantine let the curtain drop. "Excuse me? You've been doing some safe cracking? How did I miss that part before?"

Easy. She hadn't mentioned that part to him yet. Her hands were still in the back pockets of her jeans. "I thought the first safe was his. He told me that his dad had left something inside for him, and he just needed my help..." Yes, she'd been naive. Too trusting.

"A test." Constantine nodded. "I'm assuming you passed with flying colors."

She bit her lower lip. "Yes." She'd even felt a crazy rush of euphoric satisfaction when the safe swung open. Now didn't seem like the time to admit that fact. That she'd enjoyed the safe cracking. Especially since the act had led to her current nightmare.

"That safe was empty," Remy picked up the story. "The next one had a ring inside it. One he put on her finger right in front of a room full of people as the bastard told everyone they were getting married."

Constantine blinked. "That's...different."

"She's not fucking marrying him," Remy snarled.

Constantine held up his hands. "I already figured that part out. How can she marry him when she's sleeping with you?"

Heat poured into her cheeks. Not poured, wrong description. More like burned.

"Aw, damn," Constantine muttered. "Thought I might be wrong but guess not, huh?"

Remy grabbed Constantine's shoulders and pushed him back against the wall. "Watch the hell what you say to—"

Bam.

Glass shattered even as the blast of gunfire seemed to echo in the den. For a minute, Jacqueline stood there, utterly stunned. She could see chunks of broken glass on the floor, and, about four feet away, a lamp had shattered, too.

Why did the lamp shatter? Her mind was too slow. Things were processing too slowly and—

"*Shooter!*" Remy bellowed. He surged across the room, grabbed her, and slammed her down behind the couch.

CHAPTER NINE

He covered her with his body even as the echo of the gunfire slowly died away. A small shudder worked over Jacqueline as she peered fearfully up at him.

"Are you hurt?" Remy asked, heart racing. *Fucking sonofabitch.* Some bastard had shot into the cabin. Remy hadn't thought those jerks would *shoot.* They needed Jacqueline alive. A dead woman couldn't open a safe, but...

But they don't need me alive. Remy or Constantine. His best friend was back in his life for all of five minutes, and the guy was already dodging bullets. *This* was why Constantine needed to get the hell away from him. The guy wasn't gonna have any chance of living, not if he kept hanging around with Remy.

"I'm not hurt," Jacqueline whispered back as she gazed up at him with her wide, stunned eyes. "No one has ever *shot* at me before! I-I didn't even realize what was happening—"

Yes, he knew. Because she'd just been standing there, his heart had been bursting out of his chest, and he hadn't thought that he could get to her fast enough. *What if another shot had been fired before I reached her?*

"Stay here," he ordered her because he was going after the shooter. He'd break the fingers that had pulled that trigger. *You don't aim at my best friend. You don't ever try to hurt the people who matter to me.*

"Two of them," Constantine rasped. "They're separating. One is trying to circle around the back of the cabin. One fool is coming straight for the front door."

He glared down at Jacqueline. "Do not even think of coming to help me on this."

"I'll hide behind the couch," she promised.

His mouth pressed to hers. Fast. Hard. "Stay low," he growled. Then he was crouching, staying low, too, and going for his gun. The gun he'd put down while he talked with Constantine. It was no big surprise to see that his buddy had a weapon, too. Constantine's face had locked into tight, angry lines as he pressed his body against the wall.

"You okay?" Remy demanded when he closed in.

"Because you moved my ass out of the way, yeah, I'm good."

"You're not wearing a bulletproof vest." Hadn't the jerk learned anything from their time together?

"Neither are you," Constantine threw back without missing a beat. "In fact, when I first saw you, it looked like you'd just dragged your ass out of bed—"

He had. This wasn't the time for that talk. "I'll take the prick coming in the front door. You get the one in the back."

Constantine inclined his head and moved to—

Remy caught his arm. "Don't get your ass shot."

"Same, buddy, *same*."

Remy let Constantine go, and he got ready to take out the bastard coming into *his* home.

***

Nate had shot the bastard. Hell, yes. Tim practically flew toward the cabin because why worry about going in softly? Sure, sure, Nate had *said* to be cautious before his partner had bounded toward the back of the place, but they'd taken out Jacqueline's protection. No need for caution now.

They were miles from town. Miles from any other help. All they had to do was grab the woman and *go*. Nate was heading around to the back, in case she tried to run out that way, and Tim was taking the front of the cabin.

So freaking simple. He'd known that if they just waited until nightfall, it would be a piece of cake. They'd have Jacqueline back in New Orleans long before the sun rose, they'd get a fat payday, and maybe he'd hit the casinos in Biloxi and double his money.

He jumped up the porch steps. Lifted his foot and kicked at the door. The first kick didn't do anything, but the second one sent the door bounding open. "Come out, *come out!*" Tim bellowed as adrenaline surged through him. "Don't have anyone to keep you safe, but if you're nice to me, then I will—"

A chair slammed into the side of his head. The attack came from nowhere—freaking *nowhere*—and he staggered. His gun slipped from his hand and flew across the room, disappearing behind some old couch even as his knees fell and hit the wooden floor.

"I'm not going to be fucking *nice* to you," a hard voice snarled. "I'm just going to kick your ass and maybe break your fingers."

Tim's head turned slowly, and he found himself staring at the big bastard who'd answered the door when he'd come calling before. The jerk who hadn't cared at all that Tim had flashed an FBI badge at him.

The jerk who did *not* seem to be suffering from any gunshot injury. "Hell," Tim groused. "Nate missed."

The bastard brought up a gun and aimed it right at Tim's forehead. "He did, but I won't."

Tim froze.

***

Constantine decided to use Remy's trick. He opened the back door, stepped to the side, and he let his prey rush right inside the cabin. And the fool didn't even hesitate. He barreled in like he owned the place.

The intruder thundered, "Jacqueline! Come out and make this easy on—"

"Why do it easy?" Constantine drawled. "I prefer the hard way."

The sonofabitch whirled toward him, gaping. "Who—who—"

Constantine plowed a fist into his jaw. The guy staggered back, tried to raise his weapon, so Constantine just brought up his own gun, much faster. "Nope." He smiled at the intruder. "I can squeeze my trigger faster than you can. And I've got you targeted. *Drop it.*"

The intruder looked at him, looked at his gun—and didn't drop it. Even as the man's face twisted into a snarl, Constantine knew the fool was about to fire.

Hell.

Distantly, he heard what sounded like the front door being kicked in.

"That's my partner," the jerk told him. "He's gonna come in here and kick your ass!"

"I'm shaking." Nope. Not even a little. Constantine wasn't. He had nerves of steel. The bastard hadn't dropped his gun, so maybe he had a few nerves, too. Time to break those nerves. *Break him.* "Where do you want me to shoot you? The dick or the heart?"

"*What?*" The man blanched in horror.

"Dick, it is."

"No! No!" He dropped the gun. *Fast.*

That was the usual response to that particular question. Constantine had asked the same question three times, and always, that was the answer.

Constantine collected the gun and shoved it into the back waistband of his jeans. And he smiled. "Lift up your hands." A creep like him—a hired thug—would have more weapons. Maybe a knife. Maybe another gun.

"My partner is gonna shoot you," the man snarled. "In *your* dick—"

"Doubtful." Constantine did a swift pat down and relieved the jerk of *two* knives and one phone. "*My* partner probably already has him either unconscious or begging for mercy."

"Your...your partner?"

"Um." The other room had gone deadly quiet. "How about we go join their party, shall we?" He got behind the thug and shoved him forward.

***

How long was she supposed to stay behind the couch?

Jacqueline's hands pressed to the wooden floor. She had rolled over and positioned her head so that she could see beneath the couch. All that view gave her, though, was a glimpse of feet. Remy's boot-covered feet. The loafers that his attacker wore. She could also make out shattered chunks of a chair that littered the floor near them.

"I'm not going to be fucking nice to you." That was Remy's voice. *"I'm going to kick your ass and maybe break your fingers."*

A chill skated over her body. He sounded so—so dangerous. So deadly. When Remy spoke like that, she wanted to believe his words. But, surely, they were a lie. Not like he'd really just casually break someone's fingers.

"Incoming!" Constantine called out. She heard the pad of his feet. "Hope you patted down your guy, because mine came carrying two wickedly sharp knives. Wonder what he planned to do with those?"

The cold settled even heavier around her body. Men had come after her with guns and knives?

"Which asshole fired the shot?" Remy asked. His voice still held that deadly edge. The one that made him sound like a stranger. A stranger, and not the man who'd sent her tumbling headfirst into the best sex of her life.

In response to Remy's question, a man's voice blasted back, "Who the hell are you?"

She didn't know that voice. Jacqueline wanted to lift her head. She couldn't crouch there forever. "Is it safe?" she called.

"Safe enough," Constantine answered. "Just don't get close to the bastards."

Right. Like she'd planned to cuddle up with them. Cautiously, Jacqueline shifted position and popped her head from behind the shelter of the couch so she could take in the scene.

Constantine and Remy were both armed. Both held their guns like they'd done this scene a thousand times before. And the scene? It consisted of two men who had been shoved to their knees a few feet away. The men had their hands pulled behind their bodies. She straightened to her full height as she studied them.

"They're cuffed and unarmed," Constantine continued in his clear, unruffled voice. The voice that said all of this was totally normal. Only it wasn't.

Where had he gotten handcuffs? Had he been carrying them? Had Remy just had cuffs stashed at his cabin?

"But don't get close to them," he added.

Again with that warning. Why did he seem to have this obsession with her running *toward* the men who wanted to hurt her? "Not planning on it." Jacqueline blew out a heavy breath. She pointed to the man on the right, the one with slightly long, shaggy hair. The man wearing a motorcycle jacket and a glare. "I've seen him with Preston a few times. I-I think his name is Nate. He's supposed to be a security guard."

Nate's glare hardened even more. "You could have done this the easy way."

"Dude is obsessed with easy," Constantine said with a shake of his head. "Weird as hell. I already told him I wanted to do things the hard way." He pointed at the other guy. "Are you the brains of the operation or is it Nate?"

"I don't think either of them have brains," Remy announced, keeping his gun steady. "If they did, they wouldn't have shot into *my* cabin. That's attempted murder, dumbasses. In case you didn't notice, you're not in New Orleans anymore. Maybe the fact that we're in the mountains and not, I don't know, below sea level, didn't tip you off, but you're not on Preston's turf. Your asses are going to jail."

"No! No!" It was the man with the buzzcut and the black-framed glasses. The glasses sat slightly askew on his nose. "I didn't shoot—that was Nate—"

"Tim, shut the hell up," Nate snapped. "These guys aren't the cops. Don't you get it? They're just like Preston."

Just like Preston. Oh, he was so wrong. Remy wasn't some criminal pretending to be an upstanding citizen.

"Thanks for the helpful info, *Tim*," Remy said. "Good to know that you put your real first name on that fake ID of yours. Though, within about two or three hours, once I get some government agents I know to do a few favors for me, we'll have run your prints and we'll know everything there is to know about you. For your sake, I do hope those prints haven't turned up at the locations of any unsolved crimes."

"Oh, God." Tim's head sagged forward.

"Shut the fuck up," Nate snarled at him.

Remy sidled closer to Nate. He slapped his left hand on Nate's right shoulder. "Did you fire that shot?"

"Didn't hit anyone," Nate sniffed. "So what the hell does it matter?"

Jacqueline swallowed at the look on Remy's face. He lowered his head and put his mouth near Nate's ear. "It matters a fucking hell of a lot. You could have hit my friend. You could have hit *her*."

"Wasn't aiming for the woman!" Nate cried out. "We only get paid if she comes back alive! Why the hell would I shoot her?"

Her heart seemed to squeeze in her chest. These two men were spilling everything to Remy and Constantine.

"I thought—thought it was you in the window!" Sweat dampened the hair near Nate's brow. "Didn't know anyone else was here! Just trying to get you out of the way."

"Sorry, you failed in that endeavor. I can assure you, I will be very much *in* your way from here on out. Your boss's way, too. Because no one is taking Jacqueline from me. She doesn't get delivered anywhere, you understand?"

Apparently, Nate didn't understand. He chose that moment to try and headbutt Remy. Remy jerked to the side and back, so the attack failed, but Nate let out a guttural roar and sprang to his feet. His frantic gaze flew around the room, locked on Jacqueline, and he charged for her.

"*No.*" Remy's growl. He slammed into Nate, and they hit the floor with a bone-jarring thud. He grabbed for Nate's cuffed hands, and Nate screamed.

"Oh, sorry," Remy said, not sounding even mildly apologetic. "Did you break something? Or, did I? Did I just break your hand?"

Nate screamed again.

Remy rose and stared down at him as the other man twisted on the floor. "I had a gun," Remy informed him. "I could have just shot your crazy ass. Consider yourself lucky to just get a few broken fingers."

Jacqueline felt rooted to the spot.

"Because I guess I didn't make myself clear before..." Remy's voice still held that dangerous, intense edge.

Nate gagged and twisted.

"So I will say it one final time. Listen carefully, would you? You don't threaten Jacqueline. You try, and I will make you *hurt*. Understand?"

Nate lifted his head. Tears filled his eyes.

"Do we understand each other?" Remy repeated.

Nate bobbed his head in agreement.

"I think he gets it." Constantine hadn't moved from his position. "I also think they might be in the mood to talk even more now."

"Yes! Yes!" Tim inched away from Nate's body. "What do you want to know? I'll tell you, you can let us go, and we can all never, ever see each other again. Good plan, right?"

Jacqueline swallowed because her throat felt desert dry and because a really big lump had seemed to be choking her.

"How much are you getting paid to bring Jacqueline back?" Remy asked.

"F-fifty grand. Twenty-five for me, twenty-five for Nate."

"Dumbass." Remy exhaled. "She is worth so much more."

"Why does your boss want her?" It was Constantine's turn to ask a question.

"I-I don't know," Tim rushed to reply. "They're engaged, so, uh, maybe he just misses her."

She could have sworn her skin crawled at that response. "We're not engaged."

Tim darted his gaze toward her. He blinked behind his glasses. "Boss says you are. Boss says you're the key for him. That you're everything he needs."

"Your boss is crazy." The flatness of her voice surprised her, especially since she felt as if she was shaking apart on the inside. "I don't want to have anything to do with Preston. I ran away from him."

Constantine pursed his lips. "Some guys just can't take a clue."

"Does he have another safe?" Remy snapped.

Nate and Tim looked at each other. Then back at Remy. "What safe?"

Remy smiled at Nate. "Want me to break the other hand?"

Nate curled in on himself. "I don't know about a safe! He didn't tell me anything! He just—he wants her back! He needs her. Boss is freaking obsessed with her."

Wonderful. Just what she didn't need in her life.

Constantine reached into his pocket and hauled out a phone. "Our new friend Nate had this on him. A little scroll through his contact list showed me that his boss was listed. Want to make the call, or shall I?"

What were they talking about? Surely, they weren't going to *call* Preston?

"I will." Remy held out his left hand. Constantine tossed the phone to him.

"Man, you are making a mistake," Tim warned. "You do not want to come up on his radar. The boss is powerful. He's got more friends than you can guess."

"I've got a few friends. They tend to be useful. I've also got some people who *aren't* friends, but they still owe me. So I'm sure they'll be useful, too. We'll get to all those individuals soon enough. But first..." He scrolled through the phone. "Here we go. How helpful. You don't even have him listed under a fake name." He tapped the screen and a moment later, she could hear the sound of a ringing phone filling the room. Remy had put the call on speaker.

"Your funeral," Nate muttered.

"Doubtful."

The phone was answered on the third ring. "Nate, tell me you have her."

She flinched at the sound of Preston's voice.

Nate opened his mouth.

Remy shook his head.

Nate's mouth instantly snapped closed.

"Nate can't come to the phone right now. He's too busy trying not to get his other hand broken. He's also cuffed at my feet so...*Busy*." Remy seemed oddly cheerful.

"Who the fuck is this?"

"I'm the man who is calling to tell you that your obsession with Jacqueline is over. You aren't going to send anyone else after her. You aren't going to look for her at all. If you want to keep breathing, you'll forget that she even exists."

"Jacqueline is *my* fiancée! I don't know who the hell you think you are—"

"I just told you who I was. Weren't you listening?" A long sigh.

"*OhGod, OhGod, OhGod,*" Tim quietly chanted.

"Your two men made the mistake of attacking me while they were hunting Jacqueline. Foolish choice, and one they'll pay dearly for."

"I didn't tell *anyone* to attack—"

"She isn't your obsession any longer." Not so cheerful. More cutting-like-a-knife. "This is your warning. Jacqueline is protected now. She isn't on her own. You won't touch her again, and you sure as shit will never bruise her skin. Are we clear?"

Preston hung up.

"I don't know if you're clear," Constantine warned. "That didn't sound like a yes to me."

Remy stared straight at Jacqueline. "He *will* never hurt you again, I promise."

***

"They broke into your place, you say?" Sheriff Dewayne Jenkins put his hands on his hips and glared at the two cuffed men. "*And* they took a shot at you?"

The men kept their mouths clamped shut and didn't say a word back in response.

"I've got some federal agent acquaintances who will be showing up soon to take them off your hands," Remy said smoothly. "The CIA will probably arrive first. Ty is a punctual prick, uh, agent."

"The CIA?" Now Tim's mouth flopped open. "Why the hell would the CIA be coming after us? That's national security shit! We don't have anything to do with the CIA—this is just...I mean, at best, it's a B&E."

Dewayne's brows beetled. The sheriff wanted to know, "That a confession?"

"Shut up," Nate ordered Tim. He winced. "Can I get some freaking medical treatment? Some ice for my hand? Something?"

"He attacked me." Remy shrugged at Dewayne's questioning glance. "What was I supposed to do? Had to defend myself."

"Well, yeah, guess you do have to do that. A man breaks into your place, comes with a gun..." Dewayne's hands were still on his hips. "Don't like it when people break the law in my county."

Nope, Remy knew that the man did not. He and Dewayne had a sort of understanding. One they'd reached shortly after Remy took up temporary residence in the cabin. The cabin had been an old safe house, one he'd decided to use for a bit. The truck had come along with the house. Not his usual style, but he was coming to like it.

His first order of business in town had been a meet and greet with the sheriff. It had seemed like a good idea to get on the right side of the sheriff early on. To his surprise, he'd actually liked Dewayne. The man took his job seriously and just wanted to protect the people who called his area home.

So when Remy had needed these two bozos locked up, he'd known that Dewayne could handle the job. But he *hadn't* known that Dewayne would be out of town and that it would take the guy forever to get out to the cabin.

So he'd also called in a favor from a—well, a semi-friend—at the CIA. "The CIA is involved," he explained to a shaking Tim, "because I'm pretty sure the ring your boss gave Jacqueline was stolen property."

"Still not really a matter for the CIA," Dewayne said.

Really? Now the man was gonna chime in with that?

"It *is* their affair," Remy continued doggedly, "if the ring once belonged to a queen and was part of a major, unsolved international theft that occurred years ago. A theft that happened right after an assassination attempt." As soon as Jacqueline had described the ring to him, he'd known why Preston had been so pleased to get it out of the safe.

A very, very important piece of history. One that had been stolen long ago.

Not just anyone would have recognized the description of the ring. Good thing Remy wasn't just anyone.

Good thing he was a *good* thief on his own.

"Where might this ring be now?" Dewayne asked as he glanced around the den. Technically, the place was a crime scene.

Dewayne didn't seem too worried about technicalities.

Remy pulled the ring from his pocket. "Found this on Tim there—the guy who likes to impersonate a federal agent—when I was searching him." Remy had taken the liberty of putting the ring in a little plastic bag for the sheriff. "The CIA will be retrieving it as fast as possible, but I assured them it would be safe in your capable hands until they could arrive."

Dewayne straightened his shoulders. "Hell, yes, it will be." He took the ring.

Tim wilted. "We're going to jail forever."

The sheriff had come with a deputy, and they took Tim and Nate out to the waiting patrol car.

Remy followed and watched them from the porch, aware that Jacqueline hadn't said much at all to the sheriff. In fact, she'd seemed to freeze up during their conversation.

The sheriff promised to come back with questions—at a decent hour. Of course, Remy and Jacqueline wouldn't be there when he returned, but there was no sense in telling the sheriff that. The CIA—and maybe even some Feds—would be swooping in soon enough on Dewayne's small town.

"I stole the ring." Jacqueline spoke up just as the sheriff drove away. "You know that."

"No, you *retrieved* the ring," Remy corrected her as the stars glittered overhead. Thousands of stars. That was what he liked about being at the cabin. He could look up, and, without the bright lights of a big city, the sky put on a beautiful show for him every single night. "You weren't the one who stole it from an exiled queen. Or actually, if the rumors are true, she may have used that ring to try and finance the assassination attempt on her ex."

Jacqueline stumbled back a step.

Afraid she'd fall, he caught her arm.

"This...it's not real," she said.

Unfortunately, it was. Jacqueline was in one clusterfuck of an international incident.

"A queen and a ring...and guys shooting at us. This isn't my life."

"It is now," he assured her grimly. Constantine had vanished for a bit. No doubt, he'd gone to check in with his new boss. *Working for Wilde.* That was probably a good place for him to be. The Wilde agents were the best, no bullshit, and Remy knew that Eric looked after all his employees.

Constantine—with all his assorted and deadly skills—would fit right in at Wilde. As for Remy, well, there had never been a place where he did fit.

His hand slid down to clasp hers. Jacqueline's fingers immediately twined with his. *Fit.*

Remy stiffened.

"I get this is way more than you bargained for," she said, misinterpreting his tension. "You've done enough for me. You've gone above and beyond. I get it."

"It?" Remy repeated as he turned his body toward her.

"I mean to say, I understand if you would rather I slipped out of your life now."

That was fucking *not* what he wanted. "Preston isn't going to drop his obsession." No way was Preston going to be that smart. Mostly because...

It's all linked together. The ring. The missing twenty million. Jacqueline. His back teeth had clenched. Dammit. "There are some things you need to know," he began.

She surged forward and grabbed his shoulders. In a flash, Jacqueline pulled Remy down to her and pressed a kiss to his lips. "I am going to miss you." She tried to step back.

He didn't let her go. "Sweetness, you aren't going anywhere without me."

"But—"

This time, he kissed her. A deep, open-mouthed, drugging kiss. One that reminded him that he'd *been* inside her, been in the hot, tight paradise of her sex, and he wanted to be in again. He wanted to feel her come around him. To taste every single inch of her. To make her come for him over and over until they both collapsed in exhaustion. Then he wanted to sleep with her in his arms, wake up, and do everything again.

"Ahem."

But he couldn't do that. Because his buddy Con had decided this was the best moment to appear once again.

"Just gonna hang out on the porch and make out? That the new plan?" Constantine drawled. "Because, sure, that's one option, I suppose, but I'm not sure it solves the major problem we all have."

Remy lifted his head.

"You have the flunkies being taken away by the sheriff—and then, presumably, being handled by some of your mysterious agent friends." One of the boards on the porch squeaked beneath Constantine's feet. "But she isn't going to be safe, not until Preston is the one being driven away in a patrol car."

"Either that or he's in the ground." There were technically *two* ways she'd be safe.

Jacqueline sucked in a sharp breath. Whoops. His bad. That bit about the ground had probably been something one of the good guys wouldn't say.

Sue me. I can only pretend to be good for so long.

"I'm thinking a trip to New Orleans is in order," Constantine added. "Good thing I live for road trips."

A total lie. "You hate them. You get motion sick when anyone drives a car but you."

"You are not wrong."

He didn't look at his friend. Jacqueline remained his focus. "This is going to be a major clusterfuck. You're looking at several big players who are going to want Preston Guidry taken down."

"Feds have been after him for a long time." Constantine crept closer. "At least that's what Eric just told me when I called to update him. He did some of his own digging. The kind of digging where he calls in favors from the dozens of people in power who owe him. Turns out that Jacqueline's fiancé—"

"Not my fiancé," Jacqueline hotly denied.

"Not," Remy growled even though he knew Constantine had only said that to jerk his chain.

"Well, it turns out the not-her-fiancé guy is suspected of money laundering. You know how the FBI hates that. So they've been trying to pin him down for lots of assorted naughty deeds. Now you go tossing that long-lost ring around and pulling some random CIA assholes in this..."

"Ty isn't random. We can count on him." Remy had recently worked a job with the operative.

"Since when the fuck are we teaming up with the CIA so eagerly?" Constantine fired back. "Wasn't it bad enough when we had the Feds forcing us to do their dirty work?"

Shit. "Constantine. Enough."

But it was too late. Clearly. The porch light fell on Jacqueline and revealed the confusion on her face.

"Why would you be doing their dirty work?" she asked with a shake of her head. Her hair slid over her shoulders. "*You're* FBI. Why would they have to force you to do anything?"

Oh, damn. Was it time to give her the truth?

Because, sweetheart, I'm a criminal, and the only way I could keep my freedom was to make a deal with them.

CHAPTER TEN

So, the way he figured it, Remy had two options. He could come clean. That would be the right thing to do. He could tell Jacqueline that, well, technically, he *had* been forced to do the bidding of the FBI, the CIA, and even a few other groups that weren't supposed to exist. Why?

Because I'm a criminal. Not just any criminal, though. He prided himself on being an *extraordinary* criminal. After all, he'd been raised to be the best art forger in the world. He'd been trained to be a master thief. He could infiltrate any organization, any residence, any business. He could get in and out and take what he wanted without leaving a shred of evidence behind.

But...

He'd bartered for his sister's protection long ago. Started down a slippery slope that had involved more bad deals than he wanted to think about. Unloading all that on Jacqueline right then just didn't seem right.

I am such a fucking liar. I just don't want her to stop looking at me like I saved the damn day.

And that meant...option two seemed like the better choice. Option two meant he kept lying his ass off to her. Obviously, a great way to forge a relationship.

What the hell? Not like he was in a relationship. They'd had sex. He was helping her. That was all. Remy opened his mouth to tell her… "Sweetness, I'm not who you think." Shit. Wrong words. Again. Why did the wrong words sometimes fly out of his mouth when he spoke to her? Remy tried again. "I'm—"

"Out of the FBI lifestyle," Constantine inserted smoothly. "Believe me, that lifestyle is all about dirty work. The cases we handled, the people we hunted—none of that makes for casual dinner conversation." He locked a hand around Remy's shoulder and hauled him back from Jacqueline. "I recently switched employers, myself, and I've got to say it's been an improvement so far. But I'm sure our old pals at the Bureau will be appearing in no time at all, so how about we beat them to the punch?"

"Uh, Con," Remy began.

"Exactly. A con. That's what we need to work." His hold tightened on Remy's shoulder. "This Preston individual doesn't know me. He's only heard Remy's voice on the phone. He has no idea what we are capable of doing."

Most people didn't know. They had no idea just how dangerous Remy and Constantine could be.

Constantine's voice warmed as he added more details of his plan. "So we offer the guy a deal. Pretend that we're going to trade you, Jacqueline, for some cash."

She took a tiny step back.

"*Not* going to happen," Remy swore.

Constantine didn't let him go. His grip tightened on Remy. "Of course, not. That's why it's a con. Just gives us a chance to get an up-close and personal visit with Preston Guidry. You know, allowing us to ever-so-easily slip past all the guards he has. We get close to him, we potentially help the Feds with their money laundering issue, and we make Jacqueline's problem vanish."

Remy turned his head to look at his friend.

"You *do* want the problem to vanish, don't you?" Constantine pushed.

Remy swallowed. "You know I do." *I want him vanishing permanently.*

"Then let's make that magic happen. You know we can do it. A team-up just like in the old days."

Not like the *old* days were ancient history.

"Remy?" Jacqueline crept toward him. The wood creaked. "Do you really think we can get Preston locked away?"

Locked away. Buried in the ground. Sure. Something along those lines. Preston needed to understand exactly who he was facing. This wasn't amateur hour. And Jacqueline was *not* his obsession any longer. "Absolutely."

"Then I'm in." A brisk nod. "I'll find a way to repay you both, I promise. But if we can get this mess to end, if I can get my life back..."

Her safe life. Her quiet life. Her life *away from me.*

"I want to do it," she finished in a rush.

Constantine released Remy. "Excellent. I'll put in some calls, make sure we have support waiting in the wings, and we'll bring this bastard to his knees. Sound like a game plan to everyone?"

It sounded like Constantine was skipping about a million details and giving Jacqueline a majorly abbreviated version of events. Remy wanted to talk to her, alone. But first... "Mind if I talk to my partner for just a bit?" Remy asked her. "You can go ahead and get ready. Grab any supplies you need from inside. We'll want to leave in the next thirty minutes." The sooner they got moving, the better.

Instead of rushing inside, Jacqueline hurried forward and gave him a hug. "Thank you," she murmured. "I will never be able to repay you." She pulled back. Stared up at him. "You are seriously my hero."

The hell he was.

She let go. Gave Constantine a quick, slightly awkward hug. Thanked him, too. Then hurried inside. Since the door was broken—courtesy of Tim's clumsy kicks—Remy could watch her as she rushed up the stairs.

"Hero." Constantine seemed to taste the word, though he kept his voice very, very low. So low it would only carry to Remy's ears. "That's a new one."

"I'm *not* trading her."

"Oh, clearly. Not ever gonna happen. Because you're as obsessed with her as this Preston jerk appears to be." He propped one shoulder against a post on the porch. "Though I wonder if it's for different reasons or for the same reason."

"Don't dance around with me. You got something to say, say it." In the past, they'd always been blunt with each other. Honest as hell.

"Fine." Constantine continued to relax against the post. "You using her for the twenty million?"

His eyes narrowed. "That what you think?"

"I think you're fucking her."

Remy took a hard step forward.

Constantine's hands flew up. "Easy. Not looking to fight, though, the last time you came at me, you did save me from a bullet so...thank you."

"When you're around me, bullets will always be coming at you."

"Oh, right. Like you get to be the only one to enjoy an adrenaline rush. Asshole, do me a favor and stop blaming yourself for my choices."

His choices? Bullshit. "You had to deal with my family—with me—for too long. I am the one who pulled you into my world." When they'd first met, Constantine *had* actually been an FBI agent. Green as hell and in way, way over his head, but he'd been on the right side of the law. "I'm the one who got you involved in my nightmare. If you hadn't met me, then you would have been fine. You could've had an entirely different life. I screwed that up for you." Might as well clear the air now. "You want to know why I cut out and took those CIA gigs on my own? First, because I didn't have a choice. When the CIA gives you the option to play ball or pay for your crimes, you learn to be the best pitcher in the world."

Constantine didn't speak.

So Remy kept going. Maybe this shit was long overdue. "Second, I thought you'd been killed a while back. When we were trying to help my sister, I thought *you'd* been taken out. Taken out because you were helping me, just like you always do. When I realized you were alive, I knew right then that you had to get away from me. You deserved more than the trouble that I will always bring with me." There. Done. "So be pissed if you want, but at least you're alive and pissed, and not cold and rotting in the ground." He spun and marched for the broken door.

A slow clap stopped him. A slow clap. Seriously? He flipped off Constantine and kept going.

"If you're such trouble, why are you playing hero for her? Oh, wait, that goes back to the twenty million, doesn't it?"

Remy stopped. "It has nothing to do with the money."

"No? Then what is it? You gonna tell me that you've fallen for her?"

He looked through the doorway. No sign of Jacqueline.

"A woman you just met. A woman who conveniently comes with twenty million—a twenty million that is supposed to be in untraceable bills, if the stories are true."

"Can't believe everything you hear."

"She's not like us." Flat. "Be careful."

Now Remy did look back. "What's that supposed to mean?"

Constantine pushed away from the post. Sauntered closer. "I couldn't help but notice you've picked up your paint brushes again."

"You mean you noticed when you went poking around my place." Something he'd expected Constantine to do.

"I might have lifted a tarp or two. At first, I thought you were up to your old tricks. That was a very nice rendition of *The Storm on the Sea of Galilee*, by the way."

"Fuck off. It was better than nice, and you know it." The oil-on-canvas had been created by Rembrandt back in 1633, but Remy knew his version was freaking spot on. "Perfection," he snapped.

Constantine paused at his side. "Wasn't as impressed by that one. I've seen you do better."

"Oh, so now you're just being a dick and insulting me. Thanks."

"In fact," he mused, "I saw better on your easel. That work that you've started of Jacqueline is quite phenomenal. When I looked into her eyes, I swear I got lost."

Hell.

"Wondering if you did, too." Even softer. "Wondering if for the first time in your life, you're lost, and you don't know what to do. Being good isn't your thing, but maybe you're trying. And maybe you're lying to Jacqueline about who you are because you know she'll run if she learns the truth."

That was the thing about a best friend. The bastard knew you too well. "Not thinking about any kind of forever. Not my deal. Just the here and now—that's my focus. Not like she can stay with me. It'd be too dangerous for her in my world. Jacqueline likes things that are safe." Hadn't she told him that over and over?

"Um. Too dangerous—that's the same line you're trying to sell about why I should stay away from you, too. Bet it's what you tell your sister— who is expecting a baby, by the way."

Yes, he knew she was. And he wanted to see Iris. To see that baby come into the world but...

I am as bad as my father was.

"Want to know what my life would be like if I hadn't met you?" Constantine suddenly asked.

He had an idea. It didn't involve international art theft rings and deals with government agencies to stay out of jail and—

"I got the shit kicked out of me every day at school by the other kids because my clothes were trash. Because I was lucky if I had a piece of bread in my lunch. Then I went home, and my dad would take swings at me, too. My life *was* hell. Then one day, my dad vanished, and I got sent to foster care. New life, that's what they told me. New school. New start." No emotion entered Constantine's voice. "But it was the same crap. No friends, taunts all the freaking time. No one who ever had my damn back. No place that ever made me belong."

Remy knew about Constantine's past. He'd done some digging years ago and learned the truth. "You deserved better than that." *And I'm trying to give you better. Just get the hell away from me.*

Constantine needed to get away, and, when it was safe, Jacqueline would need to get away, too.

"I went to college on a scholarship because I studied my ass off in school. Didn't have any friends, so what the hell else was I gonna do? Then I got pulled into the FBI Academy. Supposed to be life changing. Only on my first case, I was fucking hung out to dry by the team that should've had my back. I was jumped by five thugs in an alley—"

"You held your own pretty well," Remy remembered.

"*You* saved my ass. I'd been made as an agent—because people in the Bureau sold me out. You knew I was a Fed when you found me getting beaten to hell and back, and you didn't care. You still helped me."

"Helped? Seriously? I fucked up your world. You were supposed to bring down my family, and instead, I brought you down with me." Because Constantine had learned the truth about Remy's screwed-up father. He'd learned all about the family business, and then things had really gone to hell.

When my father was murdered and when we learned that sometimes the FBI could be dirty.

He'd spent too long tracking down the people responsible for his father's death. Constantine had helped him. *And now I'm trying to help him.*

"You want to hear something crazy? You were my first real friend." Constantine exhaled. "You included me in everything you did—"

"I included you in my madness, that was what I did. And look how that turned out for us."

"I'm talking about *family,* jackass. You had me at your house for Christmas. You made sure I had turkey on Thanksgiving."

He actually had. He'd brought Constantine home, even introduced him to Iris. Remy had always tried to make things good—*normal,* or as normal as he could—for Iris back in those days. So, yeah, they'd done the Christmas routine. Thanksgiving.

Until Remy's *family* had imploded.

"The team I was working with in those days— I couldn't trust them. They set me up to die in that alley, and *you* saved my ass. I was a complete amateur, didn't know anything, but you taught me how to fight and survive."

"Some would say I turned you into a monster."

"Better a monster than a victim." A shake of Constantine's head. "So what would my life have been like if I hadn't met you? I don't know. Can't say for certain, but I think it would have been a lot worse. Or actually, I think I might not have even *had* a life. Because if I hadn't been killed in that alley, I'm sure another attack would have followed shortly."

Maybe. Maybe not. "What if it could have been better? Don't you have dreams, man? Things that you want now? You're clear. You don't need me dragging you down. Go find some fucking happy life and get a fairytale ending."

Constantine's laugh was bitter. "Right. Because I'm the prince charming in the story. Not gonna happen."

Not for either of us. Dammit.

"Pull the I'm-a-villain bullshit with someone else," Constantine advised, voice gruff. "Despite what you want to think, *you* are not your dad. Sometimes, you do the right thing. Like when you save a young FBI agent from being beaten to death in a dirty alley...or when you help a damsel in some serious distress who has some rich guy's goons chasing her." He brushed by Remy. "Eric is bringing in a chopper for us so it looks like I don't have to worry about a road trip. The chopper probably will be landing in about thirty minutes, so the timeline you gave Jacqueline works. It will take us to a private airstrip. Eric will send a jet to pick us up from that location. We'll be down in New Orleans before you know it."

Before he knew it. Great. He'd be down in the Big Easy, pretending to turn Jacqueline over to the bastard who'd hurt her. His hands fisted as Remy followed Constantine inside.

"Make sure your control is in place," Constantine said without glancing back at him. "Something tells me that where she's concerned, you might not be your usual stoic self."

Stoic? Oh, hell, no. He wasn't. In fact, where Jacqueline was concerned, he felt far more like a powder keg that was just waiting to explode.

***

A soft knock sounded on the bedroom door. Jacqueline whirled around, clutching the small bag she held to her chest. She'd just packed the bag, stuffing in the extra clothes Constantine had brought and some toothpaste she'd borrowed from Remy.

Speak of the devil.

The door swung open, and Remy stood in the doorway. Looking intense. Undeniably sexy. And dangerous.

In other words, typical Remy. "You smolder."

He blinked. "Come again?"

She gestured toward him, raising the bag. "You smolder. I don't think you even realize you do it. But you just...do. All the time." A barely controlled sensuality that hovered beneath his surface. "You are far and away the sexiest man I've ever met."

Remy strolled into the room. "Glad to hear that."

"There is no way I will ever forget you." The bed behind her was still rumpled—wrecked—from their, ah, bout earlier.

His jaw tightened. "I should certainly expect not."

"You're a hard man to forget."

He lifted his hand and cupped her cheek. "We're not parting company just yet, sweetness. Stop trying to disappear on me."

"I wouldn't." Husky. "But I already know this is way more than you bargained for, and I just want to say—"

"If you say thank you again, I might just have to fuck you here and now."

Thank you. Say thank you. A very loud voice threw that demand into her mind.

"And we have a chopper that will be landing close by soon, so me sinking into you and fucking until oblivion takes us shouldn't be on the table." His thumb brushed over her lips. "But if you say those two words one more time..."

She *wanted* to say them. She wanted him. But Jacqueline clamped her lips together even as she thought...*Thank you.*

"But maybe you think what happened between us was a mistake." His hand dropped. He stepped back. "Maybe you'd rather I give you your old life back, ASAP, and you can move on, and we will never fuck again."

Her hand flew out and locked around his wrist. "That was the most incredible sex I've ever had. I did things with you that I've never felt confident enough to try with anyone else." No, more than that. "I *wanted* to do them with you."

"First time you went down on a man," he said, voice deepening even more than normal.

"First time a man went down on me."

He swallowed. "Sweetness..."

"I thought it would be awkward. That I'd feel shy." She wet her lower lip. "I didn't. I loved every moment. So, no, I don't think it was a mistake. I think what we did in this room was probably the most exciting thing I've ever done."

His eyes squeezed closed. His hands fisted. She was still curling her fingers around his wrist, so she felt the fast racing of his pulse. "Remy?"

"Trying to take some advice," he muttered.

"What advice might that be?"

"Control." His eyes flew open. The darkness *burned.* "But with you, that's damn hard."

Her breath came faster. Jacqueline found herself leaning toward him. "I don't regret anything we did." She never wanted him to think that she had regrets.

"Neither the hell do I."

"Very glad to hear that. I'm sure that you're used to partners with a lot more experience—"

"Can't remember a single one of them."

Her breath caught. "Excuse me?"

"All I can think about is you. Having you again. And again." He lifted his hand—and hers, since she continued to hold his wrist. But then he took her hand off him. Brought it to his mouth and turned it over. He lightly bit down on the pad of her palm.

A shudder slid over her.

"I'll have you again," he promised as his eyes seemed to go even darker. "Before you leave me, I'll have you and you'll scream for me over and over. I might not be the guy who gets forever with you, but I will be the man you remember forever."

She surged toward him.

His head was already lowering.

Their mouths met. Hot. Wild. The lust seemed to explode between them. A desire that was fiercer than anything she'd known before. A craving that should have made her worried, but it didn't. Because when she had Remy holding her, how could she be scared? The passion between them only brought pleasure, not pain. There was nothing to fear with Remy.

She could feel his dick shoving against her through their clothes. He was fully aroused. So was she. Her nipples were tight and aching, and Jacqueline's panties were getting wet. Completely embarrassing but...

I don't have control with him, either. She didn't want control. For the first time in her life, she just wanted to stop caring about restraint and doing what was right. And with him, she could. She could let go of everything else, hold tight to Remy, and the world would be okay.

He kicked the door shut. She heard it slam.

"Fast," he growled before kissing her again. "Baby, we have to be fast."

Jacqueline already felt like she was about to come. She was pretty sure the *fast* part would be no problem for her.

His hands pushed between their bodies. He shoved down her new jeans and underwear. She kicked out of her shoes. Her hands darted between them, too, as she tried to reach for the snap of his jeans. Their fingers tangled, and a ragged laugh tore from her.

But his mouth took hers again, and there was no more laughing. He walked her backwards, and when she would have stumbled, he just curled his hands around her waist and lifted her up. A moment later, she felt a wall against her back. They were close to the nightstand, and he held her with one hand on her waist as he pulled away and used his other hand to haul a condom out of the top nightstand drawer.

This was crazy. Jacqueline knew it. The sudden, driving lust had swept her away. They should be packing. Planning.

But...

"Put it on," he ordered.

She did. First, she stroked the thick dick that shoved from his now open jeans. She squeezed him. She pumped.

"*Jacqueline.*"

She rolled the condom down his cock, and he lifted her up, moving her so that she was positioned higher. It was the most natural thing in the world for her legs to wrap around him. His cock pushed at the entrance to her body, and for just a moment, she tensed.

He stopped.

"No, I want you." Her legs tightened around him. "I've never wanted anyone like this." So much that if she didn't get him inside soon, she'd go mad. *Want him so much. Past sanity. Past restraint. Past—*

He drove into her.

Past all reason and thought. Because there was no more thought. There was only the frantic drive of their bodies. Fast, deep thrusts. Drugging kisses that fed her desire even more. Her heart pounded, her breath shuddered, and her inner muscles gripped him as tightly as she could.

His hand eased between them. Plucked her clit. Pressed. Stroked. *Demanded.*

His mouth kissed a hot trail over her neck. She could hear her own moans and gasps, and when he bit her lightly on her throat, when he sucked her skin...

Her hips jerked. Her climax surged through her body, and her head tipped back against the wall as she cried out his name. Her eyes squeezed shut and pleasure slammed along her nerve endings. Pleasure that stole her breath.

He kept thrusting. Deep. Hard. His hands seemed to be brands on her. Forget him? Never. She would remember his touch forever.

He seemed to get even bigger inside of her. *How is that possible?* And...

He came. She opened her eyes, and Jacqueline saw the pleasure flash across his face. She'd done that. *She'd* given him that much pleasure. So much pleasure his body shuddered over and over again against hers.

He held her tight.

She held him just as fiercely.

The drumbeat of her heart filled her ears and quaked through her body. Her throat felt dry so she swallowed—twice—and moistened her lips. She could taste him. He surrounded her. There was no part of her body that didn't feel as if it belonged to him.

And he belonged to her. In that one instance, she knew he did. Things would change soon enough—they would be leaving. Facing the monster that waited back in New Orleans. But for this moment, this time...

She curled her arms around him. Nestled her head in the crook of his neck. Pressed her lips over his racing pulse point.

Remy belongs to me.

And she belonged to him.

***

Remy exited and pulled the bedroom door shut.

"Uh, yeah," Constantine said as he appeared at the top of the stairs. "That loud whoop-whoop-whoop you heard a few moments ago was the chopper landing."

He hadn't heard it. He'd been too busy exploding inside of Jacqueline and hearing her cry out his name. "Right. The chopper. Jacqueline is just grabbing a few more things, and she'll be out." He had his bag in his hand. All he'd needed to do was pluck it from the closet. Remy always kept a go-bag at the ready. With his life, it paid to be prepared.

Constantine squinted at him. "Shit."

"Problem?"

"Oh, I think we both know there is a problem." His lips tightened as he pointed an accusing finger at Remy. "You're gonna break her heart."

"That's the last thing I want to do."

"Then maybe try keeping your dick out of—"

The bedroom door swung open. "I'm ready," Jacqueline announced, a little breathlessly. Her hair fell in tousled waves and her lips were swollen and pink from his mouth. She also had the faintest red mark on her neck.

Seeing it, Remy stiffened.

Jacqueline glanced at the two men. "Am I interrupting? Were you saying to keep out of something, Constantine?"

Constantine choked. Covered his mouth. Coughed. "That ship has sailed. Clearly. Probably on its way to Europe right now."

She just looked confused. And freaking adorable.

Constantine coughed again. "In case you missed it, too, the chopper is outside." He swung away and headed back down the steps. "Oh, and I took care of locking away your art while you were busy *packing*, Remy. You're welcome."

Remy reached for her bag. "I'm sorry," he said, voice quiet as his eyes lingered on the small mark he'd left on her neck. "I never meant to hurt you." His fingers brushed over hers.

A little line appeared between her brows. "You didn't."

"I left a mark on your neck." A mark on her body. Hell. He was no better than Preston. He should have never, *ever* hurt her. "It won't happen again."

"A mark?" She let him take the bag, and her fingers rose to flutter around her neck. But she didn't seem upset. Instead, she smiled. "Does it look like the one I gave you?"

He had no idea what she meant.

Then her fingers slid along his neck and lingered over his racing pulse. "Because it's right here, and you know what? I'm not sorry it's there. Maybe I wanted to give you something to remember me by."

Like he'd ever forget her. She was going to haunt the rest of his days.

"If I don't apologize, then you don't, either." Her fingers brushed over his neck once more. "You don't have to look so sad, I promise, you didn't hurt me."

Sad? Had she just said he looked *sad?*

But...

Maybe he was sad. Because he'd just realized that soon, he would be giving her the safe life she wanted once more, and there was no place for someone like him in her world.

But I can make sure her world is as safe as possible. That was the one thing he could do. He could eliminate the threats to her. When it came to threat elimination, that was an area in which he excelled.

"I've never ridden in a helicopter before," she confessed as they made their way outside. The chopper waited in the clearing near the front of the cabin. Lights shone from it, illuminating the area. "Is it weird that I'm a little bit scared?"

"Nothing about you is weird." As far as he was concerned, she was pretty damn perfect. "But you don't need to be scared. I'll be with you every second."

"Promise?"

He inclined his head and helped her into the chopper. Before he could jump in after her...

"Better watch it, buddy," Constantine whispered from behind him. "I could be wrong. It could be *your* heart that gets broken."

"Impossible." He sent Constantine a bitter smile. "Ask any of my enemies, I don't have a heart." If you didn't have one, there was no way it could ever break.

CHAPTER ELEVEN

Home, sweet home. Or rather, *bookstore, sweet bookstore.* Jacqueline and Remy had reached her pride and joy—the sweet little bookshop that was all hers, and the first thing she noticed was that the front door wasn't locked.

It should have been locked. The building should have been sealed up tightly. The bookstore was on the first floor, and her apartment was above it. Her space. Her place.

But the front door was ajar.

Jacqueline pushed the door open a bit more, heard the little bell overhead give its happy jingle, but then she froze in her tracks.

Destruction.

Her shelves had all been knocked over. Dozens and dozens of books littered the floor. The pictures and lights she'd painstakingly hung had all been ripped down. Smashed. Broken shards of glass and pottery littered the floor.

Her mouth opened, but she couldn't even speak. This had been *hers.* She'd renovated the space herself. Painted the walls. Installed the counters. Reupholstered the chairs that she'd installed in the reading nook. It had taken her months to get everything organized and now...

Now garish red spray paint covered the once cheerful light blue walls. Her place had been destroyed.

"He's a dead man," Remy snarled, voice coming from behind her. "Count on it."

She whirled toward him even as she swiped at her cheeks. She couldn't cry now. They'd flown on a private jet to New Orleans and arrived just as the sun rose. On the trip, she'd barely managed thirty minutes of sleep. Jacqueline was pretty sure fumes were keeping her going. Fumes and now fury because she knew exactly who had destroyed her store.

Preston.

But Remy had to be careful, he couldn't just growl out that he wanted to kill someone. "You know you don't mean those words. You're mad. I'm mad. I get it."

"Mad?" Remy's brows rose even as he slid past her and into her bookstore. He turned around slowly, seeming to take in everything. "Mad isn't how I feel."

Constantine wasn't with them. He'd vanished after disembarking the plane, though Jacqueline was sure he'd be turning up again soon. An SUV, a rental, had been waiting for her and Remy.

"Is *mad* how you feel?" he pushed. "Because I'm more enraged. More like flooded with killing fury. This shit..." He waved to indicate the chaos around them. "This was done to hurt you. He wanted to destroy something you cared about." A hard shake of his head. "No one gets away with that."

She knew Preston *had* ordered her place wrecked to hurt her. He'd probably searched the bookstore for her first, and when she hadn't been there, he'd let his goons loose to tear the place apart. "We'll send him to jail. I know you're not actually intending to kill him." Not like Remy would kill a man for her. Not like she wanted him to do that.

He sent her a small smile. One that didn't reach his eyes or make his face appear any softer. "How certain are you of that?"

"I—"

But he'd turned away. "You have an apartment upstairs, yes?"

Yes, she'd mentioned her place to him on the plane ride. Nothing fancy, but her home was cozy and had a great view of the city below. Located on Magazine Street, she'd fallen in love with the old building the moment she'd seen it. She'd scraped and saved and poured her soul into the business.

Now...

"I'll fix things," she said, setting her shoulders. "Messes can be cleaned up. Walls can be repainted. Books can be..." Some were ripped apart. Her chest burned. "I can fix it." She *would*.

He'd paused near the door at the rear of the shop. The door that opened to a staircase that led to the second level. "You always this positive?"

"No, I'm just trying to hold myself together so I don't break down in front of you. I don't want you thinking I'm weak."

At her reply, he jerked a little. As if she'd surprised him. "Don't think I'd ever consider you weak."

If she collapsed into a sobbing mass on the floor, he might. *Do not collapse. Do not.* She pulled in a breath. Let it out. Pulled in another. "Maybe they didn't touch my apartment upstairs." She hurried past him. She kept a spare key to her apartment hidden in the base of a flowerpot upstairs, right near the door.

As soon as she reached the second level, Jacqueline saw that the pot had been smashed. There was no sign of the key, and her apartment door hung open. She swallowed, twice, and nudged the door open a little bit more.

Even worse than downstairs. Her knees trembled as she took in the destruction. *Everything* had been destroyed. Family photos of her and her grandfather were smashed. Food from her refrigerator had been thrown on the floor—and the smell reeked. She should have noticed the foul odor sooner. Maybe she had and she'd just ignored it on her way inside. She fought the urge to gag as she stumbled toward the scattered food. "I need to clean up—"

"No." Remy's arm wrapped around her stomach, and he pulled Jacqueline back against his body. "Don't touch a damn thing in here. We're leaving. I'll get an analysis team in here, and they can search for prints. Whoever did this— either Preston or the jerks who answer to him— they will pay. After the team is done, I'll get a clean-up crew out here. You tell me how you want the place to look, and I will make it perfect for you, I swear it."

She sagged against him. No, no, she couldn't do that. Couldn't just shudder and sag. She spun in his arms. "I'm more than mad."

His dark eyes had narrowed to slits. "So the hell am I."

"You were right, he did this to hurt *me*."

"I'll make him pay." A grim promise.

"No, *we* will." She'd run from Preston, and she'd been hunted down. He'd destroyed her home. Her business. Preston thought he was going to destroy her. He thought he'd take everything away from her so that she had nothing left.

He was wrong.

"We need to work on our plan," she told Remy even as she hated the faint catch in her voice. "Whatever you need me to do, whatever orders you have for me to follow, I won't hesitate. I can do this. I will." She might not have his experience or skills when it came to this kind of thing, but she was all in.

"The first step is simple, sweetness. You just have to trust me."

A soft sigh slipped from her. "That's easy. I've done that from the moment we met." Blind trust? Maybe. But Remy felt right to her. "You've been honest with me all along. Solid. You've protected me and helped me, and I am so glad that I found you."

He looked away from her. "I'm glad you found me, too. If you'd stepped into another bar, who knows what kind of lowlife might have been waiting for you?"

She shuddered. "Maybe someone even worse than Preston. Like that's possible."

Remy's lips pressed together. "Let's get out of here. We'll get a hotel room, and I'll tell you the plan I've got spinning around. Be warned, though, you might not like it."

"If it brings down Preston, I will *love* it." She didn't let any tears fall as they left. She held her fury tight. *You don't get to destroy me.*

Instead, she would destroy Preston.

***

"The next part of our masterplan is simple," Remy informed her a few hours later as he unlocked the door to what had to be the swankiest hotel room in the city. Top floor. Massive. And costing *way* too much money, she was sure. "You sleep, you eat, you regroup. This hotel has top-notch security, and Constantine also texted to say he's coming by to watch over you. You'll be perfectly safe here."

He'd just delivered a whole lot of "you" statements. While she was sleeping and eating... "What are *you* going to be doing, Remy?" He needed to sleep, too. And eat.

He sent her a smile that held a hard edge. "I'm going to have a friendly little chat with Preston Guidry." He put their bags on the floor.

She gaped at him. "You're not."

"Oh, but I am. I can do friendly, I assure you. Or, at least, my version of friendly." His head tilted to the right. "Though by the time I'm done with him, Preston may not agree."

"You can't just confront him on your own! You don't know what he'll do!"

Remy laughed. *Laughed.* "Of course, I can. According to Constantine and his many connections, Preston is currently having brunch at his country club. The man is hardly going to get violent with everyone watching. He'll have an image to maintain in that environment." Remy tapped his chin. "I, however, will have no image to maintain, so if I feel the urge to get violent, who the hell will stop me?"

Bad plan. Bad. "Remy! No! You can't—"

"I can. Ever so easily."

"No, I don't want you getting hurt! You go in there, and he will have every security guard in the place swarm you." This was bad. No way could Remy face off against Preston *alone.*

The back of Remy's hand slid over her cheek in a gentle caress. "Ah, sweetness, where is the trust?"

This wasn't about trust. This was about safety. This was about him not getting attacked. *"I don't want you hurt!"*

"I do the hurting. Never fear. I can handle him."

A light knock sounded at the hotel room door. Jacqueline didn't even remember Remy closing the door. She'd been so distracted by his plan to confront Preston *on his own.*

"That will be Constantine." Remy strolled toward the door, paused to peer through the peephole, then swung open the door. "Right on time."

Constantine shrugged. "You know it's my thing. Always punctual."

"Keep an eye on Jacqueline for me, will you? I'm off for a chat with Preston."

"Sure." An easy reply. Like this was *normal*. "See you soon."

And Remy walked out the door.

"*No!*" Jacqueline yelled. Yes, she yelled in the swankiest room she'd even stepped foot inside.

Remy glanced back. "Problem?"

A major one. "You can't do this! If he hurts you, what will I do? We were supposed to come up with a real plan, together. You aren't supposed to go off on some suicide mission."

"No trust." A shake of his head. "It's easy to say the words, isn't it? But when the time comes, few can actually give the trust that's needed."

Was he serious? She stalked toward him. "I happen to have grown exceedingly fond of you, very, very quickly. So excuse the hell out of me if I don't want to see you getting that perfect face of yours wrecked. My bad, but *you* matter to me a whole lot more than my bookstore or my apartment. You matter more than—" Jacqueline broke off, right in the nick of time. Just before she'd said something she shouldn't. Something along the lines of...

You matter more than anything else.

Because that should be impossible. They'd just met. But...

There it is.

"Fond of me, huh?" His nostrils flared as he fully faced her. "I suppose that's a start."

"What?"

"This isn't the big attack scene, if that is what has you so worried. As I told you, Preston is in a very public place. No one will get murdered today."

God, she hoped not.

"Super public," Constantine chimed in. "The mayor is there. So are three city council members, according to my sources. It's some charity brunch. Not like the guy will throw down there."

"He won't," Remy agreed. "I will."

He wasn't listening to her. At all. Her hands fisted on her hips. "You can be quite infuriating."

Constantine laughed. Hard. "You notice it too, right? It's that thing where he thinks he knows best. Super annoying."

Remy's gaze whipped to Constantine. "Are you helping?"

"I think I am. Doesn't it seem like I am?" He scratched his chin. "My bad."

So Remy and Constantine both had a tendency to be a little insane. She actually thought their insanity might fuel each other. And maybe their unique brand of craziness was catching because she opened her mouth and flatly stated, "You are not going anywhere without me."

Some of the faint amusement left Remy's face. "Didn't we talk about this being *my* area of expertise? I'm the one used to handling the bad guys. You're the one who only recently picked up a gun for the first time."

Fair enough. "You're the one who just said Preston wouldn't pull anything in a public place. If that's really the case, then I'll be perfectly safe."

"*Oh.* She has a point. You did say that." Constantine sounded impressed. "Is this like one of those checkmate situations?"

"Not *helping*," Remy growled.

"Probably because I happen to think she's right. Why go in alone? She can be at your side. I can be watching from a safe distance. This way, we're all working together, and no one say...goes off *alone* to potentially lose control and do something he shouldn't."

A muscle jerked along Remy's jaw. "You think that will happen?"

"I think I already told you where your weakness in control lies. This guy says the wrong thing to you, and it would be nice if you had some safeguards in place, so you didn't go full volcanic explosion on him. If you *do* attack him in a public place—with all those big, local players watching— even your connections to the Feds and the CIA might not stop you from getting tossed into a New Orleans jail, at least for a bit."

Her hands were still on her hips. Tension hummed through her. "This is my fight."

He stepped closer to her. "I'm fighting for you."

I'm fighting for you, too, Remy. "If it's really safe, then I go, too. Constantine is your backup and I'm—" Heck, what was she? "The distraction," Jacqueline decided. "Preston won't know what to think if I walk up to him like I'm not afraid."

He edged even closer. "But you are afraid."

Yes, she was. "I'm less afraid when I'm with you."

"Fuck."

Was that good? Or bad?

"Fine," Remy snapped. "But you stay at my side the whole time. You go along with *every* word I say."

Her heart slammed into her chest.

"And if I say...*Exit,* if I tell you to hit the exit at any time, you run like the devil himself is chasing you, got me?"

Sure, yes, she did. Got it. One hundred percent.

"Promise me," he pushed. "No questions. When I give that code word, you leave, immediately, understand?"

"I do. And you'll be leaving then, too, right?"

"Sure." His gaze swept over her. "You know, if we're going to the country club, how about we look the part?"

"I—" Her mind raced. "There are some dress pants and a sweater in my bag. Part of the stuff Constantine brought me. Pumps, too. I'll go change." She whirled away. Had almost reached the bags again when she stopped. She spun right back toward him. "This isn't a trick? You're not going to leave while my back is turned?"

"I'm waiting for you."

"I'll be fast." She grabbed her bag and disappeared into the bathroom.

***

"You might want to change, too. If you're so worried about clothing and all," Constantine murmured. "I know how much of a concern *fashion* is for you."

"Fuck off."

Constantine grinned. But after studying Remy a moment, his grin faded. "What is it? You obviously sent her away so that we could talk." He motioned toward Remy. "Talk."

Remy glanced toward the closed bathroom door. "You should have just kept her here."

"So you could have no backup in an unknown situation? So I would be far away and of absolutely no use to you if things went poorly? Um, nope. I like her plan better." A pause. "Come to think of it, I really like her."

Join the freaking club.

"And she likes you. When is the last time someone—other than my glorious self—cared if you were hurt or not?"

Remy's jaw ached because he was clenching it too hard.

"Yep. That's what I thought. So how about you try *letting* someone care? Why not try letting her close and see what happens?"

When people got close to him, they tended to get hurt. Plus...*She doesn't know the real me.* Unfortunately, though, she might be about to see him. "If this thing goes sideways—or even slightly diagonal—you get her out. *She's* the priority, understand? Until we have that bastard locked away, I want you watching her six, not mine. I can handle myself."

"Famous last words."

"Con..."

"I got it, I got it. Watch the woman." His gaze turned shrewd. "Because she matters so much it would wreck you if something happened to her?"

"Because she's a nice person who deserves a nice life. There. Good enough for you?" He did need to change. He grabbed his bag.

"Not quite. But maybe you'll get there."

No, he wouldn't. Because it honestly didn't matter what he did. It didn't matter how many times Remy *pretended* to be the hero, he would never be good enough. Not for someone like Jacqueline.

She needed the white knight.

Not the devil.

But, in some circumstances, the devil was exactly who you could use at your side. He was about to show Preston—and any other bastards on the guy's payroll—that you didn't screw with the devil. And you sure as hell didn't hurt the woman who belonged to him.

CHAPTER TWELVE

"Are you a member, sir?" The woman near the entrance to the country club's restaurant offered Remy a beaming smile. "Because I don't think I've had the pleasure of meeting you yet. And I always like to personally greet all our new members."

Oh, *please.* Jacqueline barely contained an eye roll. The lady needed to watch it. Another minute or two, and she'd be practically drooling over Remy. Yes, he certainly looked good. Better than good. He'd dressed in black pants and a black dress shirt. The dark colors just made him look even sexier and dangerous than usual.

"Not a new member. Not yet. You could say I'm just browsing." He reached for the woman's hand. Held it.

Jacqueline narrowed her eyes.

Then she realized that Remy had just put some cash into the woman's palm. A casual little hand-off.

"I'm looking for Preston Guidry," he added with a charming smile of his own. "It would be great if you could take us right to him."

The woman pulled her hand back and discretely tucked the cash into the pocket of her dress. "Of course! I should have suspected you were one of Preston's guests. He always has the most interesting people in his circles." Her gaze darted toward Jacqueline. Chilled. "Usually."

Jacqueline sent her a tight smile. She also took Remy's arm and brought her body close to his.

"This way." The hostess turned and marched away on her three-inch heels.

"You sure about this?" Remy asked softly before they followed her.

"Absolutely." Maybe he couldn't tell that she was shaking. Jacqueline hoped he couldn't tell, at any rate. She was trying to play this scene in a cool and collected manner.

He nodded, and they were off. She kept her chin up as they navigated past the tables and the people buzzing in the large dining area, and soon enough, they were turning to the left. About ten feet away, she caught sight of Preston. Seated at a round table, with a champagne flute of orange juice—*no, it's probably a mimosa*—next to him, Preston was laughing at something the man with him had just said. That man seated by him? He was one of the city council members.

But at that moment, Preston turned his head, noticed her, and his laughter froze. For an instant, she saw rage glitter in the depths of his icy blue eyes, then it vanished. He rose to his feet. A broad smile spread over his face. "Jacqueline!" Warmth poured from his voice. Such a deceptive warmth. He extended his hands toward her. "Darling, I've missed you." He rushed straight to her, his hands still extended, as if he'd pull her in for an exuberant hug.

She tensed.

But Remy stepped into Preston's path. "The hell that will happen."

Preston stopped. He attempted to crane around Remy in order to see Jacqueline "But...darling..."

"Yeah, cut the bull. I am not in the mood for it." Remy's voice was mild and fairly low, yet the other patrons were still curiously glancing their way. Mostly because Preston's tone had been so booming that *he'd* drawn their attention. "Save the crap for the dumbass at your table."

Preston looked over his shoulder. "Do you know Councilman Griffin Bass—"

"Don't want to know him." Again, Remy's voice remained low. "And if you don't want him to hear what I'm about to say, then I suggest you bid your buddy an immediate farewell."

Preston leaned closer to Remy. "Do you know who *I* am?"

"Yeah, you're another dumbass who is in my way. Better question, do *you* know who I am?"

Preston took a step to the side and glanced around Remy. Rage flashed in his eyes as he locked his stare on Jacqueline.

A shiver skated down her spine.

"I do recognize the voice from our previous chat on the phone," Preston allowed. "But I'm hardly what you'd call impressed."

"Don't worry. You will be. Ditch the councilman, or I air all your dirty laundry right now."

Preston laughed, as if Remy had just told the most hilarious joke in the world. He also slapped a hand on Remy's shoulder. "I have no dirty laundry," he said, *his* voice low. Then he turned back toward the table. Louder now, he said, "Griffin, I'm afraid I need to have a private business chat with my associate. It's been fabulous catching up with you, and we will definitely talk more later."

Griffin paused with his champagne flute half-way to his mouth. Then he took the hint. Or order or whatever it had been. He drained the flute and shot to his feet. "Right. Understand those chats. Got some scheduled for the day myself." His head bobbed. "Be seeing you later." He straightened his suit coat. When he ambled away, he had a charming smile on his face that he sent toward several tables and country club members.

"Breathe," Remy whispered to Jacqueline.

Her breath expelled. Had she seriously been *holding* her breath? Crap, she had. But now she was sucking air in and out, and Remy's hand was at the base of her back as he guided her toward the waiting table.

Preston had already taken his seat once again, and his gaze noted the proprietary move of Remy's hand.

"Awful considerate of you to bring her back to me," Preston said, his voice carrying only to them. "After our little phone chat, I did not expect this to be your next move."

Remy pulled out a chair for Jacqueline. Gratefully, she sank into it. Much better to sit than to stand on trembling knees.

Remy took a seat right next to her.

"How much?" Preston wanted to know as he sipped his mimosa. "Of course, I'm appreciative.

Glad you could do the job that Nate and Tim couldn't, but I'm sure there is a price tag involved."

It looked as if Preston was going to take the bait. Remy was supposed to be conning the guy, so she kept her game face on. *Remy isn't here to sell me out.* He was on her side, and they were taking Preston *down.*

"Twenty million," Remy announced quietly.

Her mouth opened. Remained open. Twenty million seemed like far too much.

"You can't be serious," Preston snapped. "She's hardly worth that much money."

Remy turned his head. He sent Jacqueline a warm, intimate smile. "I happen to think," he said, voice smooth and soft, "that she's worth *exactly* that much money. And so..." His head angled back toward a glowering Preston. "So do you."

Preston slammed his champagne flute down on the table. "You sonofabitch."

Remy's head moved in a disappointed shake. "That is not the way to go about making new friends."

"I am not paying you twenty million dollars!" A hiss.

"Fine. Then just give me the safe...because clearly, I have my *own* safecracker. She can get the money for me."

The safe. Wasn't that why Preston must want her? He had another safe for her to crack. But the twenty-million talk was throwing her. She managed to snap her mouth closed. Jacqueline tried to school her expression.

"What safe?" Preston's brow furrowed. "I have no idea what you're talking about. My fiancée got a case of bridal jitters, and she ran away. I was terribly concerned about her well-being, so I sent my security team out to make certain she was all right and that she came home again." His lips curled down as his stare swept over Jacqueline. "Darling, you have nothing to fear from me. Like I told you before, you'll always belong to me."

Beneath the table, her hands curled into fists.

"The fuck she will," Remy returned pleasantly. "And bullshit really gets on my nerves. How about we drop it? I'm not a man who wastes time. You have something I want. Give it to me, or I'll destroy you."

"Excuse me?" Preston laughed.

Remy, she noticed, did not.

Remy *did* lean forward and swipe a croissant from the tray in the middle of the table. He proceeded to eat it slowly, as if he didn't have a care in the world.

"Jacqueline."

Her gaze jumped to Preston.

"Who is this jerk?"

"He's—"

"The new boyfriend." Remy had finished his croissant. He reached for her hand and brought it to his mouth. His lips feathered over her knuckles. "So you can see why I get pissy when you start doing annoying things like call her 'darling' or say she's your 'fiancée'—when clearly, she's not."

"Boyfriend?" Once more, Preston's laughter boomed. "Now who is dealing in bullshit?" He pointed at Jacqueline. "You've barely been gone a few days. You seriously expect me to think you found this creep and fell in love with him so—"

"Yes, she did find me. She fell for me. Now I'm standing between her and the rest of the world. Deal with it." Flat. "I want the fucking safe."

Preston wasn't laughing any longer. He leaned forward, and his tie dipped into the food on his plate. "How do you even know about it?"

"I have my ways," Remy responded.

"Who are you?" Preston breathed.

Remy shrugged. "I've gone by quite a few names."

He had? Oh, sure. He'd probably done a ton of undercover work when he'd been with the FBI.

"I've been Michael Vermeer. I've been Paul Seurat. I've been Henri Delacroix."

Who were those people? Were those just random aliases? They didn't seem to mean anything to Preston. He just kept frowning.

"But when I was born, my father named me Rembrandt. These days, I'm Remy to my friends and to my enemies." He smiled. "My last name doesn't matter. It's no more real than most of my aliases."

Preston's eyes widened. "Rembrandt?"

"Um. That's what I said. Named after my father's favorite artist. God rest his soul. The artist, not my father so much. I'm pretty sure my father's long list of crimes means that he doesn't get a whole lot of rest."

Preston swallowed. His Adam's apple bobbed. "You're not *that* Rembrandt."

"Which one?" Remy released her hand. "The famous artist who died so long ago? Clearly, I am not. Though I do like to think that I am a talented artist in my own right. Even if some of my work is well...forgeries."

"Fuck me, you are him." Stunned, Preston sagged against his chair.

She looked between the two men, aware of a frisson of alarm coursing through her veins. *Don't be worried. Relax. Remy is probably just delivering one of his old cover stories. No big deal.* She'd wanted to come along for this ride. So she needed to pull up her big girl panties and play along. And not flip out needlessly.

"Him?" Remy murmured.

Preston's stare flew around the dining area. Sweat dotted his brow. Was he trying to make sure they weren't being overheard? No one seemed overly close, and it looked like most people had gone back to their meals.

"Him," Preston whispered. He reached for his mimosa again. Drained it in one long gulp. When he put the flute down, his fingers were trembling. He sent Jacqueline a pitying glance. "What happened? You decide to jump straight into the fire?"

"I have no idea what you mean." She didn't. Truly.

"He's worse than me. Do you have any idea of the things he's done? If half the stories about him are true..." Preston heaved out a long sigh. "You fucking found yourself a monster."

"*Stop it,*" she snapped. Anger vibrated in her voice. "You know nothing about him, so how dare you say—"

"You're the one who seems to know nothing." Speculation showed on Preston's face. "Where the hell did you find him?"

A bar in the middle of nowhere.

"Or..." Even more speculation. "Did he find *you?*"

No, she'd found Remy. She'd begged for his help.

"Because you know about the safe." He focused on Remy again. Preston sucked his lower lip. Nodded. "You know about the twenty million that is supposedly inside of it, and you think, because you managed to seduce her and get her on your side, that you'll get the big payday."

"Is that what I think?" Remy didn't seem concerned. "Thanks for telling me. Here I was, with no clue of the thoughts running through my own mind."

"*Not* going to happen," Preston blasted. Then he caught himself and lowered his voice. "There is no way I'm turning over the safe to you."

"So you do have it. Wonderful. You have it, while *I* have the means of opening it."

Her spine was so stiff it hurt as she sat in that chair.

"I can find someone else." Preston's chin jutted up. "I don't need the bitch."

She sucked in a quick breath.

Remy reached for a glass of water. So easy. So casual. She didn't feel even a little bit causal about this whole situation, but he could truly have just been having a breakfast chat with an old friend—

Remy splashed the entire contents of the glass right in Preston's face.

Preston sputtered and gasped.

Nearby patrons turned to gawk.

"Whoops, butterfingers!" Remy called out. "No worries. I can help him." He rose, picked up a napkin, and headed around the table.

Preston jumped to his feet. "Security—"

Remy slammed the napkin over his face. The napkin and Remy's fist—they both plowed into Preston's jaw. Preston rocked back on his heels. He probably would have even fallen, but Remy's other hand grabbed him and held the guy still.

She couldn't move.

"Don't call her a bitch," Remy ordered softly. "I don't like that term and neither does she." He lifted his hand—and the napkin—from Preston's mouth and jaw. "Where is my safe?"

Preston's head turned. His wide eyes found her. "See...what he is?"

"Don't look at her. I'm the one talking to you." Vicious. Low. "Is it at your home?"

"Screw off."

Remy gripped Preston's shoulder, and she knew it looked to everyone else like a gesture of camaraderie. But she was close enough to see how tightly Remy held him.

Remy will leave marks on him.

The same way Preston had left marks on her. Deliberate. Remy was paying him back.

"Not your home." Remy nodded. He also shoved Preston back down into his chair. "Your business?"

"Not telling you a damn thing!" A harsh whisper.

"Um, let's see. You have your home in the French Quarter. You have the business in the warehouse area. You have that bar on Bourbon that you recently opened..."

Preston flinched and swallowed. "How do you know this stuff?"

Remy lowered his head. Put his mouth close to Preston's ear. "Because I make it a point of knowing my enemies, and jackass, let me tell you, you are in way over your head." He released his grip on Preston's shoulder. Sauntered back around the table and took his seat as if nothing had happened.

Preston rubbed his jaw. His *red* jaw. His eyes glittered. "You don't come to my town—"

"And punch you in the face at your fancy, boring club? Sure, I do. I just did. I also stole your girl, and I'm going to steal your safe. Kinda my thing, you know? They don't say I'm the best thief in the world for nothing."

Who said that?

"Of course, I do have other talents." Remy buttered some toast. Turned to her. "Aren't you hungry, sweetness?"

Not even a little. She shook her head no.

His strong, white teeth bit into the toast.

Preston stopped rubbing his jaw. "I'm not turning over the safe to you."

"You don't have to turn it over. I'll take it. Just like I took her."

So cold. So casual. But, he was lying. She'd gone to him for help. He'd had no idea who she was and—

Twenty million dollars. Her stomach knotted. "The first two safes were tests. So that I could prove I knew that I was doing. The third one—it has twenty million dollars inside it?"

Preston didn't reply.

Remy did. "That's how the story goes. Your dear grandfather put the money inside a safe that only he could open. He hid it—apparently, very, very well. Everyone thought they had to just kiss that cash goodbye. But now, new story."

A lump in her throat wanted to choke her. She forced it down. "My grandfather didn't have twenty million."

"Your grandfather," Remy said, "had an affair with an exiled queen. That was *her* ring that you so easily gave to the truck driver. A ring valued at a few hundred grand, by the way, so you seriously overpaid for that road trip."

A few hundred grand. He'd mentioned a queen before, but...

"No worries, though, we did retrieve the ring," he added easily.

And she was brought right back to reality. Remy was just feeding lines to Preston. They'd turned over the ring to the sheriff, with the promise that the CIA would be coming along to collect the item. Remy wasn't really some criminal mastermind who was using her. He was just playing the role perfectly, and, obviously, his CIA buddies must have tipped him off about her grandfather and this mystery safe, and Remy simply hadn't gotten the opportunity to brief her on everything.

If she was going to be Remy's partner, she needed to get with the program. She rolled back her shoulders. "Yes, we did retrieve it." She directed a cool smile at Preston. "Just as we will be retrieving my grandfather's twenty million."

"I *knew* it!" His fist slammed down onto the table. "You are as dirty as they come."

Remy tensed. "Oh, my new enemy, you need to watch what you say."

Preston ignored his advice and kept glaring at Jacqueline. "You acted so innocent. But, no, you were conning *me*. Lying to me, all along. You knew I had the safe, didn't you? *Sonofabitch*. Were you and your boyfriend scamming *me* all along? You fucking whore—"

Heads snapped toward them.

So much for playing things the quiet way.

Remy reached over and patted her hand. "Sweetness, I do believe this is the moment where you make a grand and glorious exit."

But...but they hadn't learned *where* the safe was, and Preston definitely didn't seem to be in the mood to back off and—

Remy winked. "No worries. I'll be right behind you. Just like we agreed."

A glance around showed that every eye in the place was on them. With as much dignity as she could muster, Jacqueline rose to her feet. She inclined her head toward Remy. "I'll see you outside." *Because you're not going to do anything that causes you to get arrested.*

Though, technically, he already *had* punched Preston. A punch he'd hidden with the napkin, but still...

"Oh, you certainly will see me out there. Don't worry, I know how to be good."

Right. She turned on her heel, kept her head up, and began marching through the array of tables. Lots of whispers surrounded her.

"The problem is...I don't *want* to be good right now."

At those low words from Remy, Jacqueline spun back around. She spun just in time to see Remy's hand fly across the table and fist in Preston's fancy tie. Using that fierce grip, Remy jerked Preston forward—and down—and Preston's face slammed into the table.

Her mouth dropped open.

Right at that moment, the sprinklers went off overhead. A fast, furious spray that poured out, and she lifted her hands over her head instinctively.

Desperate cries broke from the patrons. The women jumped to their feet and their high heels clicked as they rushed for the exits. Some of the men tried to cover the fleeing ladies with their expensive coats. General chaos ensued.

Someone shoved into Jacqueline, and she staggered back a step even as her wet clothes began to stick to her body. Her eyes narrowed against the fall of water, and she saw that Remy had leapt from his chair and hauled Preston to his feet.

They were—

"I believe the word 'exit' was your cue, Jacqueline," a man's voice said from right beside her as strong fingers curled around her elbow. "And when I create a glorious distraction like all of these sprinklers exploding with water, that's a sign that you need to *move*."

Constantine didn't give her a chance to argue. He used his grip to pull her along in his wake, even as he made a production of grousing and muttering about the sprinklers, acting just like all the other men who were rushing from the room.

Everyone was rushing out. Everyone but Remy and Preston.

***

Remy blinked the water out of his eyes and glared at his prey. Preston Guidry was a sniveling bastard of a man, and he would love nothing more than to give the guy the ass kicking he so richly deserved. "She's not a whore. Just because she didn't want to fuck you, it doesn't mean you get to talk shit about her."

"Guards!" Preston yelled. "Security!"

"Get a clue, would you? Everyone ran out. It's just you and me, and no one is coming to your rescue." At least, not within the next few minutes. Remy knew that he had Constantine to thank for the timely distraction.

He knew I lost my control, so he sent the water to cool my ass down. And to clear the room, so there would be no pesky witnesses to what Remy was about to say or do.

Preston grabbed his champagne flute and smashed it on the side of the table. Then he shoved the broken end straight toward Remy.

"Are you freaking kidding me?" Remy dodged, grabbed Preston's wrist, and twisted until the other man howled.

The broken glass fell onto the table.

"You are out of your league," Remy told him. "I give nightmares to men a hell of a lot tougher than you."

"Help!" Preston cried.

"So used to your hired guns protecting you. Here's a life lesson. I can get past them. Look around, I'm past them right now." Though he knew they'd be charging in soon. *So I need to hurry along.* "You try to hurt Jacqueline ever again, and I will get past them once more. I'll come for you."

Water poured down Preston's cheeks. Soaked his expensive clothes. "I'm not scared of you," he whispered.

"That just means you're not smart enough to realize that you should be terrified."

But Preston's gaze jumped to something—someone?—right over Remy's shoulder.

Preston smiled. "You're a lowlife piece of shit. When I take *you* out, I'll be legend."

Someone is behind me. "Only in your tiny mind, jackass." He released Preston, grabbed the broken champagne flute, and spun around just as a giant fist came flying toward his face.

Since he knew Jacqueline had specifically worried about his face—and because he was rather partial to it, himself—he ducked, then sliced out with the broken flute.

"Aaaah!" His attacker stumbled back and slipped, his feet skidding in the water on the floor. The man slammed down on his ass.

That's how you handle guys who like to attack when your back is turned. Remy whirled back for Preston and shoved the broken flute against his neck. "I could slit your throat in less time than it would take for your goon to get back to his feet."

Preston's eyes were the size of saucers.

"Where is the safe?"

"M-my house! Second floor. Hidden room behind a bookcase."

Remy smiled at him. "Was that so hard? I don't think it was." He threw the broken flute. Heard it shatter when it hit the wall. "Nice doing business with you." Remy stepped away, and his hand slicked back his wet hair. Whistling, he turned for the door.

"Does she know what you are?" Preston called after him.

Remy paused next to the bleeding goon who was still on the floor. "It's gonna need stitches. Probably should put some pressure on that." Whistling, he continued on his way.

"She thought I was scary, but *you're* the real psycho!"

Ah, now they were getting somewhere. Remy looked back. "And don't you ever forget it."

The sprinklers shut off. Waiters and waitresses ran back into the restaurant.

Remy casually walked out.

***

"Boss?"

Preston glared at the bastard who was *strolling* away and whistling.

"Mr. Guidry? I-I think I do need a doctor."

He ignored the idiot on the floor. Useless. Utterly *useless*. Preston swiped at the water that soaked his face and his hair.

The hostess—a woman he'd fucked a few times—ran up to him. "Are you all right? You should have left with the others. There—there could have been a fire!"

There had been no fire. He strongly suspected *Rembrandt* had set the scene. He'd made it so no witnesses would be there to see his threats.

She reached for him, trying to dot up some of the water on his face with a napkin. A wet napkin.

He swatted her hand away. Rembrandt was gone. Jacqueline was gone. His useless guard clutched his hand and kept moaning about doctors. This scene had gone straight to hell.

Luckily, things could still be salvaged.

Luckily.

Because despite what Jacqueline and her new associate believed, he was not someone who could be so easily threatened *or* played. No, he was the one who played the games. He was the mastermind.

He knew exactly what Rembrandt's next target would be. *My home.* So he would just make completely sure that he had an appropriate greeting party awaiting the man. Once Rembrandt was removed from the equation,

Preston would make Jacqueline open the safe for him. He hadn't worked this hard, for this long, to get his treasure, only to have the prize stolen by some two-bit thief.

Oh, hell, no. He'd see Rembrandt dead first.

Actually, I'll see him dead very, very soon.

CHAPTER THIRTEEN

Remy stalked toward the limo that waited near the corner. The driver opened the back door, and Remy slid inside. Instantly, his gaze went to Jacqueline. When he saw her, he couldn't help but tense.

She smiled at him and surged forward. "You're okay!" Her arms wrapped around him as her body collided with his.

He was soaking wet, but not like he could complain about that situation. He squeezed her tighter. Wanted to haul her onto his lap, take her mouth, and never let go. But...

"Ahem."

Constantine.

Constantine was the reason they were currently making their getaway in the limo. Remy had hoped for something less in-your-face, but when you put Constantine in charge of getaway vehicles, you often just had to go with whatever crazy ride he came up with. In this instance, it was a limo. One that hopefully sported bulletproof glass because Remy understood he'd just made a new enemy. An enemy who would not hesitate to take him out.

"I thought we talked about you keeping control," Constantine chided. "What happened to that goal? Did you decide that being violent was too much fun?"

Punching the jerk in the face had been fun. "He called her a whore."

Jacqueline's head lifted. She slowly pulled away from Remy and settled back in her seat. "That's why you went after him?"

"Sweetness, I had plenty of reasons. That one just pushed me a little too far." His gaze didn't leave her. "No one gets to talk to you that way. Pour on the fact that he was the bastard who laid hands on you, and the way I see it, the man deserved one hell of a lot more than I gave him." *Don't worry. I plan to give Preston exactly what he has coming to him.*

Constantine leaned forward and gave orders to the driver. Then he raised the privacy screen. "Well, while you were playing the pissed and protective lover..."

Oh, he hadn't been *playing*.

"Did you learn anything useful?" Constantine continued as he crossed his arms over his chest and lounged back against the seat.

Lots of useful things. "According to Preston, the safe is in his French Quarter house, on the second floor. It's hidden behind a bookshelf that actually leads to a hidden room. Very Scooby Doo-like."

"The safe with twenty million inside it." Jacqueline's voice was small. Quiet. "Your CIA friends told you about it? That's how you knew why he wanted me so badly?"

Constantine stared straight at Remy. Obviously, he was waiting for Remy to lie.

Remy opened his mouth... "No, sweetness. I knew the truth as soon as I learned you were Fabian's granddaughter."

Constantine gaped.

Sonofabitch. He'd just done that thing again. That thing where he fully intended to lie and tell Jacqueline some BS, but instead, he'd offered up the truth.

"Oh." Even softer. "Why didn't you tell me before?"

He could feel Constantine watching them.

Remy ignored his friend. His hand lifted, and the back of his knuckles skimmed over her silken cheek. "There was a chance I could have been wrong. Most people think the story of the safe is just legend. Hell, I believed that, too, until recently. I needed to get all my facts lined up. I tossed out my suspicion to Preston, and his reaction was the confirmation I needed." Remy forced himself to stop touching her. "Somehow, Preston recovered the lost safe. He knew it had been Fabian's, and he found *you* so he could get inside it."

"Uh, yeah, hate to mention the obvious here," Constantine interrupted. "But there are tons of ways to open a safe. He doesn't need her. I mean, seriously, grab a blow torch or a drill and just get to work."

"Preston does need her, if he's afraid the safe is booby trapped." A roll of one shoulder as the limo cut through the city. "That's the other part of the story, you see." A part that Constantine clearly hadn't heard before. "Fabian was reputed to be a suspicious, secretive bast—uh, man. Word was that he'd put a few little tricks in his safe. If someone tried to force it open, the contents were supposed to be destroyed."

Constantine laughed. "That is clearly bullshit."

"Maybe. Probably," Remy allowed. "But Preston believes it to be true. That's why he wants her. Could be that he's afraid Fabian rigged the safe with a dye pack." That was the most likely scenario for Remy. "If someone tries to force the safe open, all that wonderful cash will be stained a bright, bright red. How is untraceable cash supposed to be any good to Preston if the money is permanently stained? Easy enough to rig a dye pack with a magnetic plate. I'm certain Fabian had the know how to do it. Preston is probably sure of that, too. So he's not taking chances." His lips twisted. "With twenty million on the line, I can't say I blame him."

"Oh, no." Quiet. Horrified. From Jacqueline.

Remy narrowed his eyes. "There a problem, sweetness?"

"He showed me how to disarm it," she whispered in a rush.

"What?" Constantine barked.

"When he was so sick at the end, my grandfather said he had a science experiment for me. Wanted to show me something...something special." Her hands pressed to the top of her thighs. "There was this red dye that exploded in a small safe he had in his office. It was a glass safe, so I could see straight through it. I could see the dye exploding. And you are right, it was on some kind of metal—magnetic?—plate. After you opened the safe, a transmitter was instantly activated. He told me that he'd made it himself, a little gadget that he was so proud of creating. I would only have five seconds to deactivate the transmitter..."

"Or?" Constantine demanded when she trailed away.

"Or the red dye exploded." Her hands clenched into fists.

So this part might not be just a legend, either. Remy tucked a lock of hair behind her left ear. "And can you disarm the little transmitter in five seconds?"

A nod. "When we practiced before, I could do it in four."

Of course, she could. *And now I know why Preston will not stop until he has her.* One wrong move by some amateur—or even another professional safecracker—and the money would be ruined.

Remy blew out a hard breath. He needed to get into that safe. Get the cash. As long as Preston had the money, he would want Jacqueline.

So I just need to relieve him of the twenty million.

"What's the next agenda item?" Constantine asked. "We planning a little B&E for the house in the French Quarter? After giving up the location to you, the man is going to have it heavily guarded."

"I'm sure he will." His hand lingered on her cheek. He kept touching her. Kept going back to her over and over again. The truth was that he was drawn to her. Remy felt better when he was near her.

But soon enough, he'd be walking away.

Not until she's safe. Not until the threats are eliminated.

Her head turned. Her lips brushed lightly over his hand. Electricity snaked up his arm and went straight to his heart. *Damn.*

"Earth to Remy?" A prompt from Constantine.

Once more, he forced himself to stop touching her. His head angled toward Constantine. "He'll have a ton of guards there. Probably armed to the teeth."

Constantine nodded grimly.

"So..." Remy continued musingly. "It's probably a good thing that I'm not planning to break into that place in the Quarter."

"What?"

"*What?*"

Twin cries from Constantine and Jacqueline.

"The safe isn't there," Remy told them simply. It wasn't. "I watched his reaction when I listed the main possible locations. His house in the Quarter. The warehouse he owns. The new bar he just opened on Bourbon." And *that* had been the lucky location. "He flinched and swallowed when I mentioned the bar."

"So?" Jacqueline shook her head. "Maybe he was just doing that."

"I'm good with body language." He'd learned to read people early on. A necessary survival skill. "He didn't give anything away with the other locations. Then, later, he was going out of his way to *try* and make me believe the safe was in the French Quarter house. He might as well have just said, 'Come on over. I'll have a trap set up to kill you.'"

Jacqueline sucked in a sharp breath.

"But, if he wants to think I'm an idiot, fine with me," Remy continued easily. "While he has his men focused at the French Quarter house, I'll hit the bar on Bourbon. We'll go in and relieve him of the twenty million." A pause. He let his gaze sweep carefully over Jacqueline. "That is, of course, if you're willing to go in with me. You don't have to do it." She needed to understand that he would never force her into any situation that made her uncomfortable or scared. "If you want to go in with me, I'll have your back every moment, I swear."

They stopped at a red light. Jacqueline lightly bit her lower lip. "If we take the money out of the safe, he doesn't need me any longer."

"Right."

"But, if there truly is twenty million in there, Preston isn't going to just let us walk away with it. And, besides, it has to belong to *someone* right? Stolen money that my grandfather took and hid?" A shudder. "We have to turn it over to the authorities."

"Oh, she is a true blue one," Constantine murmured. "You could, of course, go to the authorities right now and not do anything drastic like say...sneak into a bar, try to find some hidden safe, and steal twenty million. Just a suggestion, mind you." Suspicion deepened his voice as he studied Remy and said, "Unless, you were planning to take the money, take the girl, and just disappear into the sunset. That wouldn't be on your to-do list, would it, buddy?"

The limo stopped in front of the hotel.

Remy smiled at him. "Whatever would make you ask me that?"

***

She felt icy cold. Probably because her clothes were still wet and her hair hadn't dried and because a terrible, leaden fear filled her gut.

Remy shut and locked the door to their hotel room. *Correction, suite.* Constantine hadn't followed them up. He'd stayed in the limo, said something about doing more recon work, and they'd left him. She'd walked through the lobby with her head high and her spine straight, and her heels squeaking a bit with each step that she took.

"A warm shower will have you feeling a lot better," Remy noted.

Her attention cut to him. He'd stripped off his shirt. Tossed it onto the back of a chair. Grimacing, he kicked off his shoes and ditched his socks.

"Correction," Remy amended, "I think a warm shower would make us both feel one hell of a lot better. Checked it out earlier, and I know the shower here is big enough for two." He reached for her.

She took a step back.

He frowned. "Jacqueline?"

"You told me to exit. At the country club, you used the codeword." Was that the right term? Codeword? Did it even matter?

"Right, I did."

"You wanted me gone so you could fight him?" Just what had gone down when she left?

A shrug. "I just wanted to make sure Preston understood that there were some things he couldn't say to you. Hell of a lot that he can't do, too."

She shivered.

"You should get in the shower." His voice had gone expressionless. "Alone is fine. I can dry off and change in the bedroom."

She should shower. Absolutely. But... "You're not planning to take the money and—and disappear with me, are you? Constantine was just doing some devil's advocate bit." Another little shiver chased down her body.

"You're going to catch a cold." A grumble. "We can talk about plans after you're warm and dry." He marched past her. Went into the bathroom. She hurried to follow and saw him yank on the shower. Water poured out, followed quickly by steam that danced into the air. "I feel like I'm always running showers for you." A wry grin curled his lips as he straightened and turned back to her.

Jacqueline found she couldn't smile back at him. "You didn't answer me."

"If I asked you to take the money and run with me, what would *you* say?"

"It's not my money." A whisper.

"Ah, but are you sure about that? Seems like it is in your grandfather's safe. With him gone, don't you inherit all his possessions?" His stare turned thoughtful. "I am curious about how Preston got the safe. Big coincidence that it is in his place on Bourbon while *you* are in New Orleans, too. What made you settle here?"

The lead in her gut seemed to grow heavier. "My grandfather talked about the area. We actually lived here when I was a lot younger. Before he died, he told me that he thought I could find the key to my happiness here."

Remy laughed. "Damn. Key to happiness, huh? Guessing the key is a safe loaded with cash." A smile lingered on his lips. "Fabian was clever. I would have enjoyed meeting him."

"I don't understand—why didn't he just tell me about the money? If he had just told me then I could have—" She stopped. Frowned even as she shivered. "At the end, he was trying to tell me something. Something about his past. I thought he was trying to confess to more of his crimes, and I told him it was all okay. That he didn't have to worry. I loved him no matter what."

"Lucky bastard." Hell, he hadn't meant to say that.

A furrow appeared between her brows.

"Morris Hade was supposed to notify you about the bar. For all we know, your grandfather could have even left you a note talking about the safe." A note she'd never gotten. "Fabian didn't tell you the combination to the safe." Something Remy had been curious about. "He could have done that, it would have been easy enough, but instead he trained you to unlock safes. He trained you to unlock *his* safe."

A ghost of a smile teased her lips. "My grandfather would never *tell* anyone a safe's combination. That would have been like an ultimate sin to him. He said getting into a safe took skill and finesse. That you had to earn what was inside."

And he'd taught his granddaughter how to earn the money he'd left behind.

Another shiver—a stronger one this time—had her teeth chattering.

Take care of Jacqueline. "Shower. *Now.* You can grill me when you're warm. Strip, Jacqueline."

She didn't move.

"Don't want to undress with me here? Fine. I'll be outside." He brushed past her. "I just don't want you catching a cold and getting—"

Her hand curled around his arm. "Why do you care?" About her getting a cold. About helping her deal with Preston. About *her*.

"I care because if you're coughing and sneezing and weak, then I'll have to make sure you heal."

"*Why?*"

His eyes glittered. "Don't you know?"

"No, I don't know why you care if I have a cold. Or why you want to punch a man in the face because he called me a bitch."

"Easy. Because you're not a bitch and no one gets to say otherwise."

She was on a roll, and Jacqueline kept going. "I don't know why you become enraged when you see marks on me—"

"He hurt you. I'll hurt him."

"Why do I matter so much? I haven't mattered to anyone but my grandfather in longer than I can remember, and yet you are doing so much for me." *Too much.* Steam filled the air around them. "Tell me why." Jacqueline needed to know.

The faint lines near his eyes deepened. "Do you think it's because of the twenty million?"

"You're an FBI agent, you—"

"That was one of my many lies. I'm no FBI agent. I'm a criminal, sweetness. Always have been. Always will be. Sure, I might have to work a few deals with the FBI and the CIA every now and then, but those arrangements are just so I can stay out of jail."

Jacqueline found that she couldn't move. His words seemed to echo in her head.

His teeth snapped together. "Fuck. How do you do that to me?"

I'm a criminal, sweetness. "Do what?" He hadn't meant the things he'd said. Surely, he hadn't. *That was one of my many lies.*

"I don't understand how you get me to give you the truth when I intend to offer more lies." Now his smile seemed almost sad. "Maybe it's something about your eyes. Maybe I have too much trouble looking into them and lying."

I'm a criminal, sweetness.

"But the truth has to come out sooner or later, doesn't it? I guess this is our 'sooner' moment." He pulled away. Left the bathroom.

The door closed softly behind him.

CHAPTER FOURTEEN

Well, the cat was out of the freaking bag.

I'm a criminal, sweetness. Always have been. Always will be. He was starting to think the woman might be able to perform some sort of witchcraft. Because he was sure as hell under her spell. He'd intend to lie, to manipulate, then he'd look into her eyes and randomly do the most stupid of shit, like tell the truth.

Remy had changed his clothes. Put on fresh jeans. A sweatshirt. Boots. His hair remained slightly damp, but he didn't really give a damn about that. He had more pressing problems.

Like the fact that she retreated from me. Like the fact that she knows the truth.

It had only been a matter of time until the truth had raised its ugly head. He'd been trying to find the right moment for his confession. Clearly, he had not found that moment.

The bathroom door opened. He didn't whirl around to face her. Instead, he tried to play it cool. He maintained his pose in front of the floor-to-ceiling windows that looked out over the Big Easy. "Are we warm now?"

"You're not a criminal."

His shoulders tensed. "You sound very confident of that fact."

"You're not. You've done nothing but help me from the very beginning."

Obviously, she'd forgotten that upon their first meeting, he'd tried to steer her *away*. "That night, I warned that you were confused. You had mistaken me for someone who was a helper."

"I remember the warning." Her voice was closer because she'd crept across the room "But you have helped me."

"Maybe I'm helping myself to the twenty million."

Her hand closed around his shoulder. "Why are you trying to make me think you're a bad guy?"

He turned slowly to face her. Jacqueline's hand slid over his chest before falling back to her side. "Because I am."

She shook her head. A soft, white terry-cloth robe covered her body. Her wet hair had been combed back from her face. She looked almost heartbreakingly lovely. If, you know, one happened to be the type of person who had a heart that could break.

Not me.

"Bad guys don't rescue strangers in the middle of the night," Jacqueline informed him as her chin angled up. "Bad guys don't give strangers shelter and make breakfast for them and keep trying to make sure they take warm showers."

"Ah, so you're an expert on bad guys, I see."

"Don't mock me."

He rubbed his chest because it ached. "Bad guys can do lots of things that might surprise you. They can create amazing forgeries of priceless works of art. They can conduct some of the most high-profile thefts of all time." Whoops. Had a little pride just entered his voice? Perhaps. "They can infiltrate any organization or group they want because when it comes to blending, no one does it better than your bad guy."

"Remy…"

"And when shit hits the fan, when a bad guy's father is viciously murdered, when he's killed in *your* place, when it should have been you, well, then a bad guy readjusts. He takes the deals offered by certain government agencies. He gets his sister into witness protection. Because you know what? Even a bad guy can care about someone." Can care more than most would suspect. "And the bad guy takes the jobs that he has to take. He gets his record erased, and he gets his best friend's past erased, too. He tries to start over. *Tries* to stay on the straight and narrow." A little sigh. "But that lifestyle can just be so boring. So the bad guy looks for something to entertain him. To amuse him. And a beautiful stranger walks into his bar."

"I…amuse you?"

"No, you obsess me." *Fucking fuck!* Why was she the one person he kept oversharing with? A mistake, a weakness that he'd never known before.

"Oh." Her lashes flickered. "I'm very sorry about your father."

"What?"

"Did you find the person who killed him?"

"Yes." Grim. "He got what he deserved."

Her hand reached out, and she squeezed his arm. "Good."

"Good?" Remy shook his head. "Didn't I just tell you that there isn't anything *good* about me? And why the hell are you touching me? I told you that—"

"You said I obsess you. I think you obsess me, too."

He needed to pick his jaw up off the floor.

"No, that's not really the right description." Her tongue swiped over her lower lip as she kept right on *touching* him. "I think obsession is dark. All about dark emotions and needs."

He was well familiar with the dark. He loved it.

"But I don't feel dark with you. I feel safe. I feel like I belong. I feel like I can count on you for anything."

She couldn't. No one could. How many times would he have to tell her before she understood that he just wasn't that kind of man? "You pushed me away ten minutes ago." A reminder so she would stop lying to herself. And to him.

Her brow furrowed. "No, I didn't."

"Yes, sweetness, you did. I was all about getting into that shower with you, but you backed away. You didn't want me near you. You were thinking I was after the twenty million, finally sensing that I wasn't your hero, and you wanted away from me."

"No."

He'd been right there. He *knew* what she'd done.

Her hold tightened. "Remy, I like being near you far too much. If I backed away, it was because I was scared of myself. Not you."

"Why would you be scared of yourself?"

"Because I didn't want to leave that country club with Constantine. I wanted to run back in there. Stay at your side. Fight any threat that came at you."

His head shook. No, she didn't mean that stuff.

"I'm not...a fighter. I'm not the bold one who stands out in the crowd."

Bullshit. There could be a crowd of a thousand people, and he would always see her.

"I'm different with you. I want to risk more. I want to do more." A little furrow lined her brows. "When I think you're in trouble, I go a bit crazy. I was ready to race back to be with you—I *would* have raced back if Constantine hadn't stopped me."

He'd have to remember to thank Constantine. No way should she have come back in there and seen him getting even more violent with Preston. *And why not?*

Because I don't want her to witness just how cruel I can be.

"Remy, can you really forge priceless works of art?"

"In my sleep." A bitter response. "If you'd looked under any of those sheets and tarps at the cabin, you would have seen work beautiful enough to make you cry." Was he bragging? Nope. Just truth. "I was trained to make them, from a very, very young age. Most kids have dads who teach them how to ride a bike without training wheels. My dad had a paint brush shoved into my hand for as long as I can remember. He wanted me and my sister to be absolutely perfect at our craft. The craft just so happened to be forging art that he could then swap for the real deal."

"I'm sorry."

Why did she keep saying that? "For what? You didn't make me create the forgeries." Brutal truth time. "When I got older, I knew what he was doing. I didn't stop. It took a long time..." *And the life of my sister being on the line.* "A long time before I changed things. Like I told you, I'm not the hero you want."

"I think you are."

His back teeth had snapped together. Remy gritted, "Why can't you understand what I'm telling you? You *shouldn't* be touching me. I lied to you. And maybe I will take the twenty million and vanish. Have you considered that? Maybe I'm using you right now. Other people think I am. Hell, I'm pretty sure Constantine even thinks that. I'm playing the hero, telling you all the right things, and when the time comes, when you've opened the safe and disarmed your grandfather's trap, I'll create some kind of distraction. I'll vanish, and you'll never see me or the money again."

She...shook her head. *No.*

"Jacqueline..."

"Have I told you how much I enjoy the way you say my name?" She inched closer. Her bare feet curled into the carpeting. "I used to think my name was stuffy. Kind of cold. But you make it sound beautiful."

Everything about her was beautiful. He saw that truth with stunning clarity now.

"You're not after the money." She leaned up on her tiptoes.

"How do you know?" he breathed.

"Because I don't think you'd tell me if you were planning to steal it. Doesn't really seem like the smart planning of a master thief such as yourself." Her lips were *almost* touching his. Maybe two inches separated them.

He lowered his head a bit more toward her. *Now just one inch.* "Maybe it's exactly what a master thief would do. Maybe I knew you wouldn't believe me because you're too trusting. Too naive. Preston used those traits against you, and perhaps I am, too."

"You're nothing like him."

"You don't know."

Her hand curled around the back of his neck. "Yes, I do." She pulled him down, eliminating that last inch. Her mouth was open and waiting for him.

So he took it. Greedily. Possessively. Completely. His tongue thrust past her lips, and he tasted her. Feasted. Wanted to devour her.

There was no more hiding. He'd told her everything. She hadn't slapped his face. Hadn't rightly called him a lying bastard. Instead, she'd...

Kissed him.

Was kissing him. *Why? Why?*

Remy lifted his mouth from hers. "Why?"

"Why did you want me to be your muse?" Her breath came quickly. Her lips were red and plump. *Want them again.*

But what had she asked? He struggled to think past the lust and raging need that burned so hotly. "Because you inspired me."

"To do what?"

"To fucking *be* better." He took her mouth again and when a moan slipped from her, Remy kissed his control goodbye. His hands clamped around her hips, and he hauled her even closer. His dick was hard and eager. How could it not be when the woman he wanted most in the world was in front of him and wearing a robe?

She could be wearing a garbage bag, and I'd still think she was sexy as fuck. Because it was *her* that he wanted. Her smiles. Her warmth. Her laughter.

Her trust. The too-trusting nature that he'd mocked? *Remy wanted it.*

He wanted every single bit of her, and he'd have Jacqueline.

Her hands moved to his shoulders, and her nails dug into the fabric of his shirt. She arched eagerly against him. Her tongue licked along his. She kissed him with unbanked need. Jacqueline didn't hold back. With him, she gave everything.

He lifted her up, and her legs curled around him as if they'd done this a million times before. Natural. Right. That was what it felt like to be with her.

He couldn't stop kissing her, even as he carried her to the bed. He needed her mouth too much. Wanted to taste her forever. Wanted to sink into her and never come out.

He lowered her onto the bed. Eased up just enough to yank free the belt on her terry-cloth robe. The robe gaped opened. *Completely naked.* She hadn't put on underwear beneath the robe. Her tight nipples thrust toward him. Her thighs were parted, offering him a view of her—

"*Fuck.*" He shoved down and put his mouth on her.

"Remy!"

He loved the desire in her voice. Loved having her sweetness on his tongue. He licked her clit. Fast, desperate licks. When her hips tried to fly off the bed, he used one hand to secure her while the other moved to stroke her. He pushed two fingers into her and kept licking all the while. Her thighs trembled, she moaned again, and he knew nothing in this world could have stopped him from making her come.

His fingers retreated, and he drove his tongue into her.

"Oh, God." Her breath panted.

His fingers rubbed her clit. Fingers on her clit. Tongue in her. He worked her. *Come for me, sweetness. Come. For. Me. I want to feel your pleasure against my mouth.*

A choked cry escaped her. Jacqueline's whole body went bow tight with her climax.

Yes, *yes.* Remy lifted his head so he could see the pleasure wash over her face. Incredible. He wanted to paint her this way. A painting just for him. Eyes wide and glassy with pleasure. Cheeks flushed. A sensual, sated smile on her full lips.

"Remy, if you don't get inside of me right now..."

Oh, she wanted him in, did she?

He slid up her body only to realize that he still had on his jeans. Hell. Remy yanked open the button and hauled down the zipper. His cock shot toward her, and all he wanted was to dive deep into her. To feel her come around him and sink into heaven with her.

Protect her.

He hauled the wallet from his back pocket—he'd shoved it in there when he'd changed. Remy thanked fate that he had a condom in the wallet. He rolled that baby on, *then* positioned his dick at the entrance to her body. He still had on his shirt. His jeans were undone, and his boots were on.

Screw it. Remy wasn't gonna waste any more time. He drove into her. Sank as deeply as he could go. Wet. Tight. *Hot.* He was pretty sure that fucking Jacqueline would make him lose his mind, and he didn't care.

He withdrew. Thrust back into her. Slow at first, then faster, faster as his orgasm drew closer. She had her legs locked around him again. Her hips rocked to meet each of his thrusts. Her head tipped back. Her teeth sank into her lower lip.

She is so beautiful. Not arresting. Not lovely. *Beautiful.*

He leaned forward. Took one nipple into his mouth. Licked and worshipped, and she gasped for him. Her tight core became even wetter for him.

In and out.

Fast. Deep.

"Remy!" Pleasure hummed in his name as she bucked beneath him.

Remy didn't slow down. He kept thrusting. Faster. Faster. Causing more pleasure to career through her. His climax erupted and seemed to blaze through him. The pleasure was so intense that he would have roared her name except...

She grabbed his head. Pulled him toward her. Kissed him.

And he kept coming inside of her.

***

"You're not supposed to fall asleep in the bed of a man who told you he was a dangerous criminal," Remy's voice rumbled against her.

She rolled over and cuddled closer to him. A few moments before, he'd left to ditch the condom. But he'd come back, and she'd snuggled close to him. She hadn't thought he wanted to talk, but now he was being all rumbly.

She didn't bother to open her eyes. Her whole body felt limp. So sated. How did sex with Remy just keep getting better and better? Would it always be this incredible?

"Come to think of it, you probably shouldn't have had sex with the guy who told you that, too."

But she had. Wonderful, amazing sex. "I have no regrets."

His index finger had been drawing little circles on her hip, but at her words, he stilled. "Why not?"

Oh, let me count the ways. But, maybe she wouldn't count them. She'd just start by naming the biggest item on her list. "Because I love you."

CHAPTER FIFTEEN

Silence.

She waited for him to say something. Anything. He didn't. So, even though she really wanted to drift into an orgasm-induced, bliss-filled sleep, Jacqueline slowly opened her eyes.

His stunned stare greeted her. "You..." Gruff. Raspy. "Don't."

"Oh, but I think I do."

"Jacqueline." A ragged sigh escaped him. "You're confusing good sex with love."

Jacqueline couldn't help it, she laughed. A deep, rolling, eye-tearing laugh that just tore from her. Her whole body shook because Remy was too hilarious.

"I don't think you're supposed to laugh."

"Wait." She swiped at the corner of her eye. She also pulled up the sheet to cover her breasts as she rose to a sitting position in the bed. "You were serious?"

A dip of his head. *Yes.*

"Remy, I could *not* have sex with you ever again..." What a waste that would be. "And I'd still love you."

This time, he shook his head. *No.*

"Yes," she said deliberately.

"You're grateful to me."

She fisted the sheets.

"You were scared, and you are appreciative that I stepped in to help, but, sweetness, that's not love."

"No, it isn't."

Pain flashed across his face as he looked at her.

"It isn't," she repeated. "And yes, I was scared, and I do appreciate your help, but none of that is love."

"Wouldn't know." His gaze flew to stare at the nearby wall, as if that plain, white wall contained some sort of artistic masterpiece. It didn't. "I've never been in love."

She ignored the dig into her heart. After all, she hadn't thought that he loved her. But Jacqueline knew exactly how she felt for him. She'd faced her feelings in that country club as water poured onto her when she'd wanted nothing more than to race back to Remy's side. "I hadn't, either."

His stare snapped back to her.

"Not until I met this really moody artist."

"I'm not moody."

She smiled. "He was drinking all alone in this rundown bar. I ran up to him, and he offered to take me somewhere safe."

"I told you to contact the sheriff."

"This is my story." She shrugged away his interruption. "He took me to his place. Carried me inside when I fell asleep, and he left a screwdriver by the bed so that if I woke up, I wouldn't be scared. I'd have a weapon close by to defend myself from...from whatever threat there was."

Because Remy hadn't even known why she was running at that point.

That truth was something that had blasted through to her as she stood beneath the warm spray of the hotel's shower. Remy might have learned about her grandfather and the safe later, but the first night, when she'd been a complete stranger to him, he'd just helped her. "My artist made breakfast for me the next day. He—*you* took care of me. Better care than anyone has in a very long time. And when the fake FBI agent came to the door, you never hesitated. You *still* didn't know about my connection to Fabian, yet you were protecting me."

He sat up, too, but didn't pull the covers with him. The sheets pooled near his waist, leaving all his wonderful abs exposed. "Where was I?" She'd just gotten distracted.

"You were trying to say you loved me."

"Right." *Focus.* "My moody artist protected me from the fake FBI agent, and then he called in some backup. When the real bad guys closed in, you used your own body to protect me."

His eyes narrowed.

"After the shot was fired, you ran across the room and literally jumped on top of me as you slammed me down behind the couch. I'd frozen because I had never been shot at before. I guess most people have a fight or flight response, while I have a *freeze* response."

"Work on that," he growled.

"I am." Back to business. "You didn't know whether or not another shot would come. I'm not so sure you even cared if you would get hit. You just rushed toward me."

Once more, he focused on the blank wall. "Couldn't let you get shot in front of me."

"Why not?" A deliberate test. "Isn't that something that a criminal would do?"

His lips tightened.

"A *bad* guy?" she pushed. "Would he care?"

"I knew you were Fabian's granddaughter by that time. You're no good to Preston if you're dead, and you're no good to me that way, either."

"But for different reasons."

His dark eyes darted toward her.

"For different reasons," she repeated, more certain this time. "He only wants to use me. But you want to keep me safe."

"That's what you're going with? You think you love me because you've decided I'm not using you?"

"This is why I love you." She motioned toward him.

He frowned. "Uh, *this*?"

"The very fact that you're sitting here, telling me that you don't deserve love. That you're trying to convince me you're evil and that I'm better off without you. You're so wrong." Now she put her hand on his chest. Right over his heart. "I told you once that I trusted you from the first moment we met."

"I told you that was a bad plan. Or, if I didn't tell you, I should have."

She smiled at him. "You can't have love without trust."

"You don't *know* me. Not the things I've done. Who I've had to become. I'm not the man you need."

"I'm not asking you to love me back."

He swallowed. "Why not?"

"Because you don't ask for things like that. I can't make you love me. You can't make me not love you. It is..." She still had her hand over his heart. "We feel what we feel."

Another swallow as his Adam's apple clicked. "Someone like you deserves to be loved."

He could say he was bad all day long, but Remy could also tell her the sweetest things. "I happen to think the same thing about you."

"*Don't* trust me so much." Anger thickened his voice. She could see the flash of fury glinting in his eyes. But she didn't think that the anger was directed at her. *At himself.* "I'm not worth your trust."

"Because you're a forger. A thief. A criminal." She pressed a soft kiss to his mouth. "I heard you the first time, Remy. I just can't say that I cared." Exhaustion pulled at her. "If we're breaking into a safe tonight," she figured they would strike at night, "I need a little rest." Jacqueline settled down against the mattress once again.

"How can you not care about what I was?"

Was. There it was. The real key. Didn't Remy even hear it? *Past tense. What I was.* Not...*What I am.* "Probably because my grandfather was a thief, a safecracker, and an all-around criminal. Most people thought he was the absolute worst, but for my whole life, he was the one person who treated me like I was something special."

"You *are* special."

There he went again, being all sweet and not even realizing it. "None of us are just one thing. My grandfather changed. He put that life behind him. By your own admission, you worked with government agents for years to right wrongs."

"You keep painting a pretty picture. That's *not* what I did."

"No, you don't paint pretty pictures. You paint masterpieces, ones I can't wait to see. You got freedom for your friend. You told me you got protection for your sister and justice for your father." Exhaustion pulled at her, but she needed to say one more thing. "That's all the stuff you did. Now you're helping me. Don't mean to tell you your business, but that pretty much sounds like stuff that a *hero* would do."

"Take it back," he whispered.

"Nope." A yawn. "Can't do it. When you love someone, you don't take it back. It just...is." Her eyes drifted closed again. "Love you."

***

She'd just gone to sleep. Yawned, closed her eyes, cuddled up against him, and gone to sleep. As if it was just the most natural thing in the world.

He'd told her his deep, dark secrets. Revealed all about his crimes. Instead of running, she'd made love to him. *Love*, not simple fucking because Jacqueline mistakenly believed that she loved him.

She didn't, though. Impossible. Adrenaline and fear and a mixed-up cocktail of emotions had her confused. She was grateful to him, and she must be confusing gratitude with love. Surely, that was it.

But I wish she loved me.

His phone rang, the vibration coming from the other side of the room. The place where he'd ditched his jeans after he'd gotten a bit of sanity back. The phone was probably still tucked in one of the pockets. He wanted to ignore the ringing but...

Too much trouble surrounds us.

He pressed a kiss to Jacqueline's brow and slipped out of the bed. He scooped up the jeans and the phone. A glance at the screen showed the caller to be Constantine. After hurriedly turning off the ringer, Remy crept out of the bedroom. They were in a suite, so he shut the door. When it was closed, only then did he take the call. "What's on fire now?"

"I'm outside the hotel room door. Didn't want to interrupt anything, so I thought I'd give you a courtesy call."

"Well, aren't you awesome." He jerked on his jeans, kept the phone to his ear by using his shoulder, then he stalked for the door. A quick glance through the peephole confirmed Constantine was alone and on the other side of the door. "Come on in." He hung up and unlocked the door.

Constantine didn't enter. His brow furrowed as he studied Remy's face.

"What?" Remy barked when the study session went on a little too long.

"I'm trying to figure out why you look shaken." Constantine's head tilted. "I figured you and your lady would rush up here, strip off the wet clothes, and—"

"Don't worry about what happens when Jacqueline's clothes come off." A grim warning. A possessive one.

Constantine smiled. "You have it so bad." He crossed the threshold. Shut and bolted the door. But the furrow returned to his brow. "What's wrong?"

"Nothing." *Not a damn thing. Except Jacqueline thinks that she loves me, and, clearly, she doesn't.*

"Tell that to someone who doesn't know what you look like when you discover your father was stabbed in the heart and you realize you have to abandon your kid sister in order to keep her safe."

Remy's nostrils flared.

"Because I saw pain—real pain—on your face during both of those occasions. You might like to act as if you're the big, bad, heartless thief, but you're not. Something has hurt you since I dropped you off at the hotel. You're in pain, man. I see it." A thread of worry deepened his voice even more. "Is Jacqueline all right?"

"Fine." Clipped. "She's sleeping."

A sigh of relief escaped Constantine, but he still watched Remy with concern clear to see in his expression. "So why are you hurting?"

Remy rubbed his chest. "I'm not. I feel fine."

Constantine glanced down at Remy's hand as it pressed over his heart. "Uh, huh. Sure." A hesitation. "If you can't tell your best friend, who can you tell?"

"That what we still are?" Remy swung around and headed toward a window. "Even after I deserted your ass?"

"Oh, hey, fun detail. Want to guess what I was doing while you were busy up here with Jacqueline?"

Remy tossed a glare back at him. "I'm not in the mood to guess."

"Killjoy. Fine. I'll just tell you. I was having a super fun and ever-so-informative telephone conversation with your CIA buddy, Ty Crenshaw. Remember him?"

Of course, he did. Ty had been one of the agents who owed him a favor, so he'd called in the guy to pick up the ring in Halfway, Georgia.

"Well, he had so much to tell me about you, and about the fact that you were basically willing to trade your soul so that every one of *my* sins could be erased. When you said I was free, I didn't quite understand just what you'd done to achieve that freedom." Constantine's jaw hardened.

"Ty exaggerates. Don't believe everything he says. I worked with him because he is connected to a man with a whole lot of power in the CIA. That man called me in, and I had no choice. Getting you off their radar was just a side bonus."

"Liar."

Yes. He turned to fully face Constantine. "Don't make me out to be some damn hero. I am *not.*" Why did people keep making that mistake?

"Is that what Jacqueline is doing? Trying to cast you as a hero?"

Constantine could always find weak spots with unerring accuracy. "I told her who I really am."

A wince. "Oh. Well, that explains things. Particularly, your sad-ass expression. She flipped out, huh?"

"She said she loves me." His hand returned to his side. He looked down at the floor.

"*What*?"

"I told her she was wrong."

"Tell *me* you didn't. Dude, you don't get to tell a woman how she feels, you don't—"

His head snapped up. "She's too fucking good for me, okay? She doesn't need someone like me around her long term. Yes, I can help her now. Now, while she's scared and desperate, and she needs someone who understands how to fight the monsters closing in. But when we've eliminated Preston, she wants her safe world back. *I'm* not safe. I never have been! I am not what she needs."

"Ah, man." Constantine strode forward. His hand clamped around Remy's shoulder. "Why the hell can't you realize that maybe—just maybe— she sees something good in you?"

"Because I am my father's son. I lied to her from the beginning."

"You lie to *everyone*. It's sort of your thing."

He sent Constantine a glare. "You're not helping."

"I don't know how to help! I've never seen you like this. You are—" He broke off as his eyes widened. "Oh, shit."

Remy shrugged off Constantine's hold.

"You love her, don't you?" Constantine practically pounced.

"Jeez, man, keep your voice down!" He darted a glance toward the closed bedroom door. "She's exhausted and needs to sleep."

"And you're scared she'll find out that *you love her*. Big Remy just had his heart *stolen!*"

"Okay, first, don't call me Big Remy because it's annoying."

"Yep, I can see that." A quick grin.

"Second," Remy growled, "she didn't steal my heart."

"So you...don't love her?"

"I—" Remy stopped. Just stopped.

Constantine's grin stretched. "You can't say it, can you? You can't say that you don't love her."

"I can say anything. Didn't we just discuss the fact that I lie as easily as I breathe?"

"I don't know if we said it quite that way..." Constantine rolled back his shoulders. "But maybe you just can't lie about the most important thing that has happened to you. For the first time in your life, you love someone."

"Not the first time in my life. I love my sister. I even love your annoying ass."

Constantine winked at him. "That's so sweet, and I love you like a brother, too, but you know I'm talking about romantic love. The kind of love that makes you think of forever. That has you dreaming about a home and maybe some kids and growing old as you paint in some quaint little cabin somewhere." He snapped his fingers together. "Wait, you're already doing half that stuff, aren't you?"

"Have you been watching those Hallmark movies again?" Remy snapped.

"Don't be judgy. I'm not the one who can't admit that I love someone."

Once more, he looked toward the bedroom door. Still shut. Was she still sleeping? He hoped so.

"Stop taking the weight of the world on your shoulders." Constantine's voice turned serious. "Maybe stop paying for everyone's sins. Take some joy for yourself."

If only things were that easy. "I'm not talking about this any longer."

"Sure. Like I didn't see that coming. Someone is just not comfortable with his emotions."

Time for a conversation change. "Did you really talk to Ty?"

"Yep, he has the ring, by the way. Eric gave him my number, told him that I was watching your six, as I often do. Ty is incoming, but he won't be here until at least tomorrow morning."

That's too late.

"I'm assuming we won't wait until tomorrow," Constantine added as he correctly read Remy's expression.

"Nope. We're getting into the safe tonight. Preston will have his men stationed at the French Quarter house. This is our best opportunity."

"And you're okay with taking Jacqueline into the bar on Bourbon, knowing there could be a trap there, too? I mean, if it were me, I'd have extra guards stationed at all my properties, and *particularly* at the place where I had twenty million dollars stashed away." Cool. Careful.

Remy's hands fisted. "I'm not okay with it, but we need her in there. She's priority, just like I told you before. If things go to shit—"

"As they so often can..."

"Get her out. *Carry* her out if you have to do it. She won't willingly leave me."

A nod. "Because she loves you."

Dammit. "Get her out. Her safety comes *first*. Understand? Forget about me. Focus on her."

Another nod. Slower. A little sad. "Because you love her."

He stared at Constantine. Just stared. *Hell, yes, I do. So much so that it is nearly ripping me apart.* But if he said the words out loud, he couldn't take them back. If he said them out loud, that would make everything real.

If he said them out loud...*how am I ever supposed to let her go?* And he had to let her go. Because he *did* love her so much. She needed a life without him. Remy sucked in a deep breath. "If you talked to Ty, am I to assume you talked with Eric, too?"

"Indeed, I did. The boss found out a few interesting historical tidbits for us."

"Don't keep me in suspense."

"Wouldn't dream of it." Constantine stalked across the room and peered out of the window. "Turns out that before Hurricane Katrina hit down here, Jacqueline and her grandfather called New Orleans home."

"She mentioned something about living here a long time ago."

"Did she mention that her grandfather once owned a bar on Bourbon Street?"

"Ah, no. She didn't."

Constantine sent a glance over his shoulder. "Want to guess which one?"

He didn't have to guess. "The one Preston now owns."

"Yes. Another *interesting* point. Eric managed to find out what fake last name Fabian was using before his death. Eric backtracked, using your girl and everything his techs could find on her."

You mean he had his techs tear her life apart.

"Before Fabian died, he used the last name of Carmichael, and Fabian Carmichael had a will. In that will, he left all his possessions—including his bar—to his granddaughter. But, funny thing..."

"I haven't heard a damn funny thing so far."

"The bar was never turned over to her. I'm not sure she even knew the place existed. Like I said, Fabian moved her out of here after Katrina hit, and that was back in 2005."

"I'm still waiting for the funny part."

"Here it comes." Constantine turned fully away from the window. "The lawyer that Carmichael used? That lawyer was based down here in New Orleans. Morris Hade. Good old Morris just *happens* to be working for Preston Guidry. Been the Guidry family lawyer for years, since long before little Preston grew into the big asshole that he is today."

Sonofabitch.

"Eric got his techs to pull up building permits from the city. About six months ago, Preston started remodeling work at the bar. I'm betting that's when he found the long lost safe."

The safe, and he'd known the rumored tale about the twenty million. Money that should have gone to Jacqueline. "Didn't hear a funny part." Just parts that pissed him off. The lawyer had hidden her inheritance from Jacqueline. Been crooked as hell. *On Preston's payroll.*

Remy's phone dinged.

Constantine smiled. "Once Eric started digging with the permit people, he found some old architectural designs for the bar. He compared those designs with the remodeling plans that Preston had to submit. That text you just received *should* be the schematics, courtesy of Eric."

Remy pulled out his phone. As he stared at the screen, a slow smile curved his lips.

"Consider it your treasure map. You can now see *exactly* where the safe is hidden. Did I get to the funny part? Because I thought I just did. It's the part where Preston is an idiot, and he's shown us exactly how to locate the twenty million."

Hell, yes. "I owe Eric."

"I'm sure you'll pay him back. You seem to have an obsession with doing that." A little taunt that Remy let slide. "Ready to get down to business? Just like the old days, am I right?"

Not one hundred percent but...

Close.

Remy kept staring at the building schematics as he crafted his plan. "I'm going to need some smoke bombs."

"You always do."

CHAPTER SIXTEEN

"We're just walking in?" She tugged on the hem of her dress. A dress that felt way too short and had come courtesy of the hotel. Or rather, a delivery from the hotel, from the expensive shop on the first floor. Black and tight, the dress hugged every inch of her body.

After she'd put it—and fancy new black pumps—on, she'd hurried out of the bathroom to find Remy. He'd stared at her a moment, not saying a word. When she'd prompted him, he'd finally told her, "I wish I could paint you."

From Remy, she knew that was high praise indeed, but she still felt uncomfortable as hell in the dress. Not her normal style at all. Remy, meanwhile, wore loose jeans, a tight t-shirt, a black jacket, and boots. "Tell me again," she said as the limo slowed near the intersection of Canal and Bourbon, "why I'm wearing this, and you get to be all comfortable."

"Because when you look as hot as you do, no one will expect you to be a threat. Any guards will be too distracted to think you might be dangerous."

Dangerous. That was a new way to describe her.

"You sure you don't need any tools for the job?" Remy murmured.

The job would be safe cracking, and she was trying ever so hard to play it cool. "Not like we can do any drilling." Her grandfather had always hated drilling into the weak points of a safe. He'd called the work sloppy. "A blow torch is definitely not an option." Another method not favored by her grandfather. *Too dangerous. Don't want to burn yourself, do you?* "And scoping is out."

He lifted a brow.

"That goes with drilling." Though she suspected Remy probably knew this. But she was nervous, and when she was nervous, she rambled. They had reached their location, but she couldn't quite manage to slide toward the door and get out of the limo. "With scoping, that's when you drill a small hole into the safe, and you insert a borescope. It lets you see inside."

"We already know what's inside."

Scoping let you look at the mechanisms of the lock, too, but, again, scoping wasn't an option. Not if they were right about her grandfather booby trapping this safe. "It's going to be old-school lock manipulation." Just like the other two safes she'd opened for Preston. Her hand fluttered in the air. "It's all about fingers, eyes, and ears. Not so much hearing, though, as feeling." Her grandfather had been so big on *feeling* the lock. Sensing the vibrations.

"Why didn't Preston use an auto-dialer?" Remy wanted to know.

Ah, so he *did* know his safecracking terms. "Those can take twenty-four hours or more." The computerized auto-dialers were used by the newer safecrackers, and her grandfather had scoffed at them. Said they were ruining the craft. "He always told me he could block an auto-dialer any day of the week. I suspect Preston tried them on this safe, and they didn't work."

"Probably scared to try too hard because he didn't want to damage the prize inside. Once he realized he had the legendary safe from Fingers Fabian, the man couldn't take chances."

Yes. The prize. *Twenty million.* "What happens once we get the money? Do we turn it over to the CIA? The Feds? And how are we going to stop Preston? He'll just come after us." With a vengeance.

"I like to worry about one problem at a time. Right now, we just need to get in the safe." He leaned forward and reached for the door. "You ready?"

Nope. But they were still doing this. "Constantine is close by, watching?"

"He has his orders." Remy smiled at her. "Don't worry, you will be safe."

But I want you safe, too. "We'll *both* be safe."

"Isn't that what I said?" Remy opened the door. After he stepped out, he reached back with his hand for her.

Her fingers closed around his. "No, that's not what you said."

"I'm sure it's what I meant." Remy pulled her closer. Turned toward Bourbon. She could already hear the laughter and the voices ringing out in the air.

Even though she lived in New Orleans, she didn't visit Bourbon Street very often. She'd actually only crept onto the party street once or twice with a few friends. But Remy strolled forward as if he came there every night. Confidence oozed from him, and his arm looped over her shoulders in a gesture that felt both protective and possessive.

"I did put a present or two in your bag," he said, voice soft. "Just because I wanted you to be prepared."

The little black bag that had arrived with her dress. She paused, fumbled inside, and saw...

A screwdriver.

She started to smile.

"A woman should always have her trusty screwdriver at her side," he murmured. "I also included a few things from *my* lock-picking set. Doubt they'll be of any help, but I figured they couldn't hurt."

She closed the bag. The screwdriver and the set he talked about had been nestled in a side compartment. Hidden. "You know the way to my heart."

The arm around her shoulders tensed. "And you know how to take mine."

Her eyes widened.

But before she could question him, they were moving again. Strolling past the brightly colored lights and signs that hung over the bars. People danced and called out from the second-story balconies that were all along the street. No cars, just people. People in the road. People spilling from the bars. People walking with enormous drinks in their hands.

Some people stumbling toward the curb.

It was close to eleven p.m., and the party certainly seemed to be going strong. Music blasted from the open doors they passed, and some women who appeared to be wearing nothing more than sheer negligees crooked their fingers at Remy in invitation.

She swallowed and edged ever closer to him. *Not happening, ladies.*

They kept strolling down the street, and everywhere she looked, there was something new to see. A trumpet player blasted from a corner, and a horse-drawn carriage skirted by on a crossroad.

"Did you know that your grandfather owned the bar here on Bourbon?"

"No." He'd mentioned that to her on the car ride over.

"And the attorney, Morris Hade, you've never heard of him?"

She shook her head. "When my grandfather died, there wasn't any legal paperwork or wills. I thought it was because he was living under an assumed name. Hard to legally give property to a relative when you don't have an identity."

"Um. That's probably why it made things so easy for Morris." Anger beat in his voice. "The bastard was all too eager to sell the information he possessed to Preston. Don't worry, we'll be dealing with him, too. No one takes away the things that belong to you."

The crowd had begun to thin. Not as many bars. Not as many people.

"The last bar on Bourbon street is Lafitte's," Remy murmured. "We're not going quite that far.

In fact, we're here." He turned to the right. Toward a building on the corner, two stories. Like the other buildings, it looked historic. In other words...very, very old. The white paint over the bricks had faded, and big, blue shutters surrounded what looked like four different doors that led inside from the street.

"The number of entrances and exits will work to our advantage. People will clear out fast when they see the smoke." He stepped toward the building.

She hauled him back. Though she made the gesture look more like a fierce hug than a grab. Her arms wrapped tightly around him, and she rose to whisper in his ear, "Smoke? You didn't say anything about setting a fire!"

"Relax, love," he breathed back. "It's all distraction. Just smoke bombs. A technique I learned from my father. If you want to clear a building, sometimes, you need a few special effects."

The idea still made her nervous.

"When they're running out, we'll be running for the safe. Then you can work your magic."

He seemed to have such confidence in her. Jacqueline's stomach twisted. "What if I can't do it?"

Remy eased back and stared down at her. "You can."

Too much faith. "The other two were easy. I-I think anyone with a bit of skill could have done those. This will be different. I'm *not* my grandfather. Everything could go very wrong."

He caught her hand. Brought it to his lips. "In that case, we improvise."

"Remy..."

Using his hold on her hand, he tugged her through the nearby, open door and into the dimly lit bar. Music blared. Drinks clinked. And fear iced her blood.

***

The bastard had been a no-show so far.

Preston choked back his rage as he sat in the back seat of his parked car. He'd expected Rembrandt to rush to the house in the French Quarter. To come busting in with his grand plans of theft. In return, Preston had been ready to have his guards eliminate the bastard. After all, when an intruder broke into your home, weren't you allowed to defend yourself? To do whatever was necessary if you feared for your life?

He'd already had the perfect story ready for the cops. A career thief had broken into his home, threatened him, and his guards had been given no choice but to shoot.

Except the bastard wasn't showing up.

Preston checked his watch again. A little after eleven. Yes, yes, he got that Rembrandt would probably prefer a night-time break-in. Who didn't like the cover of darkness? But this shit was taking too long.

Where is he?

"You followed him after he left the country club?" Preston snarled to the guard in the seat beside him. Jimmy Hayes. Jimmy had been with him for about a year. Jimmy didn't ask questions, he always followed orders, and he had no problem breaking the law when necessary. *Three perfect traits.*

"He left in the limo. Went to the high-priced hotel. Hell, Mr. Guidry, there were at least five other limos there when they arrived. Limos come and go all the time at that place." Nerves cracked in his voice. "We have a guy watching the hotel now, but like I said, limos come and go constantly from the place. The bastard *could* have slipped out."

Limos come and go. Which was, no doubt, why Rembrandt had chosen that ride. It was easier to blend that way. Easier to arrive and leave from the hotel in a car like the ones so many others were using.

"Where the fuck are you?" he whispered.

"Uh, boss, I'm right here," Jimmy said.

Sonofabitch. Rembrandt wasn't there. And if he wasn't taking the bait and coming to the house in the Quarter, then...*hell.* "Get me the fuck out of here," he snarled to the driver as he grabbed the edge of the front seat. "Take me to Bourbon, *now.*"

***

"So, how does this work?" Jacqueline asked. She was all wide eyes, soft skin, and sinful temptation as she stood before Remy in a dress that made him want to drool.

Perhaps the dress hadn't been the best idea. But, oh, it looked good.

He curled his hands around her waist as he pulled her closer. They were on what passed for the dance floor. They'd come into the bar about fifteen minutes ago. The plan wasn't to immediately jump into action. They needed to blend a bit first. So he'd grabbed a drink. Gotten one for her, too.

Jacqueline had barely sipped hers. He could feel the nervous energy pouring from her. Since they were still in the blending portion of the event, he'd tugged her onto the dance floor.

"Relax," he urged. "I've got you."

"Even with you holding me, relaxing is a complete impossibility at this point." She looked up at him through her lashes. "What if I can't do it?"

"Then you trigger the safe so that the ink explodes. Preston is not gonna get the cash." One way or the other, they'd eliminate that possibility before they left. "We trigger it, we get the hell out, and then we regroup." His body swayed with hers. Her scent wrapped around him, tempted, but now wasn't the time to give in to temptation.

"When do you set the, ah, smoke bombs?" she whispered.

"I don't. Constantine is taking care of them right now."

And, as if on cue, gray smoke began to drift from behind the bar.

Shouts filled the air as the people in bar caught sight of the smoke and then...chaos. Remy pulled Jacqueline even closer, he tucked her against his body to make sure that she didn't get jostled, then he watched as the patrons flooded for the doors.

Again, good thing there were so many doors. The bottom floor was pretty much just composed of doors that had been left wide open. People rushed through them.

An alarm blared from overhead.

As everyone else hurried for the doors, he turned and guided Jacqueline to the back. He jerked open the "Staff" door and entered the waiting corridor.

He also came face-to-face with a tall, overly muscled guy in black. A man with a fierce, angry expression that screamed he was security. Fabulous.

The man began, "What the hell are you—" Then he caught sight of Jacqueline. Or rather, her dress. Her legs. Her—

Remy drove his fist into the guy's jaw. Apparently, it was a glass jaw, because the fellow went down without even a whimper.

"Is he all right?" Jacqueline cried.

Not exactly. He was unconscious. "You know what they say, the bigger they are, the less likely they can take a punch." Remy hurried her along that corridor.

"I don't think anyone says that."

"They should." Another turn. Another door. This one led into an office. One that was locked. He shoved his hand into her bag, hauled out a few lock-picking tools, and the lock snicked open about three seconds later. Luckily, no goon was waiting beyond that door. The smoke bombs always did the trick. When people saw smoke, they hauled ass.

"You're really good at picking locks."

Despite the tension that rode him, Remy sent her a smile. "I'm a good thief."

After all, he'd learned from the best. Or the worst, depending on how you wanted to look at the situation. The smoke bombs had been a tool his father loved to use. He'd clear a museum with them in moments. Then he'd take his prizes with glee.

Focus.

"Are you in?" Constantine's voice chimed in his ear. The comm was incredibly small and powerful. A bit of tech supplied by Wilde. Got to love those Wilde toys.

"In the main office now," Remy returned as he headed to the bookcase behind the overly large desk. A desk with *no* papers on top. No computer. Nothing at all. "You got eyes on the building?"

"You know it. Hurry your ass along, would you? The crowd is gathering and gawking. The fire department will be here soon, and they'll realize fast that this is just smoke and mirrors."

Right. He reached for the bookcase. Looked for a trigger mechanism. "When I studied the schematics, I realized there was extra space behind this wall. It looked like it was nothing. Not marked as any kind of room. But in my line of work, things are never what they appear to be. Preston must have realized the same thing, so he got a crew to bust in the wall." *And you put a bookshelf up to cover what you found, didn't you, Preston?* When Preston had told Remy that the safe was at the house in the French Quarter, he'd mentioned that it was hidden behind a bookshelf.

The bookshelf part had been true, but the French Quarter location had been a lie.

Remy felt the small button near the edge of the second shelf. Remy pushed it, then jumped back as the door swung out. His fingers curled around the edge of the bookshelf door, and he hauled it all the way open. "Well, well..." Another room. Just as he'd expected. And in the middle of that room? One very large, old-school safe. No gleaming keypad. No fingerprint scanner. Just a black safe, with a dial right in the middle and a handle near the top. "I'll let you do your thing." Remy waved her in.

And while Jacqueline crouched before the safe, Remy took the opportunity to look around that little room. The safe wasn't the only object inside. In fact, Remy had the feeling he was gazing at a treasure room. Expensive necklaces gleamed to the right, perched on velvet cushions. Rings that glittered with diamonds and emeralds had been positioned around the necklaces. Because he had an eye for stolen work, Remy recognized several famous pieces that had gone missing over the last decade.

You think you're a collector, Preston?

Files filled a shelf to the right. Remy wondered if maybe he was dealing with a guy who was afraid of leaving a tech trail that might point to his guilt with the whole money laundering bit. Had the guy really been enough of a dumbass to keep paper files? If so, Remy knew some federal agents who would be thrilled with this discovery.

He continued his perusal, and Remy whistled when he saw what looked like three bricks of cocaine. *Oh, yes. He's a complete dumbass. Complete and total.*

A tip to the Feds would be in order once Jacqueline and Remy finished their bit of business. Remy glanced down at his watch. "How's it coming?"

She didn't answer. Frowning, he looked over at her. She had one hand on the dial. One hand pressed to the front of the safe. Jacqueline had leaned in close, and her ear seemed to brush over the surface right above the dial. An intense look of concentration covered her face.

"I'll take that as a… 'It's coming along great, thanks, Remy,'" he murmured. His gaze slid to the open bookshelf door. He didn't hear any voices, but they had to be ready for an intruder to come in at any moment.

"*Remy.*" Constantine's voice held a hard note of tension as he used their comm link. "Company."

"The fire department is here already?" Color him impressed. The New Orleans FD had one seriously great response time.

"No, no, it's a swarm of goons. They're shoving everyone out of the way and rushing inside—*hey!*" Constantine shouted.

Remy winced. That shout had blasted straight in his ear.

"Hey, you can't go in there!" Constantine yelled to someone. "There's a fire! *Fire!* You need to exit—"

Fucking hell. "How many, Con?" Remy demanded.

"You and your seven buddies need to stay the hell back!" Constantine barked.

Eight of them. Coming in hot. His gaze slid to Jacqueline once more. "Okay, I can use as much help on them as I can get." He bent and reached down for his ankle. As was his habit before a job, he'd tucked a knife into the holster there. His fingers closed around the handle.

The bookshelf door flew open even wider. An even *bigger* goon filled that doorway, bigger than the prick Remy had knocked out earlier. This goon had a gun in his hand, and he lifted it toward Remy. "You sonofabitch. No one steals from Mr. Guidry—"

Before he could fire, Remy threw his knife. It slammed into the jerk's shoulder. The gun fell from his hand.

"I do," Remy said simply. "I steal from him." Then he launched forward and attacked with his fists.

CHAPTER SEVENTEEN

The sound of flesh hitting flesh—pounding fists—had Jacqueline spinning around. A gasp broke from her when she saw Remy drive his hand into some guy's stomach. The blow was immediately followed by a vicious upper cut that sent the stranger's head whipping back as he fell toward the corner.

"Keep working, sweetness," Remy called, barely sounding out of breath. "I've got this."

Another man burst through the entrance. Smaller, leaner, with bright red hair, he came charging at Remy with a roar.

Remy went in low and slammed into his attacker's midsection even as he locked his arms around the guy and threw him to the floor. She could have sworn the whole room shook.

"Work, sweetness," Remy growled.

Her shaking fingers went back to the safe as she turned away.

"Yes," a voice hissed. The voice that had given her nightmares and sent her running from her home and straight to Remy. "Do keep working."

Jacqueline froze.

"Keep working or I will have to put a bullet into his brain."

She broke through the ice that had captured her and leapt to her feet even as she whirled toward Remy once more. He still sprawled on top of the redhead he'd tackled to the floor, but Preston had entered the little room, too. Sure enough, he had a gun pointed at Remy's head.

"I don't like blood and gore," Preston informed her. "I'd hate to splatter your thief's brains all over my wonderful treasure room, but if you don't do exactly as I order, then you can watch him die."

"*No.*" A snarl from her. Her hand went to her bag. Pushed inside. From what she could see, Remy had left one of Preston's guards bleeding and unconscious in the corner. As for the redhead, his body was slack beneath Remy's. *He's unconscious, too.* That just left Preston. An armed Preston.

"No?" Preston frowned at her.

"If you shoot him, if you so much as *bruise* him, I won't open the safe. Ever. You shoot him, and you might as well shoot me."

"Uh, sweetness..." Remy cleared his throat. He also rose, slowly, and she noticed that Preston tracked his movements with the gun.

Had the gun just shook? Preston wasn't nearly as confident as he seemed.

"Jacqueline..." Remy lifted his hands to show Preston that he wasn't armed. "I think we need to come up with an agreement that *doesn't* involve you getting shot."

At the moment, her priority was keeping him safe. "Get the gun away from Remy!" Her voice wavered. Her fingers drove deeper into her bag. "*Now!*" This time, her yell didn't waver. It was packed with the fury she felt at seeing a gun pointed at Remy.

Remy could not get hurt.

"I think this is a good exit point," Remy murmured.

Oh, hell, no. He thought he could toss out their codeword *now?* Not happening. *He thinks I'm going to try running away and leaving him? He thinks he can drop that 'exit' bullshit to me?* "I don't go anywhere without you," she said fiercely.

He looked at her. His eyes gleamed. "I fucking love you." His mouth sort of dropped open after the confession, as if the words had just surprised him.

They didn't surprise her. "I know. I—"

Bam.

Preston had fired his gun. The bastard had fired! Blood bloomed on Remy's thigh, soaking his jeans, even as he fell to the floor.

"*Sonofabitch,*" Remy snarled as he grabbed for his leg.

Preston aimed the gun at Remy—at his chest. "I don't take orders." The gun stayed on Remy, but Preston's head turned toward Jacqueline. "Open the safe or he dies. Once he's dead, if you're still being a bitch, then I'll hurt you until you open it. I will hurt you until you beg to do everything I want."

Her fingers closed around the screwdriver. A gift of love if ever there had been one.

"Don't," Remy gritted out.

Was he going to tell her not to open the safe for Preston? He didn't need to worry. She wasn't.

She *was* terrified because that was so much blood. Remy needed help. They had to get out of there.

"Don't," Remy continued as he pressed one hand to his thigh but whipped his head up to glare at Preston, "ever call her names. *And you will not hurt her.*" He grabbed for Preston's legs. A hard dive that had Preston stumbling and waving the gun as he prepared to shoot.

"*No!*" Jacqueline yelled. She lunged and drove her screwdriver at Preston. Preston twisted, and the screwdriver sank into his shoulder. He roared in pain and slammed out with the gun in a wild blow. It hit her near the temple, and for a moment, the world swirled in a sickening fog of gray. As her body trembled, Jacqueline feared she might pass out.

***

"Open the damn safe or he dies. Once he's dead, if you're still being a bitch, then I'll hurt you until you open it. I will hurt you until you beg to do everything I want."

Constantine heard the words through his comm link even as he drove his fist at some creep in his way. He had to get to Remy and Jacqueline, and even as smoke billowed around him, he grabbed a chair and slammed it at the other goon who wanted to stop him.

"Need a hand?" A mild voice inquired from behind him.

He whirled with the chair up, ready to take another jerk down.

"Easy." The man lifted his hands. "I'm on your side. At least, if my assumption that you are Constantine is correct, then I am."

Smoke billowed, making it hard to see the guy's features. "Who the hell are you?"

"Ty Crenshaw. We spoke on the phone. Thanks for telling me where you'd be. When I arrived early, I came to join the party."

Hell, yes. "We need to get to Remy." He could no longer hear anything in his comm link, and Constantine wouldn't think about what that meant. Originally, his job had been to watch the building and bring in all the bags so they could haul out cash once Jacqueline had opened the safe. Now, his only goal was to make sure Remy and Jacqueline were alive.

"I thought you Wilde agents always worked with partners."

He did have backup from Wilde on scene. The other agent was taking care of the jerks who'd tried to bust in the back of the bar. But beyond Wilde... "Remy is my partner." Always had been. "And he needs us. *Now*." Spinning away, he ran toward the main office. He'd studied the building plans with Remy, and he knew where the safe should be located. Remy should be there, too.

And his best friend had better be alive.

***

The sonofabitch had just hit Jacqueline. She staggered back, then fell to her knees. Her head tipped forward.

"*Open the fucking safe!*" Preston bellowed. He slammed the gun down on the desk, and he curled his fingers around the handle of the screwdriver that Jacqueline had driven into him. "You have one purpose, one small bit of usefulness. You *open* the safe for me, and you do it now!"

Ignoring the fire in his thigh, Remy slowly rose. Preston wasn't looking at him. The SOB was too busy snarling at Jacqueline. *I warned you about that.* "Sweetness?"

Her head lifted. Her gaze was dazed, and her temple and cheek were bright red.

You are a dead man, Preston.

"Open it!" Preston screamed.

"I-I..." Her hand feathered around her temple. "I don't...feel well."

I will rip his heart from his chest.

"I had one m-more number..."

Remy hated the weakness in her voice. He wanted to pull her into his arms and hold tight.

Preston had yanked the screwdriver out. *Bad move. You should have left it in.* Now blood soaked *his* clothes. Preston slapped the screwdriver down on the desk and immediately scooped up the gun. He pointed it at Remy, then Jacqueline, weaving it back and forth.

"Remember what I said would happen if you couldn't open the safe," Remy told her. He ignored the gun. Ignored Preston. He needed Jacqueline to get this message.

"I think I'm gonna be sick." Her head sagged forward again.

His hands fisted. *Sweetness, stay strong, just a moment longer.*

Jacqueline turned toward the safe. "I remember." A whisper.

He didn't think Jacqueline meant that she remembered the last number. He thought she remembered what he'd told her before when she'd feared that she might not be able to open the safe. *You trigger the safe so that the ink explodes. Preston is not gonna get the cash.*

"Hurry," Preston snapped at her. "Hurry, hurry!"

The gun swung back toward Jacqueline.

Remy sagged against the desk. His hand slid toward the screwdriver.

Jacqueline's fingers fluttered over the surface of the safe. Her other hand went to the dial. She turned it a little to the right.

Remy could have sworn even he heard the faint snick.

Jacqueline grabbed for the long, metal handle. She wrenched it down, and the safe swung open.

Money. Piles and piles of cold cash stacked high. Ice cold cash that was—

Her hand slammed into the side of the safe, right along the now open safe door, and red exploded. A burst of red smoke spat from the safe.

"Guess it still works," Remy said, satisfaction filling him. "Even after all this time."

"*What in the hell have you done?*" Preston screamed. He had the gun aimed at Jacqueline. The smoke billowed around her as she swayed. Her black dress had turned pinkish red in spots, but the dye didn't appear to hit her body. "I will *kill—*"

"No, you won't." Remy drove the screwdriver into his upper back. A hard plunge, as if it were a knife.

When Preston screamed again, the sound held pain. *Oh, I will make you feel so much pain.* "Exit, sweetness," Remy bellowed. "Now!" He hauled the screwdriver out.

Preston spun toward him. He still had the gun.

So Remy drove the screwdriver into Preston's hand.

Preston's scream threatened to shatter his ear drums. The gun fell. Remy yanked the screwdriver back out. "Warned you...don't call her names...don't hurt her..." This time, the screwdriver slammed into Preston's gut. Remy twisted it.

Preston *howled.*

Remy yanked the screwdriver out.

Preston hit the floor. Remy leaned over him to strike again.

"Exit," Jacqueline cried. "Exit, Remy! Let's exit together!"

His head whipped up.

She hadn't left. "Together." Swaying more, she held out her hand to him.

All he wanted to do was plunge his weapon into Preston's heart. To eliminate him once and for all. It would be so easy to stab him and to leave him in his own blood and to...

My father was stabbed in the chest. In the heart. Left in his own blood to die.

"Remy…" She still reached for him. "Together."

Remy's breath shuddered out. Preston had curled in on himself. Blood was all around him, and the fire in Remy's thigh burned hotter. *Killing him isn't all I want.*

No, he wanted something else. Someone else. *I want Jacqueline.* And if she saw him kill, if she saw him take that step…

"Remy, come with me."

He would go with her anywhere. His right hand held tight to the screwdriver, but his left took hers. With a cry, she flew toward him. Her body was warm and soft as she hit him, and he knew he had to get her out of there. Jacqueline mattered. She was the priority. She was everything.

"Sorry about the money," she whispered.

"Fuck it." He didn't care. He had plenty of his own money. The twenty million had *never* been for him. But Jacqueline, she *was* his. Always. Forever. Everything else in the world could be replaced. But not her.

He pulled her toward the door. Kept tight to the screwdriver. Saw the gleaming edge of a gun on the floor and he started to snag that weapon.

But two figures burst through the doorway before he could. The reddish smoke was every damn where, so he could barely see them, and he brought up the screwdriver with a roar.

"Is that any way to greet your best friend?" Constantine demanded.

A shudder rippled over Remy.

"And a CIA agent," a familiar voice added. "Couldn't very well let you have a party without me. You know how I love tagging along on your adventures."

Ty. The guy Remy had once thought of as a junior CIA operative. But the man had come into his own during their last assignment. In that moment, Remy had never been happier to see two people in his life. Mostly because...

Yeah, he'd had a shit ton of blood loss from his thigh. *Did that bastard hit something vital?* Remy sure as hell hoped not. But, just in case... "Priority," Remy gasped out. "J-Jacqueline..."

"Yeah, I remember," Constantine assured him as he waved a hand against the smoke that drifted in the small room. "She's the center of your universe, and I swear I'll get her out for you, buddy."

Excellent. Because with that promise, Remy's injured leg gave way, and he slammed into the floor.

***

"Remy!" Jacqueline jerked upright, his name a scream on her lips.

"It's all right. You're safe." A woman in green scrubs leaned over and gave Jacqueline a reassuring pat on the shoulder. "You're in the hospital, and everything is just fine."

But things didn't feel fine. Things felt incredibly blurry. She remembered being in the bar on Bourbon. Red smoke spilling from the exploding dye in the safe. And blood. A lot of blood.

Much of that blood had been streaming down Remy's thigh. Jacqueline grabbed the hand of the woman—the nurse?—and held on tightly. "Where is Remy?"

The woman's blond eyebrows rose. "Who is that? A friend of yours?"

"He—he's..." *Everything*. "He should have been brought in with me." Because he'd been hurt, and hurt people were taken to the hospital.

Concern flashed on the woman's face but was quickly hidden. "My name is Debra," she said. "I'm your nurse. You came in with a concussion. You took quite the blow to your temple, so it is understandable if you're suffering a bit of confusion." She tugged her hand free of Jacqueline's grip. "Don't worry. Your vitals all look great. The doctor is very pleased with your healing rate." She gave a little hum. "Do you remember seeing the doctor?"

No, she didn't. The last thing she remembered was seeing Remy collapse in front of her. "Where. Is. Remy?"

Debra darted back a step. "You weren't brought in with anyone else. Some federal agents have been in and out, but no family. No friends."

She didn't have family. "Remy was hurt."

Debra licked her lips. "If your friend was hurt, he wasn't brought here. At least, not with you."

"Remy. *Rembrandt*. I need to see him." She had to make sure that he was all right. Her temples began to throb. Especially the one on the left. It throbbed hard with every beat of her heart.

"I'm sorry." The nurse paused near the door. "But I don't know about any Remy or Rembrandt. You were brought in alone, and federal agents said...they said that was how they found you. You were alone when they rescued you. Well, you were with Preston Guidry. It turns out that he was a very dangerous man."

He was dangerous. But she hadn't been alone with him. Remy had been there.

"I want Remy," she said.

The door closed behind the nurse.

I need Remy.

CHAPTER EIGHTEEN

The door jingled when the new customer stepped inside her bookstore. It had been two weeks since Jacqueline had woken up in the hospital, desperate for Remy, only to be told that...

No one knew who he was. No one knew where he was.

She'd tried calling Wilde. She'd spoken with Eric Wilde personally, and though there had been sympathy in his voice, Eric had said he couldn't help her.

Constantine seemed to have vanished along with Remy. They'd both disappeared, as if they'd never been in her life at all.

Her life. Things were back to normal. Predictable. Safe. When she'd gotten out of the hospital, she'd discovered that her bookstore and her apartment had been cleaned. No, not just cleaned. The chaos had turned back into order. New books had replaced the savaged ones. The lights had been hung once more. Fresh paint had covered her walls. She had new furniture in her apartment. The framed photos of her grandfather hung on her walls.

Everything in her life was *almost* as it had been before.

So why did it seem as if a giant, gaping hole filled her heart?

The customer, a man with a baseball cap pulled low over his brow, ambled toward the counter. She put on a fake smile for him. "Is there something I can help you find?" He wore khakis. A button down. He walked with ease but...

But when his stare locked on her, she saw the shrewd intelligence in his eyes. Something about him set off a little bell of alarm. *No, not alarm. Recognition.* Behind the counter, Jacqueline tensed. "Do I know you?"

"I have one of those faces." He smiled at her. "People always think they know me." He glanced around the shop. "Nice place you have here."

He hadn't answered her question. That faint alarm in her mind rang again. "I know your face."

His head tilted as his focus shifted back to her. "Do you?"

She just didn't know *where* she'd seen him.

He ambled closer. "Could be because I helped carry you out of the bar on Bourbon that night. Wasn't sure if you'd be able to recall that part or not. You were drifting in and out. A blow to the head can make things a little foggy."

She shot off the stool. "Who are you?"

One shoulder moved in a shrug. "We have a friend in common. He was losing his mind worrying about you, and since I didn't want to jeopardize a ton of cases that are in play, I said I'd come and see about you myself." His gaze swept over her. "You seem good. Recovered from that concussion, have you?"

"Who. Are. You?" Her finger was inching toward the alarm button that she'd had installed beneath her counter.

"Don't press that button." He shook his head. "No need to notify the cops or anyone else. I'm not here to cause any trouble."

We have a friend in common. Her heart surged so hard in her chest. "Do you know Remy? Is he the one who sent you?"

"Remy." He seemed to test the name. *"Rembrandt."*

"Remy...Rembrandt—that person doesn't exist." A sad smile curled his lips. "Part of the message that I have to deliver, I'm afraid. Make sure you don't go talking about him to the media...or anyone else who should ever ask, understand? As I said, a lot of cases could be jeopardized."

Her breath came faster. "You're one of the agents he worked with."

Another shrug.

"FBI?" she guessed.

"Hardly. Have you seen the shitty suits they wear?"

Who was this guy? Who—

"Friends call me Ty," he said.

The name clicked. "Ty Crenshaw. Remy told me about you." Not a lot. Not enough.

"Um. All good things, I hope?" Once more, he surveyed the shop. "This is seriously a nice place you have here. A nice life. Quiet. Safe, I bet. Well, safer now, especially since Preston Guidry won't be seeing daylight anytime soon."

"No one would talk to me about him, either." Her finger still hovered over the alarm button. "Some Feds did come to see me when I was in the hospital, but they just told me they were taking over the case. That they would be contacting me again, and they left me with *nothing*."

That was how she felt. As if everything had been ripped away.

"Well, then how about I help with some closure? I'll recap for you, shall I?"

I want more than a recap. I want Remy.

"Preston Guidry sent two men to hunt you and abduct you in Halfway, Georgia. Those two individuals have become quite cooperative and are planning to testify against him. During the course of my investigation into Guidry, I discovered that he had forced you into a hidden room at his bar."

He hadn't forced her in there. She and Remy had snuck inside—

"At gunpoint, Guidry made you open the safe. A trigger inside caused the cash—twenty million, by the way, in case you didn't know—a trigger caused the cash to be permanently dyed with red ink."

She wet her lips. She still had a small dot of red on the tip of one finger.

"You fought him off when he was distracted by the dye. Stabbed him with a handy screwdriver."

She had stabbed him, but so had Remy. They'd fought him together.

"I burst in and saw you trying to escape. You collapsed. I carried you to safety, then went back inside to discover that secret room was filled with stolen jewels, cocaine, and a whole lot of evidence that tied Guidry to money laundering schemes. The fool should have known better than to leave an actual paper trail in this day and age." A disgusted shake of his head. "And, to tie things up in an even nicer bow, his ex-lawyer is begging for deals from anyone who will glance his way. Morris Hade was involved in the money laundering up to his beady eyes. The FBI and the CIA have a joint task force that is working on the long list of crimes tied to Guidry. By the way, in case you were wondering, the local authorities are *not* involved."

Because he'd had so many cops in his pocket.

"As I said, Guidry will not be seeing daylight again."

In that whole story, he hadn't mentioned Remy, and she now understood why. When he talked about cases that could be jeopardized, he meant Preston's crimes...and more. Because Remy had worked undercover for so long. Because he'd done all of his "favors" for the Feds and the CIA and for everyone else who'd used him.

I used him, too. The knowledge settled heavily around her. Was that why he'd left? Because Remy felt like she was just another in a long line to use his skills? "Tell me he's all right."

"Guidry is perfectly fine. Had some fairly serious wounds, don't get me wrong. You must have been quite enraged when you went after him. But we stitched him up."

"*Remy.* How is he?"

"Remy doesn't exist. He never has."

Screw this. She rushed around the counter and grabbed his shirt. Her hands fisted as she yanked him close. "Nod if he's okay because I have a terrible memory of him falling before me. Just...*nod*. Please."

He nodded.

Her breath choked out. "Good. Good." The choking of her breath had sounded like a sob. "You're delivering messages to me, so can I get you to deliver one *for* me?"

He stared at her.

"I love you." There. "Just tell him...I love you. I don't care what came before. I don't care what kind of life we have to lead, I love Remy."

"Remy doesn't—"

"He exists to me! And he always will." She was about to rip his shirt. Jacqueline let him go. Stepped back. "I love him. Just tell him, will you? And if he loves me, then he can come find me. He knows where I am. He can come back to me, and I will be here, waiting on him."

His lips pursed. "That it?"

What else could she say? Jacqueline nodded.

"Nice to meet you, you know, when you're not on the verge of losing consciousness." He turned away. Started his slow walk for the door. He pulled the door open. The bell jingled. "Why would you wait?"

"Excuse me?"

"If you want something, I was always taught you fight for it. You don't just *wait*."

"He's not here. How can I fight for him when he's *gone?*" Gone and breaking her heart.

"Some guys have an MO."

What on earth was Ty talking about now?

"Seen this before. Seen a guy seemingly abandon his sister, but he did it just so she could stay safe. So she could go into witness protection, and he could face the enemies who wanted to hurt her."

The moisture dried in her mouth.

"Seen the same fool turn away from his best friend because he wanted the guy to have a better life. And he thought that would never happen as long as they were tied together."

Her heartbeat shook her body.

"Same guy," Ty Crenshaw continued, "would leave the love of his life, the woman he would both die for and *kill* for, because he thought she deserved to have the safe home she wanted. Because he didn't want her having to pretend like he does. Didn't want her giving up her apartment and her business and the life she needed. Didn't want her to lose anything, not for him. Fool did that because he thought it was best." He looked back. "My opinion? Screw all that shit. When you want something badly enough, you fight for it."

"I want to fight."

"Thought you might."

"*Where* is he?"

"Afraid I don't know who you're talking about, but...you found yourself a thief once. Something tells me you already know exactly where to look if you want to find him again." He walked out.

She didn't know, dammit! The first time she'd found Remy, it had been in the middle of nowhere.

You already know exactly where to...
Jacqueline smiled.

No, she hadn't found him in the middle of nowhere. She'd found him in Halfway, Georgia.

CHAPTER NINETEEN

"Did you see her?" Remy gripped the phone so tightly he feared it might shatter in his hand. "Did you actually see her with your own eyes and talk to Jacqueline?"

"Can't hear you so well," Ty Crenshaw drawled. "Must have a bad connection. Are you back in the mountains?"

Yes, he was back in the freaking mountains. Back in the same low-rent bar and back to being ignored by Rodney as the guy watched his game. Remy was even at the same damn table he'd sat at before. *Before* Jacqueline had entered his life and changed everything.

Mostly she changed me.

"You had one job," he snapped. "See Jacqueline. Make sure she is all right. You and your asshole agents hauled me out of the hospital before I could see her for myself."

"Ah, you mean we *saved* you when you collapsed, and we got you out of there before your identity could be compromised. Happy to help. No problem. Don't mention it."

"You were supposed to call me yesterday." The connection was crystal clear. What had Ty been moaning about? "Did you see her or not?" The fingers of his left hand drummed on the tabletop. A beer sat in front of him because

Rodney had insisted he buy one in order to sit at the freaking table.

And *why* was Remy even in that bar? Because his cabin had felt too damn empty. Because he'd spent the last five days frantically painting image after image of Jacqueline. Because he missed her and if he hadn't gotten out of that cabin, he might have lost the little bit of his mind that remained.

"I might have seen her," Ty returned slowly.

The bar door opened with a creak.

Automatically, Remy's gaze jumped toward the door and to the woman who slowly peeked inside.

Wrong bar, sweetness. Wrong man. Wrong night.

"The real question," Ty continued in his ear, "is have *you* seen her? Because I think you might be seeing—"

Remy hung up on him. Slammed down the phone. Sent the beer bottle toppling and spilling over his table even as he jumped to his feet.

The woman who peeked inside didn't belong in the bar. She didn't belong in his world at all. She was too good for him. Too perfect and kind and beautiful. Her angelic face was filled with ethereal beauty that he'd captured frantically— over and over—on his canvases. A beauty that haunted him. And even across the room, when her gaze locked on him, the stunning clarity of her green eyes stole his breath. Her lips—unpainted, pale pink and lush—curled as she saw him.

His angel began to walk toward him.

Instinctively, he shook his head.

She kept advancing. His gaze dipped over her body, and he half expected her to be wearing a mud-stained white dress. Instead, she wore jeans. A loose sweater. Sneakers. And this time, there were no leaves in the darkness of her hair.

Turn away and run. A whisper in his mind. The same one he'd had the first time she'd come toward him in this bar. She should flee from him, but...

I don't know if I can let her go.

Jacqueline stopped at the edge of his wobbly, wooden table even as the beer drip, drip, dripped onto the floor. "I need you."

Before, she'd said...*I need your help.*

Remy cleared his throat. "How are you here?" His hands fisted and released. Fisted and released, over and over as he fought the urge to grab her and hold tight. To never let go.

"I drove here. No hitchhiking with truckers this time. Got a tip from a friend of yours that you were up here. Well, sort of a tip, I suppose. He gave a strong hint, and I figured out the rest."

Remy didn't know if he should thank Ty or kick his ass. "The agents took me out of the hospital while I was unconscious. I didn't want to leave you."

"But you stayed away when you woke up."

Yes, he had. His hands fisted. Released. "You deserve better than me."

"Better than someone who will risk his life to protect me? Better than someone who will fight to protect me even as blood is soaking him?" She shook her head. "I don't think it gets better than you. And if it does, I don't care. I love *you*. Thief, criminal, secret agent. Whatever—whoever you're currently pretending to be, I love you, and I am here to fight for you."

He swallowed. "You have a safe life at home."

"Are you sure it's so safe? The last time I checked, at *home,* I had someone who tried to kill me. It was up here in the mountains where I found safety. I walked up to this really gorgeous guy, and he became my hero."

"I'm not," Remy rasped. He was so far from being a hero. Had she missed the part where he nearly drove a screwdriver into Preston's heart? *That bastard will never get out of prison. He will never hurt her again.*

"I decide who is my hero. I decide who I love." Her hand rose. Pressed to his chest. Her lips trembled into a smile. "I saw a big, black truck outside. Tell me it's yours."

She was giving him all the words she'd said when they first met, and he could feel her fingers trembling. This time, he told her the truth. "It's not. Just some loaner. The cabin isn't mine, either, but I would love to buy a home similar to it. A place that you might like." He clamped his lips together before he could add...*A place where you'd stay with me.*

Her breath came faster. So did his. His hand also rose to curl around hers. Not to pull her hand away, but to press it closer. "I missed you," he confessed.

"I want *you,*" she told him. "I don't want safety if it means I don't have you."

She was ripping him apart. "Sweetness..."

"Tell me you don't love me, and I will walk away."

He shook his head. "Can't do that. I love you more than anything in this world." Another of those truths that she could pull so effortlessly from him.

Her smile widened. "You're in love with me?"

"Yes." *A thousand times, yes.* Yes—always. Always.

"It's been an incredibly bad few weeks," she said as her shoulders straightened. "The love of my life vanished. Everyone was saying he wasn't real, and I felt like a giant hole had been left in my chest because I missed him so much. The life around me was empty and dull, and I just wanted to see him again."

"I want you to be happy," Remy told her. "With me, you'll always have some danger lurking in the shadows."

"I don't care."

Rodney hadn't even glanced their way.

"I don't care about danger," she added with a small hitch in her voice. "I don't care about fake names or moving to new cities. I care about you, Remy. I love you."

That was it. He was done. Deal sealed. She wanted him? She'd come after him? No way could he *ever* let her go. The woman owned his very soul.

"Take me out of here," she urged him. "Take me away with you, and we can start over together."

Oh, they could definitely start over. He had plenty of money stashed away. He could give her any material thing she wanted in the world.

"I love you," she said again.

But he knew material things didn't matter to her. He mattered. And to him, she was the greatest treasure in the world. The one thing he'd sought his entire life. "I love you, sweetness." His mouth took hers. Careful. Tender. Reverently.

The greatest prize he'd ever discovered. He would guard her for the rest of his life. Protect her always.

His muse. She'd inspired him from the beginning. Taught him to be more than just a thief. She'd made him a better man. For her, he could be better.

For her, he could do anything. Put the world at her feet. Give her a new life. Surround her with joy for the rest of her days.

But the one thing he could not, would not do...

Give her up. She'd come to him. Searched for him.

And he intended to keep his precious muse close, forever. He kissed her again, deeper, hotter, and her sweet taste had him craving so much more. But he lifted his head. "You want to disappear with me?"

"Yes."

"Where do you want to go? Got a destination in mind?"

"I don't care." Her smile lit up the bar. It lit up his whole world. "I'm really just looking forward to the trip."

His mouth opened... "Marry me." Hell. He had meant to slowly build up to that part, but no, the Jacqueline effect had struck again.

"Absolutely."

She—

A loud laugh escaped him. More like a cry of joy and he scooped her into his arms and spun her around. He barely felt the pull of mending muscles in his thigh.

"Hey, hey, man! What is happening over there?" Rodney called.

He kept spinning her. "Rodney, you can come to the wedding."

"What wedding?" Rodney demanded to know.

"Mine." He stared at her. Slowly lowered Jacqueline to her feet. "My wedding." A wedding and a new life and some long-forgotten dreams coming true. That was what he'd get with Jacqueline.

That was *everything*.

She laughed and kissed him again. The sweetest kiss in the world.

EPILOGUE

"So, I hear you're gonna need some time off for the wedding." Eric Wilde leaned back in his chair and studied the man who sat in the chair across from him.

Constantine Leos grinned. "Can't believe how quickly he fell." But he was happy for Remy. His best friend deserved some joy. Hadn't he told Remy to go for the happy ending?

"Your first case with Wilde has officially concluded. Your probationary period is over," Eric added with a nod.

Probationary period? Constantine hadn't even realized he'd been on one.

Eric flipped through some files on his desk. "You want a week off for the wedding? That long enough? I'm assuming you will be his best man?"

"Hell, yes, I am." He was in the process of planning the bachelor party. He'd be sure to send Eric an invite. He already knew the guy would be at the wedding.

"Okay." Eric kept looking at his files. "When you get back, you'll start the next case." Something in his tone...changed.

That change was faint. A little tightening of his voice. A little rasping note. The small shift had Constantine leaning forward in his chair. "Just what sort of case will that be?"

"Ahem."

Constantine waited. *Ahem* wasn't exactly an answer.

"So..." Eric's index finger tapped against his chin. "Do you have any experience with royalty?"

Constantine laughed.

Eric didn't. "I'll take that as a no." He stopped tapping and shoved a file toward Constantine.

Oddly nervous—when he *never* got nervous—Constantine opened the file. A whistle escaped him.

"You're about to get some experience," Eric informed him. "That's an exiled princess, and she needs our protection."

"You are shitting me."

"Nope. Get ready, Constantine, because you're about to play bodyguard to real-life royalty."

Sonofa—

THE END

A NOTE FROM THE AUTHOR

Thank you for taking the time to read THE THIEF WHO LOVE ME. I hope you enjoyed the adventure in the "Wilde Ways" world. I love writing the Wilde books because they give me a chance to balance humor, danger, and romance. These books are pure fun to write, and my wish is that they will be fun reads for you, too!

If you'd like to stay updated on my releases and sales, please join my newsletter list.

https://cynthiaeden.com/newsletter/

Again, thank you for reading THE THIEF WHO LOVE ME.

Best,
Cynthia Eden
cynthiaeden.com

ABOUT THE AUTHOR

Cynthia Eden is a *New York Times*, *USA Today*, *Digital Book World*, and *IndieReader* best-seller.

Cynthia writes sexy tales of contemporary romance, romantic suspense, and paranormal romance. Since she began writing full-time in 2005, Cynthia has written over one hundred novels and novellas.

Cynthia lives along the Alabama Gulf Coast. She loves romance novels, horror movies, and chocolate.

For More Information

- *cynthiaeden.com*
- *facebook.com/cynthiaedenfanpage*

HER OTHER WORKS

Ice Breaker Cold Case Romance
- Frozen In Ice (Book 1)
- Falling For The Ice Queen (Book 2)
- Ice Cold Saint (Book 3)

Phoenix Fury
- Hot Enough To Burn (Book 1)
- Slow Burn (Book 2)
- Burn It Down (Book 3)

Trouble For Hire
- No Escape From War (Book 1)
- Don't Play With Odin (Book 2)
- Jinx, You're It (Book 3)
- Remember Ramsey (Book 4)

Death and Moonlight Mystery
- Step Into My Web (Book 1)
- Save Me From The Dark (Book 2)

Wilde Ways
- Protecting Piper (Book 1)
- Guarding Gwen (Book 2)
- Before Ben (Book 3)
- The Heart You Break (Book 4)
- Fighting For Her (Book 5)
- Ghost Of A Chance (Book 6)
- Crossing The Line (Book 7)

- Counting On Cole (Book 8)
- Chase After Me (Book 9)
- Say I Do (Book 10)
- Roman Will Fall (Book 11)
- The One Who Got Away (Book 12)
- Pretend You Want Me (Book 13)
- Cross My Heart (Book 14)
- The Bodyguard Next Door (Book 15)
- Ex Marks The Perfect Spot (Book 17)

Dark Sins

- Don't Trust A Killer (Book 1)
- Don't Love A Liar (Book 2)

Lazarus Rising

- Never Let Go (Book One)
- Keep Me Close (Book Two)
- Stay With Me (Book Three)
- Run To Me (Book Four)
- Lie Close To Me (Book Five)
- Hold On Tight (Book Six)

Dark Obsession Series

- Watch Me (Book 1)
- Want Me (Book 2)
- Need Me (Book 3)
- Beware Of Me (Book 4)
- Only For Me (Books 1 to 4)

Mine Series

- Mine To Take (Book 1)
- Mine To Keep (Book 2)
- Mine To Hold (Book 3)
- Mine To Crave (Book 4)

- Mine To Have (Book 5)
- Mine To Protect (Book 6)
- Mine Box Set Volume 1 (Books 1-3)
- Mine Box Set Volume 2 (Books 4-6)

Bad Things

- The Devil In Disguise (Book 1)
- On The Prowl (Book 2)
- Undead Or Alive (Book 3)
- Broken Angel (Book 4)
- Heart Of Stone (Book 5)
- Tempted By Fate (Book 6)
- Wicked And Wild (Book 7)
- Saint Or Sinner (Book 8)
- Bad Things Volume One (Books 1 to 3)
- Bad Things Volume Two (Books 4 to 6)
- Bad Things Deluxe Box Set (Books 1 to 6)

Bite Series

- Forbidden Bite (Bite Book 1)
- Mating Bite (Bite Book 2)

Blood and Moonlight Series

- Bite The Dust (Book 1)
- Better Off Undead (Book 2)
- Bitter Blood (Book 3)
- Blood and Moonlight (The Complete Series)

Purgatory Series

- The Wolf Within (Book 1)
- Marked By The Vampire (Book 2)
- Charming The Beast (Book 3)

- Deal with the Devil (Book 4)
- The Beasts Inside (Books 1 to 4)

Bound Series

- Bound By Blood (Book 1)
- Bound In Darkness (Book 2)
- Bound In Sin (Book 3)
- Bound By The Night (Book 4)
- Bound in Death (Book 5)
- Forever Bound (Books 1 to 4)

Stand-Alone Romantic Suspense

- It's A Wonderful Werewolf
- Never Cry Werewolf
- Immortal Danger
- Deck The Halls
- Come Back To Me
- Put A Spell On Me
- Never Gonna Happen
- One Hot Holiday
- Slay All Day
- Midnight Bite
- Secret Admirer
- Christmas With A Spy
- Femme Fatale
- Until Death
- Sinful Secrets
- First Taste of Darkness
- A Vampire's Christmas Carol

www.ingramcontent.com/pod-product-compliance
Lightning Source LLC
Chambersburg PA
CBHW011159190726
48286CB00009B/2844